VOW OF JUSTICE

A Mara Brent Legal Thriller

ROBIN JAMES

Copyright © 2022 by Robin James Books

All Rights Reserved

No part of this book may be reproduced or transmitted in any form or by any means, electronic or mechanical including photocopying, recording, or by any information storage and retrieval system, without the written permission of the author or publisher, except where permitted by law or for the use of brief quotations in a book review.

This is a work of fiction. Names, characters, businesses, places, events, and incidents are either the products of the author's imagination or used in a fictitious manner. Any resemblance to actual persons, living or dead, or actual events is purely coincidental.

1

Everyone tries to read something in the eyes of the jurors. They file in, one by one, staring either straight ahead or letting their gaze flick to the center of the courtroom. If they look at the defendant, does it mean they believe he's innocent? If they look away, does it mean they cannot face him, knowing they voted to take his freedom or his life away? I can tell you. None of it means anything. Not until we hear those words scribbled on a sheet of paper.

Guilty. Not guilty. Every single time, no matter the answer, it sends a rush through me. A release.

Today, there were eight men. Four women. Young. Old. Everything in between.

It had taken them eight hours to decide one man's fate. They had the power to put him behind bars for the rest of his life. He would never see the sunlight except through razor-wire again. Or they could let him go so that *I* would feel like I was the one going to prison.

It wasn't what he planned, this defendant. Once upon a time, he meant to do good; I think. He'd come from nothing. An abusive father. A mother who abandoned him for her addictions when he was just a boy.

He'd starved. Fought. Survived. Suffered in ways that made him hard.

He'd done more than survive. He had thrived. He had protected his younger sister, earning enough money so that when he turned eighteen, he rescued her from foster care too.

She loved him. Still. How could she not? She sat in the corner of the courtroom, trying to hold her tears back. She didn't want him to see. Didn't want him to worry about how she might fall apart. Didn't want to trigger those old protective instincts of his.

I knew she wouldn't fall apart this time. Though he had been the one to save her, she'd learned how to survive long before.

I turned to her. She'd gone rigid as the jury filed in. Each of them found their seats and turned to face the judge.

"Have you reached a verdict?" the judge said to the foreman. An older man. A former history professor. He had wispy white hair and glasses perched at the tip of his nose.

"We have, Your Honor," he said, clearing his throat.

The judge's clerk reached for the small scrap of paper that would decide the defendant's fate.

I felt as if I'd floated outside myself. How many times had I waited for a verdict like this one? Hundreds. It never got easier. Ever.

I heard the defendant take a sharp breath. He turned his head, searching for me. Should I meet his eyes? Give him some small comfort?

In the end, I knew I couldn't. This was his fate alone. As linked as I was to him, this was his life, not mine. Not anymore.

The judge opened the folded slip of paper and read the verdict. He made a note on a pad he kept in front of him. His face betrayed nothing. Judge Cranston had sat on the bench of the United States District Court for the Northern District of Ohio for twenty years. The only member of it who hadn't sought an appointment to a higher court. One of his colleagues was now a Supreme Court Justice. They'd gone to law school together. Still played bridge together with their wives once a month.

Cranston handed the paper back to his clerk. She settled herself in front of the microphone and read the words aloud.

I didn't know I needed comfort. But when Lieutenant Sam Cruz touched my hand with his pinky, I latched on to him. I threaded my fingers through his and squeezed.

"Will the Defendant please rise," Judge Cranston said.

He did.

He was handsome, wearing a tailored three-piece suit. His thick, dark hair had gone grayer in the last year. It made him look like his father. The man who set him on the path that led him here today.

"We, the jury, in the above-entitled action, on count of one of the complaint ..."

She rattled off sections of the statutory code. Those the defendant stood accused of violating. There were seven of them all told. She would read his verdict one by one. "... find the defendant guilty as charged."

Lieutenant Cruz's grip hardened, matching my own. It got hard to breathe.

The defendant didn't move. He became a statue. His head held high, he waited as the clerk read the rest of the verdict form.

Guilty. Guilty. Guilty. Guilty. Guilty. Guilty.

Lieutenant Cruz exhaled first. "We need to get you out of here," he whispered in my ear. "It's going to be a media circus. I've got something worked out with one of the marshals. They'll clear a path for us and keep the vultures at bay."

I nodded. I couldn't feel my feet. My brain buzzed.

Guilty. All counts. Every single one. There would be a sentencing hearing in a couple of months. He would get life. There would be no other choice.

He turned to me. I should have left the moment Sam told me to. Instead, I felt rooted to my spot.

The defendant. Jason Brent. Father of my only son. The man I had once vowed to spend the rest of my life with. When he met my eyes, he lost all color.

"Mara," Sam said. "Let's go."

"Wait," Jason said. He leaned in, whispering to his lawyer, Stoney Gregg. I knew the man's retainer was more than I had made in a year. He'd successfully defended one of the mob's most notorious kingpins last year. But today, he came up short.

"Mrs. Brent," Gregg said, turning to me. "I've made arrangements. You can have five minutes to speak with your husband in private before he's taken away."

"You don't have to do this, Mara," Sam said.

"One minute," I said to Jason. "And we'll do it right here."

Jason's face hardened. He squared his shoulders.

"What are you going to tell Will?" he asked. Will. My twelve-year-old son. For months, I had tried to prepare him for this day. He knew what his father stood accused of. He'd been following the trial online, even though I tried to prevent it.

"I'll tell him the truth," I said.

"I want to see him," Jason said. "You have to let me try to explain to him ..."

Explain. How could he possibly explain in a way that would make sense to Will?

Congressman Jason Brent had just been convicted on seven counts under the RICO statute. Fraud. Money laundering. Embezzlement. And worst of all, conspiracy to commit murder. No. There was no way to explain any of this. Jason would not take responsibility for any of it.

"I'll decide if and when Will is ready to see you," I said. "On the advice of his therapist, that won't be for a long time, Jason."

"You hate me," Jason said. "You have the right, I suppose. But you did this, Mara. Don't think I don't know it."

"That's enough," Sam said. He stepped in between Jason and me. Only, I didn't need his protection. I'd taken away Jason's power to hurt me a long time ago.

"Jason?" Kat came up behind me, sobbing.

Her wife, Bree, was by her side. Bree caught my eyes. She would take care of Kat today. It would be my job to break it to Will.

"Let Kat have your five minutes," I said. "We have nothing more to talk about."

I turned my back on Jason. As I walked away, I heard him saying pretty words to his sister that she needed to hear right now.

I did not.

"This way," Sam said. He was right. The hallway thronged with reporters. It would be even worse outside.

"Thanks for this," I said. "I never even thought this far ahead."

Sam smiled. "That's what you keep me around for."

We made our way to a service elevator. As the doors opened, two maintenance workers stepped off. There was a leak in the women's bathroom. Sam gave them a terse smile, then ushered me into the elevator. He waited for the doors to close before turning to me.

"You okay?"

I looked at him. Sam. My friend. We were still trying to figure out whether we could handle being something more. Jason's trial had forced me to put my personal life on hold. My focus was on Will. Always.

"I don't know," I answered honestly. "It's not like that verdict came as a shock. The evidence against him was airtight."

"He should have taken a plea deal," Sam said.

"He'll appeal," I said.

"He'll lose."

Sam was right.

"He should man up," Sam said. "Set aside whatever money he still has to secure Will's future. Instead, he's going to blow every cent chasing freedom he'll never get. He's guilty of all of it."

"I know," I said. "But I don't want his money. Not even for Will. We're doing fine on our own."

"Well, if you need me. If Will needs me ..."

I touched Sam's sleeve. "I know. And thank you."

The elevator doors reopened. We were on the first floor. As I stepped off, Sam took my arm, guiding me down a different hallway.

He was as good as his word. As we stepped outside into an adjacent alley, an unmarked black Explorer pulled up. Sam's US marshal friend rolled down the window.

"We parked your car right over there," he told Sam. "Take the side street off the alley and you should be good."

"Thanks," Sam said. "Give us one second though."

Sam had his phone out, reading a text. He pulled me aside, frowning.

"Some reporters have camped out in front of your house. I'm gonna send a couple of deputies out there to try to scare them off."

"If they're on the road, there's nothing to be done about it. Will's not there. He's staying with my mother in North Hampton for the week."

"Good thinking," Sam said. "So ... maybe it's better if you don't go straight home either. You can ... I've got a guest room. Why don't you crash with me?"

The offer floored me. It was sweet. Generous. But also fraught with complications.

Sam smiled. "It doesn't have to ..."

Before he could finish his thought, his phone started to ring. Before he could answer it, mine also started to buzz. I'd had it on vibrate in the courtroom.

I let mine go to voicemail as Sam took a few steps away from me and answered his call.

He said hello. Then nothing for almost thirty seconds. His face, however, went through a myriad of changes. Finally, he doubled over and let out a sound that speared me.

"Sam?" the marshal said, seeing the same thing I did. He turned off the ignition and stepped out of the car.

"Sam?" I said.

"No," Sam said to his caller. "She's still with me. Just ... get the scene secured. Nobody in or out. We're on the way."

Sam's hand shook as he clicked off his call and slipped his phone into his breast pocket.

"What is it?" I said, my pulse quickening.

"We have to get back," he said, his voice breaking. "It's ... Sheriff Clancy. Bill Clancy."

He couldn't get the words out.

"Okay? Why does the sheriff need you back so quickly?"

Sam shook his head. "He's dead, Mara. They found him. Shot through the head. Sheriff Clancy's been murdered."

2

The marshal gave us an escort, then turned off as we took the exit to Waynetown. Sam was silent the entire twenty-minute drive.

We were lucky.

No one saw us. No reporters tried to close in, asking me a million questions I didn't yet know how to answer.

How do I feel? Did I know what Jason had done? Is it true I was the one to turn against him?

It didn't matter anymore. None of it. At that moment, it only mattered that Sam's world had started to crumble.

Sheriff Bill Clancy had been Sam's friend and mentor since he joined the sheriff's department nearly twenty years ago. The man who had plucked him out of field ops and given him his detective's badge. Who had relied on Sam as his right-hand man for the last three years.

As we made the final turn to our destination, Sam turned to me.

"Stay back when we get there," he said.

"Of course."

"But keep your eyes open. I can't have any mistakes out there. If you see something, tell me."

"I will."

Sam pulled into the giant parking lot of the Dollar Kart Mega-Mart off of Warren Road. The deputies had already blocked off the main entrance and were turning cars away.

Sam slowed, rolling down his window. Deputy Al Trembly approached.

"Who's keeping the logbook?" Sam asked.

Trembly pointed to a deputy standing a few feet to his left. Detective Brody Lance approached.

"No one else goes in or out," Sam said. "What's going on inside?"

"We had the manager shut everything down," Lance said. "All the employees are inside. Everyone who was on duty when the body was found. The manager's getting us a list of every employee who's been in and out in the last twenty-four hours."

Sam nodded. "What about these cameras?" He pointed to the security cameras pointed at the four corners of the parking lot and those affixed to the Dollar Kart building.

"The two front ones aren't working. Manager is pulling the footage from the last forty-eight hours."

"Good," Sam said. "Come find me when you have something on it. I want to talk to the manager."

Lance nodded.

"Sam," I said as he pulled away and started the slow drive to the back of the parking lot. There, four marked patrol cars parked at angles around a silver Dodge Durango.

I recognized it as Bill Clancy's. He had a Semper Fi bumper sticker on his tailgate.

"Sam," I said. "You told me to say something if I saw something."

Sam screeched the car to a halt and looked at me. A vein pulsed in his neck. Thin beads of sweat dotted his forehead.

"You're acting like a detective, not a lieutenant," I said. "I just want to be sure there's no issue with the chain of command ... um ... down the road."

Sam gripped the steering wheel. He took a breath and punched the center console.

"Sam ..."

"I know. Dammit. I know."

I put a hand on his arm. His bicep was hard as stone. Coiled rage. A shadow fell over him as a figure appeared at the window.

Gus Ritter, Maumee County's longest-serving detective, tapped on the window. Sam collected himself and rolled it down.

Gus clocked me in the front seat, giving me a grim nod. "Hey, Mara."

"What the hell's happening, Gus?" Sam asked. Gus stepped away from the window and gestured Sam forward. Hesitantly, I unclipped my seatbelt, too.

My phone buzzed. I'd ignored it before, thinking it would be any number of well-meaning friends wanting to know how I was doing after the verdict.

I looked at the screen. Kenya Spaulding's contact photo popped up. Maumee County Prosecutor and my boss, I knew Kenya would want to know everything I did. I made eye contact with Gus as Sam stepped out of the car and walked up to Clancy's taped-off car.

"Hi," I said into the phone.

"Where are you?" Kenya asked.

"Out at the scene," I said, knowing Kenya would have already been fully briefed on the discovery of Bill Clancy's body. "Sam got the call right after Jason's verdict came in. We came straight here."

"Oh boy," Kenya said. "You holding up okay?"

"I'm fine," I said, knowing it would be the first of at least a hundred times I'd say those words over the next few days. "None of that matters right now."

"I'm glad you're out there," she said. "I want oversight on this."

"It's looking like Gus is lead detective," I said. "He doesn't need my oversight, Kenya."

"Gus Ritter played Euchre with Bill Clancy every Wednesday," she said. "Everyone out at that scene loves him and is going to take this thing personally."

"Good," I said as I stepped out of the car. I walked a good distance away from the crime scene tape. "Gus is exactly who we want on this case."

"Just ..." she said. "Tell them ... make sure they know ... anything they need. Expedited warrants. Anything."

"I will," I said. "For now, I'm just going to do my best to stay out of the way."

I clicked off. I knew Kenya meant well. She knew Bill. He'd been one of her biggest supporters. His recent personal endorsement of her bid for re-election would sway a giant chunk of critical voters. He'd gone against the endorsement of the command union and ruffled plenty of feathers. But he was also her friend. And mine.

I pocketed my phone and walked to the edge of the crime scene tape. Bill Clancy's car was parked at the outer edge of the Dollar Kart parking lot, straddling a yellow line and taking up two spaces. That alone seemed odd and not Bill's style.

Sam peered into the passenger window. I followed his line of sight.

Bill Clancy sat slumped over the steering wheel. The right side of his head was caked with blood. The smell of it hit me, metallic, sour. Instinctively, I covered my mouth and nose with the back of my hand.

"Through and through," Gus said, his voice cold, clinical. He shined a pen light on the wound.

"He wasn't shot here," Sam said.

"How do you know?" I asked.

Gus moved the light to the driver's side window. "The car's clean. No spatter."

My stomach turned. I took a few steps back. From that distance, I could almost convince myself that Bill was only sleeping. His buzzed blond hair glittered a bit in the direct sunlight. His hands hung slack at his sides.

Car tires squealed. A white Ford Focus pulled alongside Sam's car, the Channel 8 logo emblazoned on his side. I recognized Dave Reese behind the wheel.

"You tell that son of a bitch to turn around," Gus shouted. I saw his whole posture change. He took a ready stance.

"Let me handle it," I said, putting a hand up. Sam caught my eye and mouthed a thank you.

"Reese," I said, storming toward his car. "You can't be here right now. This is an active investigation."

Two deputies were running toward Reese's car at top speed. I knew Gus and Sam would want heads for whoever allowed Reese to slip through the checkpoint.

"That's the sheriff," Reese said. "This is a matter of public interest."

"The public's interest is served by not having you traipsing through here and potentially compromising a crime scene."

"Was he murdered?" Reese asked. "Are you going on record with that?"

"Dave," I said. "Not now. Let the deputies do their job."

"Can you confirm that's Bill Clancy in that car?" Reese asked.

"I can confirm no such thing," I said. "And if you don't get right back in your car and turn around, you're going to end up in cuffs and arrested for obstruction. I'll write the arrest warrant for them myself."

"I'm not leaving," he said. "Not until I can confirm who that is."

"Who that is," I said, "is someone with a family who hasn't yet been notified. Do you understand what I'm telling you? You're not going to get what you want out here. You're only going to end up cuffed in the back of a patrol car."

To prove my point, the two deputies flanked Reese. A quick gesture from Sam and one of them started pulling out his cuffs. Reese had his cell phone out, recording the entire exchange.

"Put that away," I said.

"Give me a reason," Reese said, challenging me.

I looked back at Sam and Gus. Red-eared, both of them. I knew this would quickly escalate into a circus if I didn't do something.

"Listen," I turned to Reese. "I'll give you a different scoop, okay?"

Reese kept his phone up, recording me. I looked helplessly back at Gus and Sam. The last thing any of us needed was a scuffle twenty feet away from an active crime scene.

"I'll give you an exclusive," I said. "You know where I just came from. You know there was a team of reporters on the federal courthouse steps waiting to get a quote from me. So,

I'll give it to you. Sixty seconds. You can record it and post it online. But not here. Point that thing somewhere else."

Reese looked behind him. There was a small, reflecting pond with a footbridge and benches at the north edge of the lot. A concession made by Dollar Kart corporate to the neighborhood abutting their parking lot. Reese put down his phone and waved me over to the benches. I straightened my jacket and followed him.

"Sixty seconds," I said. "That's all. Then you'll turn that thing off, drive away, and keep your mouth shut until the victim's family can be notified. We clear?"

Reese took his phone back out, pointed it at me, and started recording.

"Mrs. Brent," he said. "Can you comment on the verdict rendered today in your husband's RICO trial?"

"I'm glad that justice was served," I said. "My ex-husband isn't above the law any more than the rest of us. It was a difficult day for my family, but once again, I'm heartened by the fact that the criminal justice system worked in this case."

"So you're happy he's going to jail?" Reese asked. I kept a neutral smile in place.

"I'll reiterate. I'm satisfied that justice was served. I'm never happy when someone goes to jail."

"Have you spoken to your husband since the verdict?"

"Jason Brent and I are no longer married," I said. "And no. We have not spoken."

"But you were in the courtroom when the verdict was rendered. You were there to show your support for him, weren't you?"

"I was there at the request of the federal prosecutor," I said.

"How is your son taking the news?" Reese asked. I wanted to slap him.

"My son is a minor. And I would hope that people would respect his and my privacy during this difficult time."

"Are you planning to take him back?" Reese asked.

"What?"

"Jason. Are you planning to forgive him and take him back after all of this?"

"I'm focused on raising my son," I said. "And I'm focused on serving the people of Maumee County in my role as an assistant prosecutor. As I always have."

"How are you going to do that if you end up indicted, too?"

"What?"

I saw Sam starting to walk toward us. If he heard Reese's question, I knew Sam might not be able to hold his temper. I took a breath and found my center.

"Your sixty seconds are up, Mr. Reese."

"Do you still love him?" Reese asked. He hadn't yet turned off his camera.

"Enough," I said. Sam's deputies moved in.

Reese put down his phone. With a smarmy smile, he pocketed it and walked back to his car.

19

I waited until he'd rolled up the window and drove off before turning to Sam.

"I'll kill that little weasel," Sam said. "What did he say to you?"

"Nothing I can't handle," I said. "He's spoiling for a fight though. And he knows it's Bill Clancy lying dead in that car, Sam. He promised he wouldn't run with it until you've had a chance to inform the family. I'm not sure I trust him."

Sam nodded. "I need to get to Shanna, Bill's wife. I need to tell her what happened in person."

God. Shanna Clancy. I couldn't imagine how difficult it would be if she opened her phone and saw the news leaked of Bill's death. It was unconscionable.

"Come on," Sam said. "It might be good if you were there for her when I tell her. She likes you."

Nodding, I took Sam's offered hand. As rough a day as it had been for me, Shanna Clancy was about to have her worst nightmare come true.

3

In law school, you learn how to analyze and argue. But they never teach you how to actually be a lawyer. They never teach you the single most important skill we must master. How to counsel ... or simply *be* with someone on the very worst day of their life. That you can only learn by doing it. And it never gets easier. Never.

Bill Clancy lived down a quiet country road in the middle of Maumee County. The kind of place you'd never find with your GPS. The kind of place you probably passed by a thousand times yet never knew anyone lived back there. Not even the mailman stopped here.

Sam slowed his car and pulled up on the side of the road.

"I want to wait for our chaplain," he said. His voice was flat, emotionless. He white-knuckled the steering wheel. He'd been like that since the moment we arrived in that Dollar Kart parking lot.

"Sam," I said. "Look at me."

He didn't. He simply stared straight ahead.

"Sam ..." I said quietly. Finally, he at least let go of the steering wheel.

"Thank you for what you did back there," he said.

"What I did?"

"With Reese. I know that cost you something, letting him put you on camera. I know you didn't want to."

"It was a fair price," I said. "And a small one. Shanna Clancy shouldn't have to hear this from anyone but you."

Sam squeezed his eyes shut. It was just a moment. A wave of grief seemed to go through him. He took a breath and gripped the steering wheel again.

"Not now," he said. "I don't have time for that now. Bill ... years ago ... there's a form we have to fill out. In case ..."

"Sam, you don't have to ..."

"We designate someone. A family liaison in the event one of us is killed in the line of duty. It's me, Mara. For Bill, he chose me."

My heart broke for him. I knew it was taking every ounce of strength Sam had not to give in to his own pain.

A question came to mind. One I didn't yet dare ask. Sam had no family. His parents had passed away years ago. No siblings. No children. Who had he designated if something happened to him?

Gravel crunched as another car came to a stop directly behind Sam's. I looked over my shoulder. Pete Grady stepped out. Reverend Pete. He was the pastor for First Presbyterian

Church on Cleveland Street. He volunteered as the police chaplain for the Maumee County Sheriff's Department. His father, Pete Sr., had served as sheriff more than thirty years ago.

Reverend Pete was forty years old but looked perpetually twenty, with thick blond hair that stuck up in a swirl of cowlicks. He had rosy cheeks and a broad face with lips that curled, making him look happy even when he wasn't. His was a comforting face. Not especially handsome, but kind.

He slipped out of his suit jacket and laid it on the front seat as he walked up to Sam's car.

"Hop in," Sam said. "We'll go up there together."

Reverend Pete gave me a tight-lipped smile. "Good morning, Mara. It's good you're here."

I reached over the back seat and shook Pete's hand as he slid in. Sam put his car in gear and made the slow drive up Bill Clancy's quarter mile wooded driveway.

Clancy had lived in a cabin for most of his life, having inherited the land from his father. Bill had never wanted more than the one-bedroom house built here over a hundred years ago. Then, a decade or so ago, Bachelor Bill met the love of his life and built a beautiful, two-story home for her.

"They meant to have kids," Sam said, as if he could read my thoughts. "God. I never thought Bill would be that guy. He swore he wanted to just live in that cabin alone."

The cabin was still there, down a deeper trail behind the main house.

Reverend Pete got out first. He came around and opened my door for me. I smiled up at him and stepped out. It took Sam a moment. We could be there, Pete and me. But it would fall to Sam to deliver the news.

He got out, rising to his full height, squaring his shoulders. Sam walked up to the front door. He rang the bell.

Pete and I fell in step behind Sam. I let out a breath, feeling my palms sweat.

It took a moment, but finally, Shanna Clancy peered out of a side window. Her face lit up when she saw Sam. From her vantage point, I didn't think she could see Pete or me yet.

The door swung open. Shanna Clancy was pretty. Light-brown hair that framed her face. Deep dimples and a ready smile. She and Bill couldn't have seemed more different on the outside. He was gruff, silent, an old-school marine who said what he thought, even if it wasn't the most diplomatic. Shanna was bright, bubbly, loving the local limelight that came with being the wife of a small-town sheriff. Her smiling wave as she sat in the lead car in every town parade had become a familiar, welcoming sight.

Today, Shanna wore a purple terry-cloth jumpsuit, her hair pulled back in a ponytail. Her cheeks were flushed as if she'd just stepped off the treadmill. She likely had.

"Sam," she said. "Bill's not back yet. I'm so sorry if you're looking for him."

Just then, a stocky little chocolate-colored French Bulldog raced down the hallway. She skidded to a halt at Shanna's feet. Shanna leaned down to pick her up. The dog started licking her face.

"Have you met Daisy?" Shanna said. "She's a lover not a fighter."

"Shanna," Sam said. "Do you mind if we come in?"

It was then she noticed Reverend Pete and me. There was just a small flicker, the tiniest quiver in her smile. She kept it in place though.

"Mara! Oh my. You poor thing. Oh. Come inside. I was watching the news during my morning spin class. You two were at the courthouse. Can I ... oh. Oh dear."

We stepped inside. Bill had installed a beautiful, black slate tile floor in the two-story foyer. Shanna led us into the kitchen.

"Can I get you something to drink?" she asked. She had not yet reacted to the presence of Reverend Pete. Her voice had taken on a high-pitched lilt. It was as if her brain were protecting her, not allowing her to connect the dots as to why we might be here. "Let me just put Daisy outside."

Shanna opened the slider off the kitchen and let the dog out. I saw pain etched on Sam's face. He reached for Shanna and guided her to a stool at the massive granite waterfall island in the center of the room.

"Shanna," he said. "I've got something hard to tell you. It's Bill. Shanna ... he's gone."

Her lashes fluttered. Still, she kept her smile in place. She began to shake her head almost violently.

"He said he had to go into work last night. I missed him this morning when I woke up. I'll just call him. He isn't ..."

"Shanna," Sam said. "I need you to hear me. Bill is gone. He was found this morning in his car. He was shot."

"No," she said. "Nope. No."

Shanna popped off her stool. She walked away from Sam and to her farm-style sink. She took a coffee pot off the drying rack and started to fill it.

"You look like you could use some coffee," she said. "Mara, I don't know how you're handling all of this. I've been worried about you. Bill too. You know he'll be there ... anything you need. I'm sure those media vultures are going to circle."

"Shanna," I said, approaching her. "I'm so sorry. But Bill's gone. It's just as Sam said. He ..."

She went rigid. With the water still running, Shanna Clancy stepped away from the sink. A shudder went through her. A strangled cry. Then she dropped the coffee pot. It shattered all over the floor.

Sam rushed forward. He got his arms around Shanna as her legs gave out. She sank against him, letting out a moan that seared through me.

Sam led Shanna away from the broken glass. He took her to the kitchen table and helped her into a chair. She sobbed against him as I busied myself picking up the shards of glass.

After a few minutes, Shanna came back into herself. Tears streamed down her face, but she was ready to listen.

"What happened?" she asked.

"We don't know," Sam answered. "Not yet. Gus Ritter is going to handle this case."

She nodded but her eyes stayed wide.

"He was working?" she asked. "He was ... he left at like three in the morning. He got a call. He told me he'd be back late."

"Okay," Sam said. "Gus is going to come talk to you about all of that. For now, there's nothing you need to do. Okay? Reverend Pete is going to stay with you. I'm going to send a couple of deputies to stay outside the house. If you need anything ..."

"Need?" she said. "What do I need?" She made eye contact with me as she asked.

I wiped my hands on a towel and went to her, taking the chair beside her.

"What am I supposed to do?" she asked me. Shanna had turned away from Sam and Pete. Instead, she latched on to me. "What do we do?"

"For now," I said. "Nothing. You let us do it. Do you have family? Friends you'd like us to call? Can you write it down?"

Pete sprang into action. He found a pad of paper and pen on the counter and brought it over.

"I need my phone," she said.

It was sitting on a charger on the same counter. Pete grabbed that, too.

"Bill's sister," she said. "You know Olivia?"

Sam nodded. "I'll arrange for someone to get to her. She still lives in Tampa?"

Shanna nodded. "We haven't seen her in years. I only met her once after we got married. She was older. In her seventies, I think. She had a stroke. Oh. No. No. No." She buried her face in her hands. I kept a hand on her back. Her heartbeat hammered.

"I'm so sorry," she said to me. "Today of all days. You probably need to be somewhere else."

"I'm fine," I said.

"No," she said. "You're not fine. You've ... you lost your husband today too, didn't you?"

The question took me aback. My husband. I had lost him years ago. At least the man I thought he was. Shanna's day and mine weren't the same at all. And yet, in a strange way, I knew what she meant. It caught me. Took the air from my lungs for a moment.

That day, in Bill Clancy's kitchen, Shanna looked to me for comfort. At the same time, she offered it to me. I took her hand. Squeezed it.

"You'll find out who did this?" she said to Sam.

Sam's jaw went hard. "Yes," he said. One word. A promise.

"And you?" she said to me. "You promise me you'll make them pay?"

I met Sam's eyes. Our pact. Sam and I. I turned back to Shanna and gave her the answer she desperately needed. That I needed.

"Yes."

4

Kenya wouldn't sit. She stood behind her desk, gripping the back of her chair as if it were a ship's wheel and she was the captain. In a way, she was headed for an iceberg. Six months from now, she faced re-election against an opponent rising in the polls. Skip Fletcher was part of a wave of candidates promising to drain the swamp of Maumee County politicians. The message had started to resonate with voters unfairly blaming Kenya for the failings of her predecessor. I'd heard a rumor that Mayor O'Keefe secretly backed him.

"He's late," she said, letting her eyes flick to the clock on the wall.

"He's had his hands full, Kenya," I said. I sat on the leather couch against the far wall. Seated in front of Kenya's desk was Howard Jordan, the only other assistant prosecutor in the county besides me.

"They're sure he didn't just off himself?" Hojo asked. "I mean, why park way out in the corner of the Dollar Kart Mega-Mart?"

"There was no blood in the car," I said. "I saw it with my own eyes. He was ... shot through the temple. Gus thinks there would have been blood on the window if he'd done it right there. Plus, his service weapon was holstered at his side."

There was a quiet knock on the door. A young woman I didn't recognize poked her head inside. Young. Flawless skin and makeup that looked professionally done. She also looked barely older than my son, Will. For a split second, I assumed she was a reporter.

"Ms. Spaulding," she said. "Caro told me to check with you on whether you wanted me sitting in."

Kenya shot me a glance. She found a smile and looked back at the girl. "Next time," she said. "For today, just have Caro show you where to find everything."

The girl looked disappointed, but gave Kenya a smile as she quietly excused herself and shut the door.

"That's Mercedes. I suppose I should have introduced you," Kenya said to me. "We've got a new intern. Her father is ..."

My stomach dropped. "No," I said. "I don't even want to know. Not if you're gonna tell me she's a nepotism hire."

It was probably unfair of me to prejudge. But our office had been cursed where interns were concerned. The last one had ended with the need for a restraining order.

"Relax," she said. "I'll keep her out of your way for now. We've all got enough on our plates today."

"Thank you," I said. "Send her to Herc Manfield. Let her help him with appellate briefs. He could use it."

"We need more manpower here," she said. "With what's coming down the pike ... ugh. Where the hell is Sam?"

"He'll be here," I repeated.

Kenya squeezed the bridge of her nose. "I need information. I need to know who's in charge. I'm fielding calls left and right. We need to project order. Right now, we're projecting chaos."

"Kenya," I said. "Sam will be here. He said he would. Bill was his friend, too."

She tucked her head to her chest. I was afraid she'd break her chair in half with how hard she gripped it.

"I know," she said. "He was a friend to all of us. This loss is personal. But I'm afraid that might also be the problem."

"There's no problem." Sam's booming voice caught all of us off guard. He filled the door frame. I didn't like what I saw. He was clean-shaven, wearing a pressed shirt, but his eyes were hollow, his face almost gaunt. It meant he hadn't likely eaten much or slept at all in the thirty-six hours since Sheriff Bill Clancy's body had been found.

"Sam," Kenya said. "I didn't mean ..."

"I know what you meant," he said. "I also know you're under political pressure with this. But that's your problem, not mine."

Kenya came around her chair and finally sat down. She gestured to the chair beside Hojo. Sam avoided it, taking a seat on the other end of the couch from me.

"Thanks for coming down here," Kenya said. "I know there are other places you need to be."

"I'm doing my job," Sam said. "Briefing you is part of my job."

I wanted to put a calming hand on his shoulder. But Sam and I had been discreet about our budding relationship. He was in pain. It tore at me.

"Tell me what you can," Kenya said. "For starters, who's acting sheriff? That's the question I'm getting most often."

"I am," Sam said. I drew in a sharp intake of air. This was news to me. I hadn't seen or spoken to Sam since we left Shanna Clancy's house.

"Good," Kenya said. "That will go a long way toward reassuring the people ..."

"You mean the voters," Sam said.

"Sam," I said quietly. "We're all on the same team. I think Kenya wants to make sure you know you have our support."

He dropped his shoulders just a fraction. "I know. I'm sorry."

"Forget it," Kenya said. "Tensions are high. I know how much Bill meant to you on a personal level. It's understandable if ..."

"Ritter's lead," Sam said. "He's coordinating with the Ohio Bureau of Criminal Investigations. They've put Clancy's murder at the top of every priority list they have. They got out to the scene about an hour after Gus did. We're crossing every tee here."

"So you're certain we're dealing with a homicide?" Hojo asked. "There's no doubt."

"No doubt," Sam said. "No gun residue on his hands. Bullet didn't come from any of his own guns. No spatter pattern in his car. He was killed somewhere else and placed in that vehicle."

"What about security footage from the Dollar Kart?" I asked.

"We're analyzing it now," Sam said. "Bill's car was parked in a corner where the cameras don't have a clear shot."

"Someone knew what they were doing," Hojo said.

"What about the wife?" Kenya asked. "Has Gus finished interviewing her?"

"Shanna's in pretty rough shape," Sam said. "But she's been cooperating as well as she can. She said Bill got a call in the middle of the night. Like two or three in the morning. It was brief. He stepped out of the room. She woke up. He came in and told her he got a call from the office and had to go in. Told her not to worry. Gave her a kiss on the forehead, then never came back."

"I hate to say it," Kenya said. "But does his wife have an alibi?"

"Like I said, she's been cooperating. Bill had a million security cameras all throughout the house. Shanna never left. We've got footage of her letting their dog out a couple of times in the middle of the night and in the early hours of the morning. She was home last night."

"Have you traced that call that came in?" Kenya asked.

"BCI is working on it. We haven't been able to locate Bill's phone yet. Waiting on the results of Gus's subpoena to the cell phone company. I expect something by the end of the day.

But I can tell you nobody from the department called Bill that night. It was quiet. Nothing urgent that would have required hauling the sheriff out of bed in the dead of night."

"Who found the body?" I asked.

"A store employee. The kid they had running carts. Poor girl's traumatized. Fifteen years old. She went after a loose cart at the end of the lot. Happened by Bill's car."

"How awful," I said.

"Do you have any instincts on this one?" Hojo asked. "Were things good with the wife? Did he have any recent death threats?"

"He was the sheriff," Sam said. "We always get crackpots making threats. I can assure you, we're running down all of them. But to answer your question, no. I don't have any solid instincts on this one. He and Shanna were good. Happy. They suffered a blow a year or so ago trying to have a kid. But they were in a good place. Shanna's been amazing for him. Put ten years back on Bill's life if you ask me."

His voice dropped at the end. It was hard, thinking of Bill Clancy in the past tense.

"What are you doing for her?" Kenya asked. "Is there anything she needs from us?"

"She likes Mara," Sam said. "I think if you'd let her know she can reach out to you if she has any questions, that would bring her some comfort. She's got deputies with her round the clock. One of 'em's out there cutting her grass as we speak. Reverend Pete, our chaplain, has been doing most of the heavy lifting in terms of being a go-between with my office. I'm going to lean on him pretty heavily over the next few days."

"That's good," Kenya said. "And Sam, thank you. I know you're needed across the street. I won't keep you. Please, I meant what I said. Anything you need from this office, you get a hold of me or Mara. Bill deserves the best from all of us."

Sam rose. I got up too, hoping to steal a moment alone with him. Hoping he'd let me in enough to make him dinner or something tonight. Whatever I had to do to get food in him.

Sam excused himself. I followed him into the hall.

"Don't," he said.

"Don't what?"

"Don't tell me I need to eat or sleep. I know what I look like. It doesn't matter. We're in the first forty-eight hours of this thing. Every second I'm not helping Gus or doing something for Shanna ..."

"Okay. Okay. I won't say it. Just, this is me. Okay? I'm going to be keeping an eye on you."

He nodded. "Fine. I appreciate it. I have to get back."

No sooner had he said it than his phone buzzed.

"Gus," he answered, turning away from me. Sam's back went stiff as he listened to whatever Gus Ritter imparted.

"I'll be there in two minutes," Sam said, then clicked off the phone. His whole posture changed. I could almost feel an electrical charge coming off him. Something had happened. Something big.

"I've gotta go," he said.

"Sam, what is it?"

"Not now," he answered. "When I have something to tell you, I will. I promise."

There was no one in the hallway. Kenya's door was closed behind me. I took that moment to reach for Sam and pull him into a hug. It was brief, but I felt him go a little slack in my arms before he stiffened again and pulled away. His grief was there simmering below the surface. But someday soon, I knew it would explode.

He gave me a grim nod, then headed for the elevators.

5

In the three days since Jason's verdict, my son had asked me no questions. He had simply listened, motionless, expressionless, while I told him what it meant. Now, as we stood in the kitchen, two minutes before the bus was due to come, he asked his first question.

"Will you take me to see him?"

I froze, holding my coffee cup, my briefcase already slung over my shoulder.

"Is that what you want?" I asked.

He sat down at the table. From the corner of my eye, I saw the bus pull up to our circular driveway. I knew my son. I also knew what his therapist and mine had cautioned about how to handle all of this.

Let him ask the questions. Answer what he asks honestly.

I went to the front door, opened it, and made eye contact with the driver. I waved her off. Smiling, she nodded her understanding and drove away.

"Okay," I said. "Do you want to go see your dad?"

Will stared straight ahead. His face might have been made out of glass. He processed his things his own way. The hardest part, as his mother, was knowing when he wanted me to just listen, and when he wanted me to offer advice.

"I don't know," he finally said. "I suppose he wants me to want to."

"It's not about him," I said. "You're allowed to feel your own feelings. You don't have to manage his."

I reached for him, not touching him. But I put my hand next to his. It was our way. Enough that he knew I was there, but Will didn't always do well when other people initiated affection.

"I know," he said. "But do you think he's scared?"

I took a breath. "Yes. I think he probably is."

"Does he have a roommate? Er ... I mean ... a cell mate?"

"I don't know," I said. "Probably."

"There's overcrowding at the federal penitentiary in Milan. He's probably got a cellmate. Do you think he'll have to get into fights?"

The truth was, I didn't know. He was asking the questions I wondered about myself. Jason was in a maximum security federal prison. He was getting no special treatment in theory. At the same time, he was still technically a United States congressman.

"I'm not sure," I said. "I trust that the prison will try to make sure that doesn't happen."

Will nodded. "But ... how will it work? If I wanted to go see him?"

"I would arrange it with the prison. We would go to a special visitor's room. You'd sit at a table and talk to your dad. Just like normal."

"It wouldn't be through glass? With a phone on the wall?"

"No," I said. "I can make sure you'd just sit at a table and be able to talk to him. But it won't be for a while. Your dad is probably going to be moved around a little."

"Did he ask about me?" Will asked.

"I didn't get much of a chance to talk to him in court," I said. "But yes. He wants to make sure you're okay. That we're okay."

"Then he shouldn't have committed those crimes," Will said, his voice taking a hard edge.

I knew what Jason would do if given the chance. He would make excuses. Tell Will he'd been set up or framed. Or that the things they said about him were flat-out lies perpetrated by his enemies. Someday, Will would grow to understand that his father ... for whatever else he was ... was a liar. But he would never hear those words from me.

"I know," I said. "It's hard. But we're going to find our way through it. Okay?"

"Sheriff Clancy's dead," he said.

"Yes."

"Are you going to catch whoever did it?"

"Well, it won't be my job to do that. Detective Ritter is going to try."

"What about Sam?"

"He's very sad," I said. "Sheriff Clancy was his friend."

Will nodded. He furrowed his brow. Turning the puzzle over in his mind. Then he looked at me.

"I missed the bus."

"I can drive you," I said. "If we leave now, you'll still make it on time."

"You'll be late for work."

"My boss will understand."

Will grabbed his backpack off the chair, slung it over one shoulder, then walked with me out to the garage.

I let go of a breath I hadn't realized I'd been holding. This was the first of very many hard conversations I would have with Will. I just prayed he could handle all of it without regressing. He'd come so far in the last few years through the turmoil of my divorce. And then learning that his father wasn't the man either of us had thought he was.

As I pulled out of the driveway, my son reached for me. He threaded his hand through mine. I drove him left-handed, all the way to school.

6

Two hours later, I stood in the conference room on the first floor of the Maumee County Sheriff's building. It was the largest space they had, and Sam had turned it into a command center for Bill Clancy's murder investigation.

Sam sat at the head of the long conference table, holding a remote control. On the far wall, he'd mounted a giant flat-screen television. The first meeting of Sam's task force had just adjourned. He'd called me in to give me the highlights. Both the mayor and Kenya insisted we get daily briefings on the status of the investigation.

"The middle-of-the-night call came back untraceable," Gus said. "It came from a burner phone."

"A burner phone," I said. "So you're telling me Bill got a call in the middle of the night from a burner phone? Lied to his wife about it. Then left to meet probably his murderer?"

Sam clicked play on the remote control. It was security camera footage from Bill Clancy's house. It showed him leaving at 2:49 a.m. the morning he was found dead.

"He's not in uniform," I said. "Shanna said he told her he was called into work. But he's wearing jeans and a tee shirt. She didn't think to question that?"

"She was barely awake," Gus said. "She went back to sleep after he got out of bed."

Sam fast forwarded the video. Dark clouds rolled over the Clancy house after Bill sped off in his car.

"That wasn't his departmental vehicle," I said. "So he doesn't wear his uniform, and he doesn't use a county car. But he tells his wife he's heading to work?"

A few frames forward, the back door opened again and Shanna Clancy came outside to let Daisy the French bulldog out at 4:00 a.m., then again at 6:00 a.m. No vehicles came or went from the house until later that afternoon, when Sam and I pulled up. He clicked off the video right as the camera picked up Reverend Pete stepping out of Sam's car.

"Was he seeing someone?" I asked. "I know Bill and Shanna seemed happy. But how well do you really know?"

"She gave us her phone too," Gus said. "Her laptop and Bill's. All the passwords. The credit card bills. There's just nothing that raises any red flags. That doesn't mean Bill couldn't have been lying to her. His comings and goings over the few weeks prior to this ... it's boring. Normal."

"He goes to work. He comes home. That was Bill," Sam said. "He was happiest at home. Didn't play golf unless it was for a charity event. Gus says he even stopped coming to their weekly Euchre games as much. He hated going out. Hated feeling like he had to be Sheriff Clancy when he did. He told me he felt like he could never really be off duty."

"There was always some clown wanting to complain to Bill about something when he went out. He hated even going grocery shopping anymore," Gus said. "But he liked being married. I was just as surprised as anyone else. Thought Bill would stay a bachelor forever. But Shanna made him happy. She wasn't one of those wives that nagged. She let him do his thing. Pitched in at all the cop fundraisers. She volunteers with the Friends of the Police League. All that crap."

"That's going to serve her well," I said. "She has a lot of support in this community. She's not alone."

Sam picked up the remote again and clicked through to another screen. More security footage, this time from the Dollar Kart Mega-Mart parking lot.

"You don't see Bill's car coming in," Sam said.

"They knew," I said. "Whoever it was knew that corner of the lot wasn't accessible from the cameras."

"We've interviewed every store employee," Gus said. "Present and recently former. So far, I'm hitting dead ends with that."

"There's just this," Sam said. He fast forwarded to the time frame at 6:58 a.m. A beat-up, blue van could be seen entering the parking lot from the north end, closest to where Bill Clancy's car had been parked.

"What am I looking at?" I asked.

Sam paused the video.

"There," Gus said, using a red laser pointer to circle the driver's side window. I squinted, trying to make out the figure. I could only tell that he was male and that he was white.

Sam advanced the video. Five minutes and nineteen seconds later, the same vehicle could be seen exiting the parking lot on the same west side. Sam paused it. Gus used his laser pointer.

"I see," I said, tilting my head to the side. This time, I could make out two figures in the front seat.

"Store doesn't open until 8:00 a.m.," Gus said. "The first employee got there twenty minutes after that vehicle left. The delivery trucks came a few minutes after that."

"So who is it?" I asked.

"Manager requires every employee to register their vehicle. They get a parking pass for the south end of the lot. This van isn't registered to any employee."

Sam advanced the video a little more, then froze it at the clearest shot of the van's tail lights.

"It's too blurry to make out the plate," I said. "Can you have someone clear it up at all?"

"We're working on that," Sam said. "BCI works with software developed by NASA. We were told not to get our hopes up too much. There's a lot of glare from the sun. It rose at 6:53 that morning."

"Seven. Or a one? And that's maybe an X next to it," I said. I could read the two characters on the far right of the plate, but that was all.

"That's what we see too," Sam said.

Gus's phone rang. He looked at the caller ID. "That's BCI now."

He rushed out of the room to take the call.

"That's all you have, then?" I asked.

"It's a solid lead," Sam said.

"If you can find the driver of that van. You're not even sure Bill's car was parked in the lot when that van came through. How is it that the store doesn't have security cameras pointing at every single way in or out of that lot? I mean, what's the point of even having them then?"

"There's a dirt road on the west end of the lot. It's an old bike path. You're not supposed to drive cars down it. But we found tire treads matching Bill's car."

"So the killer drove him in," I said. "Maybe called a buddy to come pick him up."

"That's the working theory anyway," Sam said.

"It just doesn't make any sense. Why leave him there? Where he would for sure be found and quickly."

"It wasn't quick," Sam muttered. "It's almost three hours from when that van drove out to when he was found. The cart attendant found him just after ten. We don't know for sure when his car was driven there. Just that it was sometime after he left his house and 10:15 a.m. when he was found."

Gus walked in, cheeks flushed, chest heaving.

"We've got something," he said. "They've got a partial on the blue van. There's only one in the county. Registered to a Rick Wahl over on Broad Street."

Sam looked at me.

"Go!" I said. "Don't worry about me."

Sam twirled his coat on and raced with Gus straight out the door.

7

Ricky Wahl was about to have a very bad day. He came willingly, at least. At Kenya's request and Sam's okay, I sat behind the one-way mirror looking into the interview room as Gus Ritter made Ricky wait for him.

He was just a kid. Twenty-two. Ricky chewed on his thumbnail and wouldn't stop banging his knee against the table leg.

"He's using?" I whispered to Sam. He'd just sat down next to me. "Sam, if he's high ..."

"He's not," Sam said. "He's just nervous."

Gus walked into the room holding a yellow legal pad. He smoothed his tie over his bulging belly, then sat down across from Ricky Wahl.

"Thanks for coming in," Gus said. "I'll try and get you along your way as soon as possible."

"Do I have a choice?" Ricky asked.

"You walked in here on your own," Gus said. "You're free to walk out. I'm not stopping you. Is that what you want to do?"

"You're gonna just keep asking me the same questions," Ricky said.

"I've asked you one so far," Gus said. He pulled a color printout he had tucked into his legal pad and slid it in front of Ricky. "This is your van, isn't it?"

Ricky leaned forward. "Can't tell. Picture's too blurry."

"What kind of van do you drive?"

"That could be anyone," Ricky said.

"That's not what I asked you."

"Look," Ricky said. He started banging his knee even harder. "I know what you're doing. I saw on the news. You're trying to figure out who killed that sheriff. Is that what you brought me in here for? I had nothing to do with that."

"I'm asking you about your van, Ricky, that's all. As soon as I can clear that up, the sooner I'll be done asking questions."

"I've got a blue Uplander."

"Is this you?" Gus slid another photo in front of Ricky. Another still shot from the Dollar Kart security footage. Ricky leaned forward but didn't answer.

"Ricky," Gus said. "Do you remember your day on April 15th? Last Thursday morning?"

Ricky shrugged. "I work on Thursdays."

"That's for Braxton Windows, right? You work on the production line?"

"Yeah," he said.

"That's over in the east end of the county," Gus said, making casual notes on his pad.

"Yeah. Split shift. Sometimes second."

"What about last week?"

"I worked split," Ricky answered.

"When do you go in?"

"Depends. One o'clock is my usual start time but sometimes my boss, Mr. Hyden, has me come in at noon. I usually get off at eight unless I'm working over."

"What time did you go on Thursday?" Gus asked.

"I don't remember."

"So if I talked to Marty Hyden, he'd be able to tell me for sure? I went to high school with Marty. He's a good guy. You like working for him?"

"Good for you," Ricky said.

"Ricky, if I ask Marty Hyden whether you were late for work on Thursday, what kind of answer am I going to get?"

"How should I know what Mr. Hyden's answer will be? I was at work on Thursday. That's all I know. If anyone says different, they're lying."

"But this is your van, isn't it?" Gus said.

"I don't know," Ricky said. "I told you. It's blurry. It looks like mine but I can't say if it's mine. Where is this? When is this?"

"He's going in circles," I whispered to Sam.

"Give him time. Gus is just giving the kid a chance to lie."

"Ricky," Gus said. "I'll level with you. I already talked to Marty. He told me you didn't show up to work on time last Thursday. He told me he never saw you. He told me that you're one more screw-up away from getting fired."

Ricky started chewing his thumb again.

"Missing work isn't a crime," Ricky said.

"No. No, it's not. But lying to the cops is."

"Careful," I whispered.

"I ain't told a single lie."

"Ricky, why were you late for work Thursday morning?"

"I overslept."

"You overslept. Do you live with anybody?"

"I live with my dad."

"Was he home that morning?"

"I don't remember. I don't always see him."

"So, if I asked your dad about Thursday morning, would he be able to confirm your comings and goings?"

"You'd have to ask him," Ricky said.

Gus slammed his pen down.

"Ricky, I'm glad you came in to talk to me on your own. That's a good start. But if you don't start leveling with me about where you were Thursday morning, we're gonna have a problem."

"I don't need to say nothing to you. I know my rights."

"Good," Gus said. He shoved one of the van pictures closer to Ricky.

"Now, look again. Is that your van? Is that you driving it?"

Ricky shoved it back. "You tell me. Seems like you know the answers to the questions you're asking me. Not even sure why I had to show up at all."

"You didn't. You're right. Did your dad tell you to?"

Ricky crossed his arms in front of him and looked at the door.

"Fine," Gus said. "You're right. I should just go ask your dad about all of this. Why don't you sit tight while I go call him? Steven Wahl, right? He volunteers at the Elm Street Mission, doesn't he? I see him in there lots."

No answer from Ricky. Gus sat back and pulled out his cell phone. He punched in a number and waited.

"Hey, Bud? This is Gus Ritter down at the sheriff's department. Yeah. Hi. I know. I'll get down there next week. Promise. Hey. Is Steven Wahl volunteering this afternoon? Can you put him on? I've got his son sitting here in front of me and ..."

"I was late, okay?" Ricky shouted. "I was late for work Thursday. I told you. I overslept!"

Gus held the phone out. "Ricky, your dad's on the line. He said he wants to talk to you before he talks to me."

Gus put the phone between them and clicked on the speaker button.

"Mr. Wahl?" Gus said. "I've got Ricky here ..."

"Ricky?" Steven Wahl said other things, but from behind the one-way glass, I couldn't make it out. Whatever he said caused Ricky to scoot his chair back almost violently.

"I don't have to talk to you," Ricky said. "I told you. I know my rights."

"Sam," I said. "Gus needs to end this. If he asks for ..."

"I want a lawyer!" Ricky shouted. He walked right up to the glass and pounded on it, flat-palmed.

"You hear me?" Ricky shouted. "Lawyer! Law ... yer!"

"Sam," I said.

"What's the matter, Ricky?" Gus said. "I thought we were just having a friendly conversation?"

"I didn't do nothing wrong. I was late for work. That was it. That ain't a crime."

"Ricky!" Steven Wahl was still on the line, shouting at his son. Ricky went to the table, picked up Gus's phone. Gus got up and tried to grab it back. Ricky shoved Gus. Then he flung the phone against the far wall with enough force to shatter the screen.

Gus moved like a tornado. He grabbed Ricky, wrenched one of his arms behind him, and pushed him forward until his cheek pressed against the wall.

"Sam!"

"Gus!" Sam yelled at the same time I did.

He leapt out of his seat and stormed into the hallway. A second later, he burst through the door to the interview room.

"Gus," Sam said. Gus's face sent a cold shock of fear through me. He was incensed. Eyes red. Cheeks flaming. Ricky snorted and wheezed as Gus held him in place.

"He broke my arm! He's breaking my damn arm!"

Sam got to him. He put a hand on Gus's shoulder. For the briefest of moments, it was like Gus was in some other dimension. He was gone. Then, slowly, he loosened his grip on Ricky Wahl. Ricky slid out of his grasp and ran out the door.

I waited, letting Sam talk Gus down, but my own blood boiled.

"Gus," Sam said. "Take a breath. That kid's not worth it."

"He's lying." Gus said. "He knows something."

I straightened my suit jacket and joined Gus and Sam in the interview room. Gus took one look at me and hung his head.

"Gus," I said calmly, walking toward him. I stooped down and picked up his shattered phone. I placed it on the table.

"Don't say it," he said. "I don't even want to hear it, Mara."

"Gus," I said. "You've got to get a hold of yourself."

"I didn't do anything wrong," Gus said.

"Well, now he's asked for a lawyer. There will be no more questioning of that boy without one present. Okay? Promise me."

"He was there," Gus said. "That was him driving that van."

"Until you get a picture with a better resolution, I can't prove that," I said. "And even if it was him driving it, it's not enough.

It's too early, Gus. Any half-good defense attorney would be able to suppress that van footage at this point. You need proof that Bill's body was even in that lot when that van went through. You can't. Not yet."

"He knows something," Gus said. "I feel that in my bones."

"Your bones aren't enough to get me past a suppression hearing."

Sam shot me a look. His unspoken message was clear. He wanted me to leave so he could handle Gus on his own.

I couldn't leave things with Gus as they were.

"Gus," I said. "Emotions are running high. I get that. It's just …"

"Enough," Gus said. "Save me the lecture."

Gus shrugged Sam off, then blew past the both of us, storming into the hall.

"I think you'd better take off for now," Sam said. "Let Gus blow off some steam."

"I'm on his side," I said. "I'm on yours too. But there was a reason Kenya insisted that I sit in on this today. She's worried about Gus. So am I. If he can't get a hold of this …"

"He will," Sam said. "The kid shoved Gus and threw his phone against the wall. Gus didn't cross any lines. He didn't ask the kid a single question after he asked for a lawyer."

"He put his hands on him," I said quietly. "It's a problem, Sam. If we get that far. If it turns out he did have something to do with Bill's murder, what happened here today is going to come out on cross."

"He wasn't asked any questions after he asked for a lawyer," Sam said.

"It won't matter!" I said, flapping my hands in exasperation. "Come on. You can see the defense strategy already. Overzealous cop making a rush to judgment over the murder of his friend."

Sam didn't answer. He couldn't really. He knew I was right.

"What do you want me to do?" Sam asked.

"I want you to ask for help. We need someone impartial working with Gus."

Sam shook his head. "He won't have it. I won't have it. Mara, this was Bill."

"I know."

"You can't ask him to have some pinhead from BCI second guessing Gus's every move. Getting in his way. Mara, he's the best there is. I need Gus on this case."

"Look, you're all under unbelievable pressure with this. You're burying your friend tomorrow."

"Gus isn't compromised," Sam said. "He is on top of this. You need to trust him. And you need to trust me to keep an eye on him."

"I do," I said. "But I'm telling you. Down the road, if this goes to trial, I'm going to be the one prosecuting it. You know that. Yes. Gus is the best at what he does. But so am I. So I'm telling you. For the good of this case ... to give me the best chance to secure a conviction if that's where we're headed ... call in BCI and hand them the lead on this. It will matter. Who'd they send out to the scene?"

"Andrea Patel."

"Good. She's good. Give this to her, Sam."

Sam stood with his hands on his hips. The pain stamped across his face affected me, too. In less than twenty-four hours, this town would lay Bill Clancy to rest. Sam, Gus, and I would have to look Shanna Clancy in the eye and once again promise her that we would deliver justice for her husband. At this moment in time, I knew Gus Ritter had just made that promise harder to deliver.

8

It was cold the day we buried Sheriff Bill Clancy. The last week in April, we had a late winter storm the morning before. There was beauty in that. An inch of snow blanketed the ground at Holy Cross Cemetery. It put the rose wreaths standing beside the open grave in stark contrast with the wintry white of the rolling hills.

"She picked the perfect spot," Kenya said. She and I came together, along with Hojo and Caro. The four of us had opted to sit in the church gymnasium along with the general public at the service. The main pews of the church were taken up by all members of the Maumee County Sheriff's Department and contingents from neighboring law enforcement agencies. Now, Hojo drove us to the cemetery in a long, hundred-plus car, invite-only procession that stopped traffic all the way through Waynetown.

Thousands came to the service. The mayor spoke. Senator Brassow. And newly appointed Congressman Damon Rounds. Another reason why I chose to sit far away from the news cameras and live streams. Rounds had been tapped to fill the vacancy left by Jason. The more vulturous of the press core hoped to film my reaction when Rounds took his seat.

All through it, Shanna Clancy sat stoic, impeccably dressed in a black suit and hat with a small veil that hid half of her face.

Sam stayed by her side, quietly whispering to her so she knew what to expect, who each person was who came to pay their respects.

"She's bearing up well," Hojo said. "But I'm worried. She had some sort of breakdown last night at the funeral home."

"She's still in shock," Kenya said. Hojo could drive no more than five miles an hour in the processional. It would take us almost two hours to get to the nearby cemetery and we were the twentieth car.

Waynetown's population quadrupled that day. People lined the streets to pay their respects, waving as each car drove by.

"She's terrified," Caro said. "Shanna's been having nightmares. She keeps thinking Bill's killer is going to come back for her."

"How awful," I said.

"We're in a book club together," Caro said. "My next-door neighbor, Monica, is pretty tight with her. Everybody's been taking turns staying over at her house. I will go next week."

"She has deputies outside the house round the clock still, doesn't she?" Hojo asked.

"Yes," Kenya answered. "I'm hearing the same thing through the grapevine from them. They had her pretty heavily sedated those first couple of nights."

Finally, Hojo made the last turn into the Holy Cross Cemetery. A pair of uniformed deputies directed traffic with road flares. We parked along the curving driveway and got out together.

Though only a fraction of the people came from the church, we were still in a group of several hundred. We packed in tightly, surrounding Bill Clancy's gravesite.

In the thick of it, near the grave, I caught Sam's eye. He wore his Class A uniform. Darkest black with gold bars on his sleeves, denoting his rank. I noticed a new one. The official announcement hadn't come, but as of this morning, Sam had publicly been named acting sheriff. A job he never wanted. Perhaps not ever, but certainly not like this.

Reverend Pete held open his prayer book. "Saint Michael the Archangel, defend us in battle. Be our protection against the wickedness and snares of the devil; May God rebuke him, we humbly pray; And do thou, O Prince of the Heavenly Host, by the power of God, thrust into hell Satan and all evil spirits who wander through the world for the ruin of souls. Amen.

"Lord, please take your servant Bill Clancy into your loving care. Through your grace, send comfort to those of us left behind who loved him. Whose lives he touched."

Shanna stood beside Reverend Pete. She looked so small next to him, even though Pete wasn't particularly tall. Cameras snapped. I stiffened.

Not today, I thought. Not now. But pictures of Shanna's grief-stricken face would grace the covers of every local paper and online news page tomorrow morning.

Shanna took her seat at the head of Bill Clancy's casket. The hardest part would come next.

As a veteran, Bill Clancy would receive Marine Corps Funeral Honors. The Honor Guard, Clancy's former brothers in arms, gave him his twenty-one gun salute. Each volley cut through me and every other mourner. Shattering the peace. Punctuating the grimness of the occasion. And although that was jarring, the worst was yet to come.

Two members of the Police Pipe and Drum Corps stepped forward, one with tears streaming down his face. They began the slow, mournful notes of "Amazing Grace" on their bagpipes. Of all of it. The speeches. The flag-draped casket. The sheer number of other law enforcement agencies that had shown up to pay their respects. It was those cutting, beautiful, high-pitched notes of the bagpipes, layered with the low, continuous drone that brought these grown men and women to tears. And me as well.

"Order arms!" The command came from the guard commander standing beside Sam.

Sam stood at the head of the casket, his white gloved hand held in rigid salute, his eyes glistening. The members of the military held their weapons out toward the casket as a sign of respect.

Never again, I thought. For as long as I live, I never want to have to attend another police officer's funeral.

Beside me, Caro started to weep uncontrollably. I put an arm around her. "They were still trying for a baby," she whispered to me. "Shanna's already suffered so much. She had three miscarriages in the last five years. I just keep thinking maybe she's pregnant now and doesn't know it yet. Do you think that's possible?"

"I don't know," I said. "You're a good friend. She'll need plenty of those."

There was one person I hadn't yet laid eyes on. Not here at the cemetery. Not in the church. I scanned the crowd again.

Detective Gus Ritter hadn't joined the main group of mourners. As subtle as I could, I turned around, looking over my right shoulder, then my left.

It was then a new cold chill went through me. At the top of a hill overlooking the gravesite, I spotted a silver Ford Explorer. It was Gus. He had the window rolled down directly behind the driver's seat. From the small gap, I saw a telephoto lens.

Detective Ritter didn't have time to grieve today. Even now, he was working the case.

I grew uneasy, letting my eyes track where the high-powered camera lens pointed. I saw no one unfamiliar. No one who shouldn't be here today. And yet, it would make sense for Clancy's killer to want to witness the impact of his or her handiwork.

Two members of the Marine Honor Guard went to the casket. They began their quick, methodical removal of the flag draping Bill's coffin. Folding it tightly into its signature triangle, one member of the guard tucked the shell casings from the twenty-one gun salute inside of it.

Shanna Clancy looked up at him with hollow, shadowed eyes.

"On behalf of the President of the United States, the United States Marine Corps, the citizens of Maumee County, and a grateful nation, please accept this flag as a symbol of our appreciation for your husband's honorable and faithful service." He gently placed the folded flag in her lap. She brought it to her breast, hugging it as if it were a way to embrace her husband one last time. I suppose in one way, it was. Sam stood behind her and leaned forward, putting a gentle hand on her shoulder. He whispered something to her that made her lip quiver, but she found a smile.

A few moments later, it was over. There was a reception to follow for close friends and family at the Union Hall. We'd been invited, but hadn't decided if we'd go.

"I'm going to catch a ride with Monica," Caro said. "A group of us are going to go over to Shanna's while she's at the reception. Just to tidy up. Make sure she's got groceries for the week, that sort of thing."

"I'm sure she'll appreciate it," I said. "You're a good egg, Caro." I gave her another hug as the crowd slowly began to disperse.

Hojo went on ahead. "I'll bring the car around to the front entrance," he said. "If you two want to pay your respects. I'm sure the mayor will want to make sure he's got a picture with you, Kenya."

"He can stuff it," she said under her breath. "I'm not using Bill's funeral for a political photo op. And I'll be damned if I let him use me for the same reason."

"You probably should make an appearance at the reception though," I said.

"Not unless you're there too," she said. From the corner of my eye, I saw the main reason I wanted to fade into the woodwork. Congressman Damon Rounds was heading straight for me.

"Come on," I said. "Let's see if we can make a clean getaway."

"Don't you want to check in with Sam?" Kenya asked.

I cast a nervous glance at Kenya. We weren't at all public about our budding relationship. Least of all at an event like this. And yet, Kenya knew me well enough that there was no point lying to her face.

"Not here," I said, smiling. "Sam knows how to find me if he needs to."

Mercifully, Damon Rounds got caught up by the mayor before he could get to me. It was the perfect chance to slip away unnoticed.

Unfortunately, I wasn't that lucky. An arm shot out, touching my shoulder.

"Mrs. Brent," its owner said. I looked up and couldn't keep my jaw from dropping.

Stoney Gregg, Jason's defense attorney, had his hand on me still as he steered me away from the crowd.

"What do you want?" Kenya asked. She was tall and formidable if you had the misfortune of getting on the wrong side of Kenya Spaulding. Gregg let go of me.

"I'm sorry," he said. "I know this isn't the best time to talk. But you haven't been returning my phone calls."

"Mr. Gregg," I said. "I can't think of a single thing I'd want to talk to you about."

He produced an envelope from his coat pocket.

"Jason is still the father of your son," Gregg said. "He has rights. We're hoping not to have to resort to anything public, but ..."

"Are you kidding me?" I said, looking around. "You're threatening me? Here? About my son?"

A shadow fell over Stoney Gregg's face. Behind me, Sam appeared as if out of thin air. He was still as stone, but I sensed a fire within him. Oh Lord. If Gregg put a hand on me again. If he so much as mentioned Jason's name, I worried what Sam might do. He'd been coiled so tightly for the past two weeks.

"I've made arrangements," Gregg said. "Obviously, you can do whatever you choose. But like I said, your husband is prepared to get this in front of a judge if he has to."

"Get what in front of a judge?" I said, taking the paper from him. I wouldn't read it. Not here. Not now.

"He wants to see Will," Gregg said. "He has legitimate concerns about what your son's been told about his situation."

"From me," I said. "You're telling me Jason's worried about what I'm doing?"

"Let's go," Sam said. "Mara's done talking to you."

"This doesn't concern you," Gregg said. Damon Rounds had freed himself from the mayor and was headed my way again. This was a disaster. I regretted coming. Sam's posture drew attention. He got in Stoney Gregg's face.

"Stop," I said. "What does he want?"

"A visit," Gregg said. "I told you. I've arranged it. Tomorrow afternoon. Just go see him. Jason's confident the two of you can work out your differences with just a conversation."

Cameras clicked in my direction. It had even drawn Shanna Clancy's attention. She caught my eye as she finished hugging the mayor's wife.

"Fine," I snapped. "Tell him I'll be there. Just ... leave. Quickly."

With that, I turned my back and tried to disappear from view of any more cameras.

9

Someone pulled some strings. As the corrections officer led me into the common visitors' room, I quickly realized we would have the place to ourselves. In the fifteen years I'd served as an assistant prosecutor, I'd never seen anything like it. Even here, Jason Brent wielded a certain level of power. As I took a seat at the largest table in the center of the room, I knew his power over me had ended. But there was Will to consider.

"You'll have about twenty minutes," the officer said. He'd introduced himself as Officer Bryans. Lord, these guys kept on getting younger, it seemed. Bryans couldn't have been more than twenty-five. He was big, well-muscled to the point his uniform shirt stretched over his biceps. He had a look about him that made me suspect he'd used performance enhancers. Large veins in his neck and forearms.

"No touching," he said. "Don't try to pass anything to him. When you leave, you're not permitted to hug the prisoner."

"You don't need to worry," I said. "If you see the prisoner trying to hug me, that's your cue to put a stop to it."

Bryans showed no reaction. He simply turned on his heel and took his post by the door. He spoke into his shoulder radio, instructing another officer to bring the "prisoner" in.

I didn't know how I'd feel. Surely, I'd spent the better part of the last year imagining what it would be like to see Jason in his khaki prison jumpsuit. I couldn't recall the last time I'd seen him wearing anything but the most impeccably tailored suit, sporting a two-hundred-dollar haircut.

The door opened. I resisted the urge to rise. I didn't want to give him the slightest satisfaction of seeing my nerves. But as he walked in, all of that faded away. For just an instant, I saw the man I first met sixteen years ago when I was a first year law student. A third year, he'd been assigned to mentor me.

Confident. Outwardly cocky. But as I got to know him, I saw how vulnerable he really was. A lost boy. Abandoned by his mother, abused by his father. Left in foster care and forced to fend for himself. It toughened him. Made him ruthless. Or maybe he'd been that all along. It was so strange to me. Once upon a time, I'd admired that strength in him. No matter what happened, it was easy to believe Jason Brent would always take care of things. Of me. Of our son.

"Mara," he said, breathless. Jason cast a nervous glance over his shoulder. The guard's presence reminded him of the rules he too was bound to follow. I found myself grateful for the distance of the table between us.

I didn't smile. I kept my face neutral, folding my hands in front of me. I could never forget what he'd done to us. But slowly, over the past year, I'd come to view his cheating on me as a blessing. It had given me an escape hatch. The ability to move Will and me to a safer distance while Jason's life imploded.

His face fell as he read mine. A muscle twitched in his jaw, providing a window to the simmering anger I knew he felt.

"Thanks for coming," he said.

"I didn't have a lot of choice," I said. "I don't appreciate being ambushed at Bill Clancy's funeral."

"You wouldn't return my calls. It's not like I have an unlimited chance to make them, Mara. You've won, okay? You got everything you wanted."

Now it was my own simmering rage I had to hold in check. There was no part of this that I wanted.

"Say what you need to say," I said.

"You're enjoying this, aren't you?" he said, finally taking a seat in front of me. He was too casual as he sat, folding one ankle over his knee. Somehow, even in his prison jumpsuit, he managed to seem arrogant.

"No," I said. "I'm not enjoying it. Stoney Gregg shoved a draft motion in front of my face while I was standing about twenty feet from an open grave, Jason. So here I am. You wanted a face-to-face meeting."

"I want to see Will," Jason said. "We've never talked about how this is going to work."

I wanted to argue with him. Point out that he was the one who'd been in denial for the past year. He lied to Will. Insisted he was innocent. That he'd been framed. It had been left to me to prepare my autistic son for the inevitability of his father's conviction and prison sentence.

"How do you think this is going to work?" I asked.

"He's my son. You can't erase me."

"I don't want to," I said and that was the truth. "But I'm also not going to let Will get invested in some fantasy about what's really going on. He's too smart for that. Your trial and conviction is a matter of public record now."

"And you're supposed to limit his access to the internet. That's what a responsible parent would do."

I ran my hand through my hair. It would have been so easy to be petty. The man was lecturing me on responsibility. But there was no point in it. It had taken me a long time and hours of therapy to build the boundaries I needed, or to even recognize where I needed them.

"I want to arrange regular visits," Jason said. "I'm entitled to that."

"You're not," I said.

"I have rights as Will's father."

"It's not about your rights or what you want, Jason. It's about what's in Will's best interests. Coming here ... seeing you ... here ... he's not ready. I'm barely ready. For now, if you want to write him a letter, I'll make sure he gets it."

"Right," he said. "I have zero confidence that you'll deliver it to him."

"That's all I can offer you. We're going to take this slowly. One step at a time. Will's actually drafting a letter to you.

He's been working on it in therapy. I don't know when he'll finish, but he's capable of mailing it himself when he does."

"That's not good enough." He slammed his fist to the table. "I want to see him. He needs to see me. You know how he is. Will thrives on routine. I need to be part of that routine as long as I'm in here. When I get out, we'll start over. I'll find a place closer to you. In Waynetown. I'm putting politics behind me, at least until Will's done with high school. Until he's launched and on his own. It's not that far from now. Six years."

I felt like I had whiplash. Never mind Jason's current predicament. He was talking about Will as if we were on some linear path. Our remaining few minutes wouldn't be remotely long enough to unpack everything he just said. So, I stuck with one.

"There are no guarantees on when or if you'll ever get out of here, Jason. The sentence on your least serious conviction is twenty years. You have to face the fact that you'll be incarcerated, at a minimum, until Will is in his thirties."

"I'm going to win my appeals," he said. "So get ready."

Though it was in me to argue that point, I stopped myself. I realized it was possible Jason needed to believe that, to hang on to a healthy dose of denial for his own survival. It cost me nothing to let him have that. Reality could take care of itself.

"Fine," I said. "But you know what the appellate process is like."

"That's why you're here," he said. "Because I will not allow my son to fall out of the routine of being with me. Of having me in his life in whatever version that has to take. So, tell me now. What are your intentions? Are you planning to stand in the way of that?"

I took a breath. "I know you want to paint me as the villain in this. Know this. I am fighting for Will, not against you. He's asked me if I think you did everything you were convicted of. You know that, right?"

"You say nothing," Jason said, leaning forward to close the distance between us. "You tell him I'm the one who can answer those questions for him. You tell him his father loves him."

"I do," I said. "Every single day, Jason. In spite of everything, I've never uttered a negative word about you to our son. And I never will. He can come to his own conclusions."

"Time's about up, Brent," Officer Bryons said.

"I want to see him," Jason said. "And he needs to see me. God. It's probably keeping him up at night wondering what it's like for me in here. He might put on a brave front for you, but he ruminates. I don't want him to worry."

For the first time, Jason said something that didn't center around his own feelings and experiences. It was a start.

"Write him a letter," I said. "Let's start there, okay? Tell him how you're doing. Give him a chance to process it in a way and in a place where he feels safe. That's all I'm asking. I'm not trying to erase you from his life. I'm trying to help him deal with everything that's happened in the healthiest way possible. That's all."

"Time to take you back," Bryons said, stepping up to the table.

"Five minutes!" Jason shouted. Bryons stiffened.

"It's okay," I said. "We're done for today. Write your letter, Jason. I mean it. Small steps at first, okay?"

Jason rose and put his wrists out, palms up. Officer Bryans cuffed him. I stood at the table, waiting, as Jason was led out of the common room and back to his cell.

He was right about something important. Will's imagination would be worse than anything he might see here. Once again, I felt hate rising. Jason had done this. He could say all the right words about putting Will first. But when it mattered, he had chosen something dark instead.

I walked out of the common room and back to the visitor's exit. Gathering my belongings, I felt as if I were suffocating. The air around me seemed to thicken. I just wanted to get out.

I made it all the way to my car before my phone started ringing. I unlocked the screen. Showing six missed calls, all from Sam. He was ringing me again now.

"Sam," I said, still breathless. I hadn't told him I was coming here today. If I had, he would have tried to stop me.

"We've got a break in the case," Sam said, sounding just as breathless as I was. "Ricky Wahl's father's coming down. He's asking about the reward posted for information on Bill's case."

"Oh boy," I said. "Do you have a lid on Ritter? Sam, he cannot conduct that interview by himself."

"He won't be," Sam said. "That's the other thing I wanted to tell you. Special Agent Patel is coming down from BCI. She'll be here in twenty minutes. If you're close, she's fine with letting you sit in the observation room again."

"How do you and Gus feel about that?" I asked, slipping behind the wheel. I pressed the ignition and waited two seconds for my Bluetooth speaker to take over the call.

"... leave nothing to chance," Sam's voice cut back in. "Gus knows he owes that to Bill. We both want to be as textbook an investigation as we can make it. How soon can you get here?"

I checked the dashboard clock. "Forty-five minutes," I said. "I'm in Milan."

Stony silence. Then, I heard Sam breathe. "Okay. See you when you get here, then."

10

"This is good," I said. "No. This is really good."

I stood in front of the projector screen in the sheriff's department conference room. Agent Andrea Patel sat in a chair to my right. I'd only met her once before, but found her to be an extremely calm, competent investigator. She would be the perfect complement to Gus Ritter. She could be assertive without stepping on anyone's toes.

"There," Andrea said. Gus stood on the other side of the table, shifting his weight from hip to hip. The video was hard for him to watch. Patel had gotten it enhanced, blowing up one part of the frame with remarkable detail.

"6:28 a.m.," Andrea said. She hit a button on her laptop, which blew up the image on the screen. I leaned in.

"There's a dent," Gus said. "Right front bumper."

"I see it," I said. "So there's no doubt we're looking at Bill's car. Are we sure the timestamp on the security video is accurate?"

"It is," Andrea said. She tapped the keyboard and scrolled back. "6:22 a.m., you're looking at an empty parking space."

I'd watched the raw footage of this feed at least a dozen times. Now, with the enhancements, that tiny, identifiable corner of Bill Clancy's car could be seen. It meant we had a timeline.

"So that car is driven into the lot between 6:22 and 6:28 a.m."

"And it doesn't move," Andrea said. "That same portion can be seen all the way up until 10:15 when the cart girl finds him."

"And this," Gus said. "Wahl's van is driving in and out at 6:58 and 7:04."

"There's nobody else in the lot before the employees start arriving," I said.

"And I can give you a clerk from the DMV that can testify as to the partial plate. Wahl's is the only van of that make, model, and color with those partial numbers."

"It's him," Gus said.

"I'd feel better if we could actually clearly see his face in the video," I said. "He's driving the getaway car, but we still don't know who he was there to pick up."

"It's enough to let me have a go at Ricky again," Gus said.

I met Andrea's eyes. We both knew that was the one thing we weren't going to let happen.

"We've got to come at this another way, Gus," Andrea said. "Ricky needs to understand he's running out of options. Whoever he's trying to protect isn't going to return the favor."

In the interview room behind us, Steven Wahl, Ricky's dad, sat sipping coffee from a paper cup.

"Let me do what I do," she said. "See if I can get anywhere. Then we'll figure out a plan for Ricky."

I knew how much Gus hated this. Tension practically dripped from his pores. And it was exactly the reason why he had to sit this one out. Why I hadn't ruled out physically sitting on him to keep him out of the room.

Andrea got up. She grabbed a thin file from the table and headed into the hallway.

"Come on, Gus," I said. "She's not you, but Agent Patel is good at what she does, too."

Gus said nothing. He waited a moment, then made his way to the observation room. I said a quick prayer that Andrea could deliver like I thought she could, then went to join Gus.

Andrea was just entering the interview room as I took my seat next to Gus. She slid the file folder across the table to Steven Wahl.

"I'm not going to waste your time," she said, opening the file folder. She laid three photographs across the table in front of the elder Mr. Wahl.

"Your son drives a blue Uplander. These photographs show him entering the lot at the Dollar Kart on April 15th a little before 7:00 a.m. That was a Thursday morning."

Wahl barely glanced at the photographs. "He had nothing to do with whatever happened to the sheriff."

"I hope not," Andrea said. She took her seat across from him. "I'd like to rule him out as a person of interest. If you can help me do that, I'd appreciate it."

"How much?" Wahl said.

"How much what?"

"How much do I get if I help you?"

Gus stiffened beside me. "He's a bloodsucking piece of …"

"Shh," I said. "The glass is one-way, not the walls, Gus."

"You work third shift at the refinery, isn't that right?" Andrea said. "I've already checked with the payroll department. Their records show you were at work that morning. You clocked out at seven."

"That's right," he said.

"So you can't say for sure where your son was at six or seven in the morning on the 15th, because you weren't home. Do you remember when you last saw him before you went to work that day?"

"He was lying on the couch, playing some video game. Like he always is."

A question burned through me, making my pulse skip.

"What video game does he like to play?" Andrea asked, reading my mind.

"I don't know. Some kinda thing with soldiers or elves or something. Dungeons and dragons or something. I don't know."

Andrea casually wrote something in her notebook.

"How long does he usually spend playing that game?" Andrea asked.

"All friggin' night," Wahl answered. "He's supposed to go to work at noon at the window factory on Fir Street. He's usually asleep by the time I get home. When I wake up, he's gone or he's got his face in front of the TV."

"But he wasn't home when you got home on the 15th, was he?"

"I don't remember what time he came home. It was after I did," Wahl said.

"That's not what you told Detective Ritter on the phone," Andrea said. "He says you told him you think Ricky has information to share about what happened at the Dollar Kart that morning."

"I never said that," Steven said.

Gus tensed beside me. "He's a filthy liar!"

"Gus. Please. I know how badly you want to rip that guy's face off. And that's exactly why Andrea needs to be in there right now."

"I know how to do my job," he said.

"Okay. And so does she. But if this breaks the way we think it's going to, I cannot put you on the stand alone. You can't be the only one investigating this case. We'll get torn apart."

"He sat there," Gus said. "It's been three weeks since Bill was shot. Three weeks since we put it out there where he was found. He sat there ..."

"Mr. Wahl," Andrea said. "Take a good look at that second photo. The kid driving that van ... your son's van ... he's been positively identified as Ricky by one of the store employees."

Gus went silent beside me. Andrea was bluffing, but as far as we knew, Steven Wahl didn't know that.

"Ricky has been uncooperative," she said. "Nobody thinks your son actually killed Sheriff Clancy. But we think he might have information about who did. We think he might have seen something. The longer he waits to come forward with it, the more difficult it will be for me to help him. That's what I need you to understand. Ricky's an adult. He's twenty-two years old. If he got roped into something he shouldn't have ... if he's maybe got a friend who got him in over his head, he could be tried as an accessory after the fact. Do you know what that means?"

Nothing from Steven Wahl.

"It means your son could face the same penalties as if he committed a murder himself. He could go to jail for the rest of his life. We're talking about a cop killer. The state will want to pursue the death penalty against the shooter. I get that he's just a kid ... your kid ... even if he is technically an adult. So let's try to help him, okay?"

Steven Wahl was starting to sweat. He chewed on his thumbnail in the identical way his son had just a few days ago in the same room.

"Stupid, stupid kid," Steven said.

"He's a good kid," Andrea said. "I know what it's like for this generation. Mr. Wahl, I've got a twenty-two-year-old myself. They're not like we were at that age, are they?"

"They sure as hell aren't."

"They don't plan ahead," she said. "They don't seem to think about the consequences of their actions ... or their inactions. I don't know. I read a study somewhere that it's to do with being born after 9/11. The pandemic. These kids are suffering from something like a quarter-life crisis. I've never seen anything like it."

"I try to tell him," Steven said, starting to choke up. "He can't just sit in front of a screen his whole life. But maybe he should. Goddammit. I told him maybe he should make plans with his friends in person every once in a while. I didn't mean ... he couldn't have ..."

"There's still time to help him," Andrea said. "If he comes forward. If he tells us what he knows and gets ahead of this. It's understandable that he's scared ... He can bring a lawyer with him if that makes you feel more comfortable."

"We can't afford a lawyer," Steven said.

"You belong to the union, don't you? That means you're eligible for legal services. Talk to your steward. He's your son. They can help you. But let's not let another day go by on this. Ricky's at work right now. Can he take a break? He can come straight here. I'll wait."

"He's been hanging out with this one kid in town," Wahl said. I reached over and put a hand on Gus's knee.

"Do you have a name?"

"I've never met him," Wahl said. "He calls him Turk. But I think that's just a handle. I see it on the screen when they're playing that stupid game. But they maybe went to high school together. I'm not sure."

"Well, if you can find out who Turk is. If you can get Ricky in here."

"You'll help him?" Wahl said. "I don't want him talking to that other guy. My son came home with a black eye."

"He's full of crap," Gus muttered.

"I know," I said.

"Will he answer if you call him or text him?"

Steven took out his phone. "He texts."

Andrea sat back. Wahl punched in a text and set his phone on the table between them. He waited about thirty seconds, then his phone lit up with an answer.

Steven picked up the phone and called his son.

"Ricky," he said. "Son. I need you to listen to me, okay? Tell your boss you're sick. Tell him you need to take your PTO for the rest of your shift. We've got a situation. I'm handling it, but you need to come down to the sheriff's ..."

We watched as Steven Wahl squeezed his eyes shut. He was a father, trying desperately to save his son. I understood him at that moment. His whole body shook as the gravity of Ricky's trouble really sank in.

"I know," Steven said. "Buddy. I know. But this is a way out. You gotta worry about yourself. You gotta let me worry about you. And you gotta trust me that this is the best way. Okay? Just tell your manager you got sick in the bathroom and you need to leave. He's not going to fire you. You've got time coming. And they don't wanna shut down production because some kid got sick and didn't tell nobody. He'll appreciate you taking care of yourself. Okay. Okay."

Steven was silent for another thirty seconds, then he clicked off the call and set his phone on the table.

"He'll be here in twenty minutes. He says he's ready to talk. But I wanna be here with him. That's the only way this goes down. I'm in the room."

"He's twenty-two years old," Gus said.

"Let him," I said. "Ricky needs to feel safe. He's been manipulated by whoever that friend was he went to pick up. If that's how it went down."

Gus nodded. "We've got to break that up. Yeah. Okay."

Andrea Patel shook Steven Wahl's hand. She excused herself, leaving him the room to himself. Then she came to join us.

"Good work," I said.

Andrea went straight to Gus. "I think this will work best if Ricky at least sees you when he walks into this building. He's afraid of you. Let him think his dad can save him."

"I sure as hell hope he can," Gus said. Now, there was nothing to do but wait.

11

A different Ricky Wahl showed up to the sheriff's department that afternoon. Gone was the cocky, obscenity-spewing kid who had thrown Gus's phone against the wall. Ricky sat bent-backed, practically molding himself into his father's chair beside him.

"Tell them," Steven Wahl said to his son. "These people can help you."

"I know my rights," Ricky said, but without the bluster from before.

I leaned against the wall, standing directly behind Gus. Surprisingly, Ricky insisted that he be in the room along with Agent Patel and me.

"If I tell you what I know," he said. "You have to give me immunity, right?"

"No," I said. "I don't. It depends on what you have to say, Ricky. And it depends on you being one hundred percent forthright. You have to tell us everything you know. But before we get to any of that, I need it on record that you're here of your own free will. Do you understand what that means?"

Ricky nodded. I gestured to Gus. He reached across the table and pressed the red button on the small voice recorder. The video cameras were also recording. We would leave nothing to chance today. I could already hear the objections from some defense attorney playing in my mind.

"I don't want a lawyer," Ricky said. "I know I asked for one before. But I'm ready to talk to you alone."

"Have you spoken with a lawyer?" I asked.

Ricky shook his head.

"I need you to say it out loud."

"No. Not formally. I don't have a lawyer and I don't want one at this time. I have information that might help you figure out who killed Sheriff Bill Clancy. If you can promise me I won't get in trouble ... that you won't charge me with anything ... I'll tell you what I know."

"That's not how this is going to work," Agent Patel said. "How this needs to work? You tell us what you know. Then Ms. Brent will figure out if it's within her power to make a proffer of immunity, if your information checks out. Do you understand?"

"I understand," Ricky said.

I took a seat beside Gus. He said nothing, but his solid, rock-like presence spoke plenty. He seemed to emit a low, vibrating hum of tension just by being there. But he kept his rage in check.

"All right," Agent Patel said. "First thing, I need you to sign a waiver of your right to an attorney if that's what you feel comfortable doing."

I slid the Miranda waiver across the table to her. Patel read it to Ricky, then allowed him to read it through himself. Without hesitation, he picked up a pen and signed it. Patel tore off his copy and handed it to his father.

"Okay," she said. "Now that that's out of the way. Let's hear what you have to say."

"It was me," he said. "That was me driving into the Dollar Kart lot the morning the sheriff was found dead."

"Okay," Patel said. "Why don't you start from the beginning?"

Ricky looked nervously at his father. Steven gave him a nod. "Tell them everything you did, Rick. Start from when you left the house. Who you talked to. All of it."

Ricky started chewing his thumbnail as he'd done the last time he was interviewed. I stared at him hard. He wasn't sweating or trembling. His eyes looked clear. He had none of the obvious signs of being under the influence of anything. That was encouraging. "I worked overtime the day before ... um ... Wednesday the 14th. Came home around ten, I think it was. Then I went online and started playing *Legends of Warfare*. That's what I normally do. Sometimes I go to bed around three or four. I need to wind down after work."

"That's understandable," Patel said, though I knew she had to be thinking the same thing I was. Parental frustration. "So what happened next?"

"I lost track of time. I got a text from a friend of mine at four thirty in the morning. I was just about to log off and go to bed. My friend Austin texted me."

"Austin who?" Gus asked.

"Austin Merkle," Ricky answered.

"Does he go by any other names?" Gus asked.

"Yeah. Turk. That's what he calls himself in L.O.W. I'd sent him a direct message because he hadn't logged on. He was supposed to. So that was kinda weird. Then he messaged me finally. Said he needed me to come pick him up."

"He messaged you," Patel asked. "Was this on your phone?"

"No. It was through the game. He responded to my message."

I wrote a note. Gus and Patel were going to need a warrant for Ricky's phone, computer, and gaming platform so we could verify all of this.

"What did Turk ... um ... Austin say?" Patel asked. "Exactly."

"He said he needed me to come pick him up. Said to bring my van and come get him at the Dollar Kart on Warren."

"Was that an unusual request?"

"Not really," Ricky said. "Austin doesn't have a good car. His is always breaking down. It was weird of him to ask for a ride that late at night. But I've picked him up other times."

"All right," Patel said. "Then what happened?"

"I put on a pair of jeans, grabbed a Red Bull, and went to pick him up."

"When was this?"

"I left a little after six in the morning. Drove over to the Dollar Kart. That's about a twenty-minute drive from my dad's house."

"Did you pick anyone else up? Tell anyone else where you were going?"

Ricky shook his head. At Gus's prompting, he verbalized his answer. No.

"I got to the Dollar Kart and started looking for Austin. I thought he'd be standing outside the store or next to his car. At first, I thought maybe I'd gone to the wrong place because I didn't see his car."

"Tell me step by step," Patel said. "Where did you enter?"

Gus had printed out a satellite image of the Dollar Kart parking lot. Ricky pointed to the west entrance and indicated that's where he drove in and out.

"There was a car parked here," Ricky said, pointing directly to the spot where Clancy's car had been found. "A Durango. I drove right by it and didn't see anything. Then, the passenger side opened and Austin came out. He was carrying this plastic bag and was naked except for his underwear. I thought maybe he got jumped or something."

I felt sweat begin to trickle down my spine. Beside me, Gus leaned far forward in his chair. I knew he wanted to reach across the table and shake Ricky. The hardest part of his story was coming next.

"Austin flagged me down," Ricky said. "I drove up alongside the Durango, kind of parking at an angle in this spot here. Austin walked up to my car and poked his head into the window. I rolled it down to talk to him."

"What did you see, if anything?" Patel asked.

"Well, with how Austin was dressed, I was really confused. And there was somebody in the driver's seat of the Durango, but he looked like he was sleeping. Or drunk. It was an old guy. I didn't really recognize him at first. I mean, his head was slumped over the steering wheel."

"Did Austin say anything?" Gus asked.

"He was pissed at me. Asking me what took me so long to get there. I mean, I left about as soon as he messaged me. It's not like that Dollar Kart is close. It's on the other side of town from where we live and Austin knows that. I told him to eff off. I was about to just leave him there. He was high."

"What makes you say that?" Patel asked.

"He just was all sweaty. His eyes were bugged out. Anyway, he moved out of my window and started coming around to the passenger side so he could get in. That's when I got a clear look inside that Durango. I saw blood."

"Ricky," Gus said. "We're gonna need you to describe exactly what you saw."

"The dude was dead. Not sleeping. Dead. All white and waxy and gross looking. And I saw that frigging hole in his head. He was shot. It scared the crap out of me. Austin was in the car at that point. He told me to just drive. Just keep my eyes right in front of me, and drive the hell out of there. He was saying not to speed. Not to panic. And he told me not to say anything or ask questions. Just drive."

"What did you do?" Patel asked.

"I got the hell out of there. I was like ... like I couldn't even breathe. The dude was dead! And Austin was acting like it was no big deal. I said what the hell did you do? He told me to shut up. Told me I didn't need to know. And I said, you got me into this now. I figured it was some kind of drug deal, you know? Like things went sideways and Austin was acting all weird and jumpy so I thought maybe that dude tried to rob him or rape him or pulled a gun. Cuz I did see a gun on him. In a holster. And well ... I couldn't figure out why he took his clothes off."

"Where did you go?" Patel asked.

"I took Austin home. He lives about a mile from the Dollar Kart on Canning Street. I pulled into his driveway and Austin asked me to come inside. I wouldn't. No way. I wanted to get the hell away from him. I told him not to call me again. You gotta understand I was pissed. I asked him why he didn't just call the cops if that dude pulled a gun on him. Austin started getting out of the car. And that's when he pulled a gun out of the bag with his clothes. He was laughing about it. Sounded like a hyena. He stood right outside my window and pointed a gun at my head. Told me to quit being a baby or something like that. Told me it was time for me to act like a real man and step up. I didn't know what the hell he meant."

"Do you know what kind of gun it was that he pointed at you?" Patel asked.

Ricky shook his head. "I don't know. A nine, I think. It was big and black."

"Did you notice any injuries on Austin?"

Ricky shook his head. "No. I told you, he just looked strung out. Sweaty and pale. But no scratches or bruises or anything like that, if that's what you mean. Plus I saw all of him. You know. Cuz of his clothes. Well, then he walked up to his house and threw that bag on top of this blue garbage can on the side of his house."

Patel was good. She was establishing that whatever happened between Clancy and Austin Merkle, it probably wasn't a physical fight.

"What did you do next, Ricky?" Patel asked.

"I told Austin not to call me anymore. That's when he started threatening me. He said I better keep my mouth shut if I knew what was good for me. That I was part of this thing now. I'm so stupid. I should have come right to the cops. I know that. But I didn't know who that guy was. I swear. I didn't know he was the damn sheriff. Then, like a day or two later, I saw it on the news. His picture. They said where he was found. That car he was in. And I just thought ... I didn't know what to do."

"You were scared," Patel said. "That's understandable. Ricky, Have you spoken to Austin since?"

"Not in person," he said. "He's been texting me and messaging me. Wanting to make sure I know I'm supposed to keep my mouth shut. He's crazy. If he finds out I'm here, he's gonna kill me. He made that clear."

"I'd like to see him try," Steven said. "If that little punk comes anywhere near you or the house ... I'll kill him myself."

"Mr. Wahl," I said. "I'm going to need you not to do that."

"And I'm going to need you to write down everything you just told us, Ricky."

Gus slid a pad of paper and pen across the table in front of Ricky. He picked up the pen with his left hand and started writing.

I took that opportunity to excuse myself and head into the observation room on the other side of the wall. Sam stood there along with Kenya. Sam was pacing back and forth, hands on his hips.

"You're going to need a warrant," I said.

"Already being written up," Sam said.

"Patel needs to be involved in serving it," I said. "I know Gus is going to want to be there."

"Gus will be fine," Sam said. "I'll make sure of it."

Behind us, Ricky started talking again. Patel had asked him if Austin Merkle had been acting strange in the days leading up to Bill Clancy's murder. If Merkle had any other known associates.

"Austin was always shooting his mouth off. Wanting everybody to think he was some big deal. He always had some scheme going, you know? Some shit he said was going to be the next big thing. He was dealing in stolen shoes for a while. Then he had these shots he was selling. Some type of 'roids. He's bulked up in the last year or so. It's messing with his head. Here. I'll show you."

Ricky handed over his cell phone. Patel would later upload screenshots of the entire text chain between Ricky and Austin Merkle. Austin's texts were disturbing. He bragged about women he slept with. Then it escalated. He sent Ricky picture after picture of naked women. Videos of himself having intercourse.

"It was sick," Ricky said. "Austin would bang anything. Old women. Young women. Not girls. I don't think any of these chicks were underage. I hope not."

"Christ," Sam said. "We might need to add distribution of child porn to Ricky's immunity deal if it turns out ..."

"Let's not even go there yet," I said.

"Sometimes," Ricky said. "I'm not sure these girls knew they were being recorded. He'd take videos from ... you know ... behind."

Through the glass, I could see over Agent Patel's shoulder. She pulled up at least four videos of Austin doing exactly what Ricky described. Two of the white women had tattoos on their backs. One was African-American. The fourth was too grainy to make out much.

I couldn't look anymore. It made my stomach turn.

"He's crazy," Ricky said. "It's all that crap he's putting into his body."

"Sam," I said. "You need to be careful when you serve this warrant. Promise me. If you're dealing with a pumped-up, angry ...

"Mara," he said. "Everything's going to be by the book. I promise. Nobody wants a cleaner case more than me."

Andrea Patel walked into the room, leaving Gus alone with the Wahls. Her face registered the same revulsion I felt. "There's at least a hundred different photos and videos of naked women on Ricky's phone sent to him by Merkle. I'm going to get our digital forensics team on it and see if we can identify any of them."

"What does any of that have to do with Bill?" Sam asked.

"Hopefully nothing," Patel said.

"Thank you," I said to Patel.

"He's asking if he's told us enough to get an immunity deal," Patel asked me. I looked back at Kenya. She gave me a nod.

"You keep him here," I said. "For his own protection. And as far as any deal. Tell him it will depend on what you find when you get to Austin Merkle's house."

Andrea Patel nodded. "Good. Sam?"

"Already on it," Sam said. "Let's see if we can have this thing locked down within the hour."

12

"I understand the police are about to make an arrest in the Clancy case. Can you comment on that?"

The question came from nowhere. I saw Dave Reese from the corner of my eye as I got to my car. It was five o'clock. Four hours ago, Ricky Wahl had finished his interview with Agent Patel and Detective Ritter. The warrant for Austin Merkle's house, car, and computer had been signed by Judge Ivey only two hours ago. This was bad. Very bad. It meant someone at the courthouse had likely leaked that information.

"Reese, you know I can't comment on an active sheriff's investigation. Talk to their media relations. You know how this works. My office has no involvement at this point."

"Mara," he said. "Come on. I know what's going on. I'm asking for confirmation, that's all. You've got your job to do, I've got mine."

"And I'm doing mine," I said. "I have no comment."

"Kenya Spaulding needs this," he said. "Your office is under a tremendous amount of pressure to secure a conviction in this case. Or you will be. Don't you think justice might be better served with a transfer of venue? Considering the political climate in Maumee County?"

"Reese," I said. "Quit while you're ahead, okay? I have no comment. When there's something official to announce, I'm sure there will be a press conference with all the appropriate agencies available to take questions. That time isn't now though."

He didn't relent. Instead, Reese got even closer, holding his phone out. He was recording.

"Fine, if you can't comment on the status of the Clancy investigation, maybe you can comment on a rumor I heard that you were seen visiting Congressman Brent in prison."

A flash of anger went through me. My hand shook as I reached for my car door handle. Fully aware that he was recording my reaction, I tried to keep my face neutral.

"I have no comment."

"If and when the Clancy murder goes to trial, do you feel you can handle the pressure of trying it? Considering the turmoil in your personal life."

"There is no turmoil in my personal life, Mr. Reese. And frankly, I find the suggestion slightly misogynistic. Would you care to address that?"

"So you did see your ex-husband. Have you worked out whether your son will see his father in prison? I understand the congressman has met with a family law attorney regarding his visitation rights."

I could barely see straight. White spots flashed in front of my eyes. Where the hell was he getting all of this?

I knew what he wanted. A reaction. For me to lose my temper. I'd been down this road before. I would give him none of those things.

"Mara," he said. "Your husband was just convicted for his involvement in a massive corruption scheme. The voters of this town want to know what you knew and when you knew it. Now, the sheriff is dead. If there's a chance that his murder is connected with your husband's activities ..."

"What?" I said.

"She said she had no comment, you ghoul!"

A female voice shouted to my left. I saw a flash of blonde hair. Then, Kenya's new intern stepped in front of me, blocking Dave Reese's shot of me.

"Buzz off," she said. "Shoo!"

Shockingly, with his shot ruined, David put his phone back in his pocket. "Will you grant me an interview at your convenience?" he asked.

I bit my tongue past the retort I had in mind. I had a clear idea what I'd like to do to Reese's request for an interview.

"Shoo!" she said. Reese grimaced, but turned and walked back to his own car.

"You okay?" she said, turning to me.

"I'm fine ... thank you ... um ..."

"Mercedes," she said, smiling. Lord, she looked about sixteen years old, this one. But she'd shown some backbone with the reporter, so maybe I'd written her off too quickly.

"Most people call me Mercy," she said. "Mercy Gale."

"Well, thanks, Mercy," I said. "I'm afraid that kind of thing is going to get worse before it gets better."

"Oh, I know," she said. "You really should have had security out here patrolling the parking lot to keep reporters away. It's too open here. They all know what cars everyone drives. I saw that guy taking down license plates the other day."

"I'll talk to Kenya about it," I said.

"I already did. She's actually who sent me out here to come find you. Is it true what he said? I mean, what he was questioning you about? Are they about to make an arrest in Sheriff Clancy's murder?"

"Maybe," I said. "But you understand you're bound by confidentiality. Even though you're just an intern, what happens in our office ..."

"You don't have to worry about me. I know my way around reporters. They've been buzzing around since the day I was born."

The way she said it, I got the impression I was supposed to know what she meant. Gale. Mercedes Gale. The name didn't ring any bells. But Kenya had started mentioning something about her father ...

"Mara," she said. "The reason Kenya sent me out here. She's worried word's gonna get out online before anyone has a

VOW OF JUSTICE

chance to talk to the widow. Mrs. Clancy. She thought maybe it would be better coming from you."

I smacked a hand to my forehead. "My God. Of course. In all the commotion, I'm not sure if Lieutenant Cruz had the foresight to send anyone over to Shanna's house. Tell Kenya I'll take care of it."

"Well," she said. "That's the thing. About what I said ... you know. That reporter writing down license plates and everything. There's a good chance either he or somebody on his behalf will follow you. Why don't we take my car? They don't know it. We can be at Mrs. Clancy's in fifteen minutes."

I knew Dave Reese. Mercy was exactly right. If he could scoop me before I could update Shanna Clancy on what happened today, he was just slimy enough to do it.

"Let's go," I said. "I know a shortcut to the sheriff's house."

"You want me to cut past the quarry," she said. "I already looked it up on my GPS."

Mercedes pulled up in a Lexus LC. It was a hundred-thousand-dollar car. What in the world was a starving law student doing driving a car like that? I saved my questions for later. No sooner had Mercy pulled out of the government lot than my phone rang. Sam.

"What do you have?" I said.

"Austin Merkle's being brought in for questioning," he said. "Patel's bringing him down to the station. Gus is going to stay at Merkle's house while BCI gets started there. Then he's going to head straight to Shanna's."

"I'm headed there now," I said. "What can I tell her?"

"Oh good," Sam said, relief in his voice. "She can't hear about this thirdhand."

"Reese from Channel Eight was already here sniffing around," I said. "He knows a search warrant was issued."

"Great," Sam said. "There's a courthouse leak."

"It appears so."

"Well," Sam said. "Judge Ivey is about to sign an arrest warrant, too."

"Sam," I said. "What did you find?"

"I'll tell you more later, after BCI finishes up. But we think we have the murder weapon, Mara. This kid. Merkle? He might be the world's dumbest criminal. I just can't believe it. I don't want to believe somebody like him took Bill out ..."

"I know," I said. "Let's worry about that part later. Sam, if Merkle asks for an attorney ..."

"I know," he said. "I trust Patel. And I trust Gus."

I took a breath. "So do I."

"Tell Shanna Gus will be there just as soon as he can."

I promised him I would then clicked off. Five minutes later, Mercy pulled into Shanna Clancy's driveway. She was already waiting on the front porch with the two female deputies Sam had assigned to stay with her. They knew something was up.

"Do you want me to hang back?" Mercy said as she parked the car.

"If you could wait with the deputies," I said. "Tell them what happened with Dave Reese. I can't believe he'd be bold enough to drive all the way up here."

"I can," she said. "He's looking for a reaction shot. He's not concerned about getting sound bites at this point. But a video would go viral."

It made my stomach turn. I thanked Mercy for standing by with the deputies. They cleared the way for me as I walked up to Shanna.

She looked almost child-like. Thin to begin with, I guessed she'd lost at least fifteen pounds since Bill's funeral.

"What's happening?" she said. I stepped into the house with her, not trusting that Reese or some other reporter wasn't out in the woods somewhere with a telephoto lens.

"Let's have a seat," I said.

She went to the kitchen table. Her eyelids fluttered and for a moment, the woman looked like she was about to pass out.

"There's been a break in the case," I said. "Gus Ritter is on his way here. He'll fill you in on what he can. But the media already has the first inklings of what's going on. We wanted to make sure you heard it in person."

She nodded. "Thank you for that. I've been staying off my phone. Away from the television."

"That's good."

"Who did this?" she asked. "You know, don't you? I can tell. I can see it on your face."

"There's a young man who came forward. The one who we believe picked up the shooter at the Dollar Kart parking lot. Gus has told you from the beginning, he doesn't believe Bill was killed there."

She nodded. "Gus said he thinks somebody drove Bill's car there after he ... when he was ..."

"Right," I said. "Well, the man who drove the getaway car has turned in his friend. Everything is still in flux, but an arrest warrant has been issued for this friend."

"Who is he? Can you tell me his name?"

Tears welled in her eyes.

"I'm going to leave that to Gus," I said.

"But they have him? Gus has him down at the station? He's not ... he's not out there anymore?"

I realized then what scared her. Of course it scared her. Someone had shot her husband in cold blood. For the past few weeks, Shanna Clancy had been living in the house she shared with him. She had to be wondering, what if they came back? Bill's address hadn't been a secret. Over the years, reporters and protestors had shown up at his front door.

"You're safe," I said. "Do you hear me, Shanna? You're safe. The deputies are right outside. They aren't going anywhere."

She wiped her tears. "They've been wonderful. You've all been so wonderful. And Reverend Pete. I had no idea how many people loved Bill. I mean, I knew ... but ..."

"He was a good man," I said. "And he wouldn't want you to be afraid."

"But you don't know," she said. "You don't know why this man shot him. If it was for revenge or something. Bill put a lot of bad men away, Mara. I read this story about another sheriff who was murdered near Atlanta a few years ago. They came after his family, too. They ... I just don't know how long I can stay here.'

"One thing at a time," I said. "Have you been contacted by the Silver Angels? They're a victim's advocacy group. They help people who ..."

"I'm not the victim," she said. "I wasn't raped. Nobody tried to hurt me. I thought that group was for women who have been assaulted."

"They're for women who've been victimized, Shanna. You have. They have trauma counselors. It might be good for you to talk to one of them. And if this goes to trial, they can be with you every step of the way."

"Trial," she said. "I haven't even thought that far ahead. Do I have to be there? I don't know if I can hear about all of it, Mara. What if I can't?"

"We'll worry about that later, okay?"

"But it will be you, won't it? If this person they've arrested ends up being the one who did this to Bill ... it'll be you who makes sure he goes to jail for it, right?"

"I think so," I said.

"Good. Good. I trust you."

Gravel crunched on the driveway. A moment later, the front door opened. Gus Ritter walked in. His face had gone hard.

New lines formed around his eyes and his mouth. He walked into the kitchen and froze when he saw Shanna Clancy.

Shanna rose. Gus strode toward her. Shanna ran to him and collapsed in Gus's arms.

"We think we got him, Shanna," he said. "Shh. It's going to be all right. We think we got him."

"Tell me," she said. "Gus. I want to know his name."

Gus looked at me over Shanna's head. Then he pulled her away from his body, holding her up.

"Austin Merkle," he said. "That's the bastard's name. Shanna ... we got him."

13

"Austin Merkle. A white male aged twenty-six years old. He was apprehended in the sixteen hundred block of Grantville Road after a brief foot pursuit with my deputies. Mr. Merkle was currently unemployed and moved to Waynetown three years ago. That's all the information I can share with you right now."

A chorus of questions came at Sam hard. He didn't take his eyes off the note cards in front of him. I stood to the side of the lectern, out of the camera shot. Kenya stood on one side of Sam, the mayor, Karl O'Keefe, on the other.

"Lieutenant Cruz," one reporter shouted, managing to get her voice heard over the others. She got close to the microphone.

"Is it true that your suspect, Mr. Merkle, suffered a broken nose and collarbone in the tussle with police officers? Can you comment on that?"

"That's false," Sam said, his jaw clenched. "The suspect was apprehended without injury."

"But he was tased," the reporter said, reading from her own notes.

"Also false," Sam said. "No weapons were discharged in the suspect's apprehension."

"Will body cam footage be released?"

"Listen," Sam said. "That's all the information I have for you at this time. But I can assure you, I will work with the prosecutor's office, the mayor, the media, and any other agency required with the utmost respect and transparency. As you know, this is still an ongoing investigation. You'll have more information as soon as I can share it. That is all."

Sam tilted the microphone down, angling it for Kenya's height as she took her turn facing the barrage of questions.

"What steps is your office taking to ensure Mr. Merkle receives a fair trial? Has he asked for representation?"

"Mr. Merkle is innocent until proven guilty," Kenya said. "Like all suspects. I'd like to commend acting Sheriff Cruz's office for going above and beyond to ensure transparency in this case. But like Lieutenant Cruz has stated, my office can't comment much beyond that either."

"Ms. Spaulding." Dave Reese stepped up to the microphone. Though he asked Kenya the question, he kept his focus right on me.

"Are you prepared to address the concerns people have about who might prosecute this case? Your office has come under scrutiny in the past ... and was part of a massive investigation by the Ohio Attorney General's office regarding your predecessor's corruption. Mara Brent, your assistant prosecutor, has strong ties to a corrupt congressman who was convicted in connection to criminal enterprises and obstruction of justice right here in Waynetown. How can the people of this county possibly trust this case will be handled above board?"

"Mr. Reese," Kenya said. "First of all, you're jumping ahead about fifty steps. This is an ongoing investigation at this point, not a criminal trial. We'll get there if we get there. Mara Brent's reputation as a fair prosecutor is impeccable. I have the utmost confidence in her abilities on any criminal prosecution put before her. We're lucky to have her. Which means you're lucky to have her, Reese. I won't be taking any more questions ..."

"Ms. Spaulding!"

Another man shot up and took the microphone from David Reese. "Many of your constituents have legitimate concerns about whether you can remain impartial on this case. The questions raised by Mr. Reese are only the tip of the iceberg. How do we know that your office wasn't connected to the corruption brought to light by both the Attorney General's office and during the RICO case involving your lead prosecutor's husband? This whole thing stinks to high heaven. It seems the only fair outcome is if you and your office have nothing to do with the investigation or eventual trial of any individuals connected to the murder of Bill Clancy."

Behind him, about a dozen people stood up, wearing matching blue tee shirts with white lettering. They turned so the assembled press got a clear view. "Pull the Weeds. Recall Kenya Spaulding."

Lord. These were volunteers working for Kenya's opponent, Skip Fletcher, in the upcoming election. They all began chanting in unison.

"Pull the Weeds! Pull the Weeds!"

"That's all we have for you today," Sam said, barely containing his rage. Oddly, I didn't share it. I cared more about how Kenya might react. For my part, I'd gotten used to the attacks. I only hated how my personal life might impact her professional one.

A pair of deputies opened the door behind us. We filed out of the press room and into Sam's temporary office down the hall.

Bill Clancy's office, the largest in the building, was one floor up. Sam so far refused to move into it. He used the excuse of wanting to take great care going through Bill's things while the investigation continued. Fair. But I knew it was more than that.

Gus was the last one in and slammed the door behind him. "They're gonna poison this case before we even get to trial," he said. "That out there? It was all crap. Drummed up by Fletcher. That guy is a weasel. The biggest scam artist I've ever seen."

"Forget it," Kenya said, unrattled by the shrapnel she'd just taken.

I took a seat on the couch against the wall. Sam sat behind his desk. Gus paced. Kenya stood quietly by the closed door.

"Gus," Kenya said. "What do we know about Austin Merkle?"

There was a soft knock on the door. Gus opened it. Kenya's intern, Mercy Gale, poked her head in. I'd almost forgotten that she'd been in the press room. Kenya motioned her in. She looked nervously around the room and took a seat on the other end of the couch from me.

"He's a nobody," Gus said. "Merkle's not much more than a drifter. He's lived in Waynetown maybe three years. Before that, Toledo. He's had a series of odd jobs since high school. He's some kind of fitness fanatic. He was working at one of those fitness club chains as a personal trainer before they fired him."

"Fired him for what?" I asked.

"Dealing,' Gus said. "'Roids."

From what I'd seen of Austin Merkle's mugshots, he was using performance enhancers himself. He was thick-necked, bulked up, his bulging arms covered in huge veins.

"What about friends, family," Kenya said. "Who's he been living with?"

"Other than Ricky Wahl, he doesn't seem to have too many friends in town," Gus said. "You heard what Wahl said. Merkle's always bragging about his next get-rich-quick scheme. Wahl had been loaning him money, investing in some pyramid scheme related to the drugs Merkle was selling. At one point, he convinced Wahl he had a medicinal pot-growing license and they were going to make millions. It was all a scam. Steven Wahl claims he didn't know anything about it. Ricky stole about a thousand dollars from his dad to give to Merkle."

"Do you have any indication of what his motive might have been?" I asked.

"None," Gus said. "It doesn't make any sense yet. Merkle's a punk. He didn't say anything when he was arrested. He hasn't been questioned since he asked for a lawyer. But he's been cocky as hell. Arrogant little puke. He hates cops. That much we know. Agent Patel is getting the digital forensics reports, but Merkle's made some social media posts against law enforcement over the last year or so."

"You think this was his way of protesting?" I said. "By executing Bill Clancy? How did he even get him alone?"

"We don't know yet," Sam said. "But so far Merkle's not done a very good job of covering his tracks. The phone call Bill got in the middle of the night, the one that made him leave the house. It came from a burner phone, which we knew. But we found the thing in Merkle's garbage can."

"Wow," Kenya said.

"Sam," I said. "Was he injured at all during his arrest?"

Sam leveled a stare at me. "No," he said. "I swear. Not a scratch on him. My people are well trained. The last thing anyone wants to do is open the door to something ugly."

"I wasn't suggesting ..."

"Has he hired a lawyer yet?" Mercedes spoke up. "Excuse me. I don't mean to interrupt. It's just ... this case is going to become high profile. There are certain players who may want to use it as a springboard for their own name recognition."

VOW OF JUSTICE

"Not yet," Gus said. "And that crap out there? With Skip Fletcher's people? That needs to be locked down. Sam, how the hell did they even get in?"

"Those weren't local," I said. "Did anyone in this room recognize any one of them?"

Everyone looked at each other. No one answered.

"That's kind of why I asked about Merkle's defense lawyer," Mercedes said. "That was too well orchestrated. The way they all stood up at once and showed their tee shirts. And they knew what way the cameras were facing."

"You think Fletcher hired them?" Kenya asked.

"No," Mercedes said. "I think it was more of an audition."

"By whom?" I asked.

"Austin Merkle's soon-to-be defense lawyer," she said. "Um ... that was straight out of the playbook of the Law Dogs Group. They're a legal watchdog group that engages in some guerilla tactics at times. Today's display was pretty mild. My father had dealings with them during the Jackson Smith trial."

Puzzle pieces slammed into place in my brain. Mercedes Gale. Kenya's comments about a nepotism hire. Gale. Jackson Smith trial? That was going on thirty years ago, but Smith had been an NFL player accused of killing his son or his stepson, I couldn't remember which.

"Wait," Gus said, getting there just as I did. "You're E. Thomas Gale's kid? The guy who's on all those cable news channels?"

E. Thomas Gale was one of the most famous celebrity defense lawyers in the country. Before Jackson Smith, he put himself on the map defending some Beverly Hills doctor accused of murdering his mistress. They'd made an Oscar-winning movie out of it. Then he got uber rich as one of the top legal commentators during the heyday of court television and the OJ trial. That explained how Mercy could afford the wheels she drove. But what in the world was his daughter doing interning in Maumee County, Ohio? That would be a question for another day. I had more pressing matters at hand.

"I think Mercy is right," I said. "We've got to consider the possibility that this case is plum pickings for someone to get name recognition. They're going to come for you, Kenya," I said. "They're going to come for all of us."

"Let them," Sam said. "This is Bill Clancy we're talking about. I'm not gonna let this turn into some circus."

"It already is," I said. "It just makes it that much more important that this investigation run smoothly. We can't afford a single mistake."

"There won't be," Gus said. "We have this kid dead to rights. It was his phone. He lured Bill out of his house that night. I'm going to find out why. We have the gun. It was in his damn laundry hamper with blood on it. His fingerprints were all over it. I'm waiting on ballistics, but if they come back as a match ... this case is ironclad."

When Gus said ironclad, I couldn't help but hear "too good to be true." There was something coming. I could feel it. Another shoe about to drop. A bomb about to go off.

14

On the morning of June 15th, two months to the day after Sheriff Bill Clancy was found shot dead in a parking lot, Austin Merkle was indicted on one count of first degree murder. It took the grand jury less than an hour to come back with their verdict. Kenya stood beside Sam and read her pre-written statement to the press. Skip Fletcher's supporters had come out in full force wearing their blue tee shirts. Their numbers kept growing and none of them were local to Maumee County. Mercy's hunch had been correct. The Law Dog Group had funded their trip to our little county.

As Sam, Kenya, Mercy, and I left the courtroom, a second impromptu press conference formed on the courthouse steps.

"Is that him?" Kenya whispered to me. We looked from the clerk's office window.

I saw him in profile, his blond hair gleaming in the sun. Sam grumbled beside me.

"That's him, all right," I said. I hadn't seen him in person in almost fifteen years. Not since our third year of law school.

"Alexander Nash," Mercy said. "He looks ... even taller in person."

"I am certain that once we have our day in court," Nash said, "we'll be able to shine the light on this gross miscarriage of justice and prove my client is one hundred percent innocent of the charges brought against him."

Nash faced a typical barrage of questions, but none of them harsh like what Kenya kept getting. He stepped away from the microphones and walked away from the crowd.

"Those people aren't even from Maumee County," Sam said. "They're plants, pitching so Nash gets the sound bite he wants. I can't watch it. I want to rip his throat out."

He spoke louder than he should have. Two staff members from the clerk's office went back to their desks when I gave them sharp looks. I tugged on Sam's sleeve.

"Not here," I said.

"I'll talk to you later," he said. "I need to get back to the office."

Sam excused himself. In the last two months, he looked like he'd aged ten years. Kenya, Mercy, and I started walking back to our offices. We took the service elevator, avoiding members of the public or press who might be lurking about.

"How do you suppose the likes of Austin Merkle can afford someone like Alexander Nash as his defense counsel?" Kenya asked once we'd made it back to the prosecutor's office lobby and were away from any courthouse gossips.

"Give me a day or two and I'll find out," Mercy said. "I have a hunch you're not going to like it."

"Find out for sure," Kenya said. "In the end, there's nothing we can do about it. It won't be admissible at trial anyway. But I'd like to know what we're dealing with."

"On it," Mercy said. She took a different exit, heading to the parking lot. Kenya and I walked straight to her office.

"She's a good one, I think," Kenya said. "Mercy's working angles I hadn't thought of. And she has connections that might be of help. How do you feel about me assigning her to you for the rest of the summer for trial prep on Merkle?"

My initial reaction was to say no. I had nothing personally against Mercy Gale. She had proven useful on a few things. But I couldn't ignore my recent track record with interns.

"I'll think about it," I said.

"You're gonna need eyes in the back of your head on this one, Mara," she said. "And it's good Mercy's not personally connected to Maumee County. She can look at things with a fresh perspective. She's not entrenched like ..."

"Like I am?" I smiled.

"I didn't mean ..."

"Mara?" Caro popped her head in. "Um ... I'm sorry to interrupt, but someone just showed up asking for a meeting with you. He insists you'll see him without an appointment."

"Him?" The way Caro's eyes lit up, I had a strong hunch about who she meant.

"Mr. Nash," she whispered.

I met Kenya's gaze. "Do you want to sit in on this?"

Kenya shook her head. "I trust you'll keep me in the loop."

I excused myself and headed down the hall to my office. Caro went ahead of me. She froze at my doorway. "Sir, I didn't give you permission to just march back here," she said.

"It's all right," I said, moving past her and heading through the door. "I'll take it from here."

Alexander Nash rose from my office couch. Mercy had a point. The man seemed taller than even I remembered. He offered me a firm handshake. I gestured for him to retake his seat and perched myself, leaning against the corner of my desk. For some reason, I didn't want Nash getting too comfortable. Gesturing to Caro, she smiled, then finally backed out and closed the door behind her.

"You haven't changed a bit, Mara," Nash said. "You look exactly the same as the day we graduated from law school."

I never knew how to respond to things like that. I said a polite thank you but dove into the matter.

"So, Austin Merkle," I said. "Hardly seems like the kind of small potatoes your firm would be interested in. Last I heard, you were hungry to take on Capitol Hill."

"I'm hungry to right injustices where I see them. Stepping into the gladiator ring with you just makes this a little sweeter."

"What injustice do you think you're righting, Nash?"

He just flashed me a thousand-watt smile, but didn't answer.

"Maumee County," he said, rising from the couch. Nash walked over to the wall, letting his eyes wander over the framed documents I had hung there.

"How's your mother?" he asked. "I can't imagine the great Natalie Montleroy was thrilled when you took such a low key career path. We all thought you would be the one to make a run for Congress, not Jason."

"The great Natalie Montleroy is enjoying her retirement and life as a happy grandma from her North Hampton mansion."

Nash turned to me. He stood with his hands folded behind his back.

"I want you to know. I've been thinking about you. I'm sure the last year has been rough for you. With Jason's trial. And before that ... It's commendable that you've just carried on here."

"As opposed to what?" I asked. There was a hard edge to my tone. I was beginning to resent the implication in Nash's questions.

"Sorry," he said. "I didn't mean anything negative by that. Honest. If anything, I'm trying to figure out how to apologize for not reaching out. It occurred to me you could have used an old friend during all of that turmoil with Jason. We used to be that, didn't we? Friends? Study partners, at least, right?"

I let out a breath I hadn't realized I'd been holding. Though I'd never be able to truly let my guard down when people questioned me about Jason, it was at least possible Nash's sentiment was genuine.

"Yes," I said. "We were friends. And I appreciate your concern."

Nash turned back to the wall. He tapped my law degree. "Summa Cum Laude," he said. "You know, it chapped my ass that you were always one spot ahead of me in the class standings. One spot. For three years straight. I thought I had you in that last Evidence class. And then when you booked Professor Weaver's Trial Practice class ... well, it still stings."

"Sounds like you could use a few different hobbies if you've still got time to worry about your law school grades, Nash."

He laughed. "I heard you wiped the floor with Weaver the Cleaver in the Sutter murder case. Legend."

"It was an honor trying a case against her," I said.

"She's doing well?"

"Last I saw her, she was doing quite well, yes. You should reach out. I'm sure she'd love to hear from you."

Nash finally came away from the wall and took his seat back on the couch.

"What's this really all about, Nash?" I said. "What are you doing here?"

"Well, I suppose it was time we talked. Feel each other out."

"You've filed your formal appearance," I said. "I'll have your discovery files couriered over by the end of the day. Give you a chance to get familiar, talk to your client ..."

"You planning on certifying this one as a death penalty case?"

"Austin Merkle murdered a cop," I said. "Executed him. The physical evidence in this case ... honestly? It's about as heavy as I've ever seen in all my years as a prosecutor. So what's your angle, Nash? Why get your hands dirty down here? This one's a loser for you and I think you know it."

He said nothing, his smirk the only window into his thoughts.

"I think the bigger question is why are you still down here dirtying *your* hands? It's incredible how much you've survived. You were the lead prosecutor under Phil Halsey. The taint of his corruption is going to stain this office for decades. You were married to a criminal on top of that."

His motives began to crystalize for me.

"Maumee County is politically newsworthy," I said. "There's a big election cycle coming up. There's also a bit of a power vacuum now that Jason and his affiliates' misdeeds have come to light. So what is it? You think you can make a name for yourself down here? Get some national press? I think you're wasting your time. Bill Clancy meant a lot to the people of this town. Defending the kid who murdered him isn't going to endear you to anyone. Which isn't to say Austin Merkle doesn't deserve a vigorous defense. I welcome it. But why you? Why here?"

Nash crossed his leg, making the leather couch creak. He just fixed that smirk on me. "I think your office and what's left of Bill Clancy's sheriff's department have made a rush to judgment. I think your eyes and instincts are clouded on this one, Mara."

"Are you planning on pursuing a change of venue?" I asked. "You should know, I'll fight that tooth and nail."

He shook his head. "I think this case fits right where it belongs. And I think the citizens of Maumee County deserve to know what happened to Bill Clancy and the aftermath."

"Kenya," I said. "This is about Kenya Spaulding, isn't it? Those people out there. Skip Fletcher's supporters. That transplanted crowd on the courthouse steps. You brought them in. You and whatever PAC is paying your legal fees. Is that it?"

Nothing. Stone-cold silence.

I knew I'd hit on it. It was the reason Jason had wanted to return to his hometown in the first place and eventually run for Congress. It was the reason this county held such an important position in state and ultimately national politics. We were a bellwether. A critical pocket of an even more critical swing state. And now, whoever was paying Alexander Nash's likely six-figure legal bill, was hoping to turn this trial into some kind of political statement.

"Your backers are looking to make a new king," I said. "Is that it? And the royal road runs straight over Kenya Spaulding."

Alexander Nash got to his feet. He towered over me, keeping his smile in place.

"If you came here expecting a plea deal," I said, "you should know, I'm not prepared to extend one. Austin Merkle is guilty. He murdered Bill Clancy and the people of Maumee County want to see justice done for him, despite whatever your K Street focus group might have told you."

"I'm not expecting a plea deal for my client," Nash said. "At this point, he'd never accept one. Mr. Merkle is looking forward to his day in court. So am I. And we will not be waiving his right to a speedy trial. So you'd better get ready. We'll be in trial by mid-October. This really is going to be fun, Mara. In a lot of ways, a dream come true for me. You and I finally get to do battle."

"Thanks for stopping by, Nash," I said. "Like I said, you'll have your files by the end of the week."

Alexander Nash made a courtly bow before he showed himself out of my office. A fire burned in my belly. I wanted to beat that man in court. Badly. Even as a small voice in my head told me that might be the first sign I was in trouble.

15

As the summer wore on and my trial date loomed, I finally took Kenya's advice and brought Mercy Gale on as my full-time trial assistant on the Merkle case. She was organized, dogged, and determined to solve the mystery of who was funding Alexander Nash's legal bills. While she worked on that, I met the task force over at the sheriff's department. In late August, Andrea Patel had wrapped up her report for BCI.

I stood at the head of the conference room table as Patel laid out the extensive digital forensics findings. We had a map of the cell tower hits for Merkle's burner phone as well as his personal one. In the three months prior to Bill's murder, Merkle had been using it in support of his fledgling steroid-selling enterprise. The call to Bill in the early morning of April 15th was the only one he'd made to him.

"This is the part I don't get," I said. "One call. It lasts three minutes. Whatever he said was enough to lure Bill out of the house."

I didn't want to say what I'd suspected. Not in front of Gus. He had gotten increasingly defensive anytime someone made a disparaging comment about Bill. Today, though, Gus was out with food poisoning. It was only me, Sam, and Andrea in the room.

"Sam," I said. "Gus and Bill were closer than the two of you were. In the sense, he spent more time with Bill outside the office. Yet Bill picked you to be his contact point with Shanna in the event he died. Why not Gus?"

"For the same reason you came down here today knowing he'd be out of the office," Sam said, his tone gruff.

"I didn't mean anything by that," I said, but we both knew that wasn't entirely true.

"Bill was afraid Gus would get too emotional in the event he was killed in the line of duty."

"Okay. I really wish you hadn't just said that. Or that I hadn't heard it. I can't hear that, Sam. That's exactly the kind of thing Alexander Nash will seize on at trial. The more he can paint Gus as a loose cannon, or someone too emotionally attached to this case, the easier time he'll have raising reasonable doubt."

"So don't call him," Patel said.

"What?" Sam said.

"Don't call him to testify. You don't need him. I've been lead on this case since almost the beginning. I can make sure the jury understands there's been an impartial investigator making all the major decisions."

"Except Nash will sink his teeth right into that," I said. "He'll know for sure there are problems with Gus."

"There are no problems with Gus," Sam said.

"You know what I meant," I said. "Okay. So here's what I'm really trying to ask you. Bill had a home gym built in the last year. That's where Shanna was when we showed up to tell her what happened that morning. Remember? She said it was his Christmas present to the both of them. She'd been on him to get in better shape."

Sam smiled. "That and he hated going to any of the fitness clubs around town. He didn't even like going to the one at the Union Hall. For the same reason he didn't like going out. People would bug him too much."

"Got it," I said. "So what I'm wondering, do you think there's any chance that phone call was Bill trying to buy steroids from Merkle?"

"There was no evidence of anabolic steroid use in Bill's autopsy," Patel said.

"There wouldn't have to be. If this was the first contact Bill had with Merkle," I said. But even I knew this was the longest of shots.

"I'll ask around," Sam said. "But I really doubt it. 'Roids just wouldn't be Bill's style. He didn't care what he looked like. He didn't care what people thought. He wasn't vain. And I just don't see him doing anything stupid like that. Something that might hurt his career."

"All right," I said. I moved to the other side of the table and stared at the vast array of pictures Patel had pulled from

Merkle's personal cell phone. They numbered in the hundreds. I hated looking at them.

"Any luck identifying any of these women?" I asked.

"Just these two," Patel said. She pulled up one shot of an African-American woman lying naked on her back. She smiled at the camera ... at Merkle.

"Yvonne Porter," Patel said. "She and Merkle dated briefly two years ago. She hasn't seen him since then and she's moved out to the Tampa Bay area. She worked as an exotic dancer in Toledo. That's where she met Merkle. She's the one who ended it. She said it was amicable. This picture is actually the last text he sent her before the break-up. She was pretty angry when she found out he sent this one to his friends, but said the ... um ... act leading up to it was entirely consensual."

"Are you charging him for anything in connection with these photos?" I asked.

"No," Sam said. "So far, we have no evidence that any of these women were underage. Those we've managed to speak to, like Ms. Porter, admitted the sex they had with Merkle was consensual."

"This one," Patel said, picking up another photograph. It was actually a still from a forty-second video on Merkle's phone. It showed Merkle exchanging oral sex with a red-headed woman who looked to be in her early twenties.

"Amber Kirby," she continued. "Another exotic dancer from Toledo. There was a strip club Merkle frequented up until the middle of last year. Same one where he met Yvonne Porter. Yvonne actually introduced him to Amber. From what we can tell, this was the only encounter Merkle had with her.

Same story. She admits she knew about him videotaping the um ... exchange ... but not that he shared it with anyone. This one went to Ricky Wahl. Along with all of these."

Patel had at least a dozen other photos that Merkle sent to Ricky Wahl. None of the other women's faces could be seen. In addition to the video with Amber Kirby, he had recorded two other sexual encounters. These women could only be seen from behind.

"The White Lotus and the Crown Princess," Sam quipped, referring to the tattoos they had on their lower backs.

"He was a creep," Patel said. "But none of what we found on his phone rises to the level of criminal activity."

"Dead ends," I said.

"We'll pack it up, copy it all, and send it to your office," Patel said.

"And I'll send it off to Nash."

Sam picked up the printout of yet another picture text. This one showing Merkle receiving oral sex from Amber Kirby.

"This," he said, "is why I tell all my deputies not to use their own phones to take pictures at crime scenes. The second they do it, some defense attorney is going to have the right to see every other thing on their phones."

"Believe me," Andrea said. "You don't want to know the things I've seen from cops. From this department, even."

I put a hand up. "I've seen enough. Thanks for all of this."

"But here's the stuff I think you'll like the most," she said. She pulled two stapled pages off the table and handed them to me.

They were texts from Merkle to Ricky Wahl on the afternoon of April 15th and the morning of April 16th.

Merkle had texted, "We cool?"

There was at first no answer from Ricky for almost three hours. Merkle texted again. "RU cool?"

Then the next morning, a longer text. "Dude you better not ghost me."

Ricky answered none of the texts.

"This is good," I said. "It looks like Merkle is trying to make sure Ricky's going to stay quiet."

"I know it's open to interpretation, but it fits with Ricky's story at least," Patel said. "But I just don't think I'm going to be able to deliver you a motive on this one."

"It's money or love," I said. "Most of the time anyway."

"Right. And we don't have evidence of either," Sam said. "If it weren't for that phone call, I'd say Bill was just somehow in the wrong place at the wrong time."

"Nash is the one who doesn't make sense to me," Patel said. "Punks like Austin Merkle don't get high-powered defense lawyers like that."

"I know," I said. "That's what I've got Mercy Gale working on."

"Is she really E. Thomas Gale's kid?" Patel asked.

"Yes."

"Boy, the way he defended Dr. Anton Milo? The movie they made out of it? *Deadly Affair*? It's one of the ones that got me jazzed about crime scene investigation when I was a kid. I'd love to meet him. If ... uh ... he happens to come to Waynetown for a visit, I wouldn't mind ..."

I laughed. "I'll let you know."

Patel packed up her things and excused herself. She was on her way to Fostoria to process another crime scene in a double murder.

"I've cleared my schedule for the week before trial," she said. "I'll be at your beck and call."

"I appreciate that," I said as she left.

An awkward silence fell between Sam and me as we suddenly had the room to ourselves. He looked haggard. Thinner than I'd seen in a while. I was worried.

"Sam," I said. "What we have? It's going to be enough. I don't have to prove motive."

"I'm not worried about that as far as the trial goes. It's just ... I don't know if *I* can live with not knowing. The idea that we might never know. That even if ... when ... you secure a conviction, there still won't be answers for Shanna. For Gus."

"And for you," I said. "I know. But we've got a few weeks before the trial yet. A lot can happen. Nash knows he's got a loser on his hands, potentially. We both know he's not doing this because he believes in Austin Merkle's innocence. Maybe he'll finally realize his client's facing the death penalty and convince him to cooperate."

"Mara. Be careful. Merkle's motives aren't the only ones I'm worried about."

"What do you mean?"

"Just what you said. Nash doesn't care whether Merkle is innocent. He cares that you're the one prosecuting this case. That's dangerous. He could hurt you. I don't want that. Bill sure as hell wouldn't have wanted that."

I went to him. I loved that he worried about me. But hated that he felt he had to. I went up on my toes and kissed him on the cheek. His face flushed. He stammered something, but never completed the thought. It warmed my heart to leave him speechless, to bring him outside of his own head, if only for a moment.

But as I left his office, his words kept thrumming through me. Nash was dangerous. He could try to hurt me. Well, I knew just how dangerous I could be as well.

16

"It's not what I'd call a smoking gun," Mercy said. She stood in the doorway of Kenya's office, clutching a stack of files to her chest. I'd just finished briefing Kenya on the status of the Austin Merkle trial prep. After three months of discovery, and Nash's decision not to waive Merkle's right to a speedy trial, we were only two weeks away from selecting a jury.

"Show me what you have," Kenya asked. Mercy came fully into the room. She pulled a single sheet of paper off the top of the stack she held and set it on Kenya's desk. It took far longer than we thought, but she'd come up with the answers on Merkle's legal defense fund.

"The Cerberus Justice Project," she said. "CJP. Their funding is buried under several other non-profits. But they're ultimately part of the Legacy Foundation. That's who's writing the checks for Alexander Nash's six-figure retainer."

"You think Nash's got political aspirations of his own?" Kenya asked.

"Maybe," I said. "Maybe he's being a good soldier for the party. Or maybe he just loved the idea of getting to try a case against me. We were competitive in law school. He's the kind of guy that still smarts from the idea that I ended up higher in the class rankings than he did. He made a point of telling me that when we met in my office a few months ago."

"What?" Mercy said. "That's nuts."

"It wasn't about me so much," I said. "He and Jason were bigger rivals than Nash and I were. It was your typical alpha male crap. Now Jason's in prison. The icing on the cake for Nash would be to best me in court. I'm sure he jumped at the chance when the case came up."

"Fine," Kenya said. "So it'll be that much sweeter when you wipe the floor with him."

I wasn't so sure. Though I said nothing, something must have registered on my face.

"What?" Kenya said. "What wheels are turning in that brain of yours?"

"I just ..." Kenya trained her eyes on me. I looked at her. Really looked at her. We'd worked together for more than a decade. She'd been one of the first friends I made in Waynetown when I moved here with Jason. It hadn't always been easy. Kenya didn't let that many people in. I suppose I didn't either. This was the twenty-first century, but Maumee County was still stuck in the past in a lot of respects. Kenya often had to work ten times as hard to get twice as far and earn the respect of the people here. She came from nothing. I had the backing of an affluent family. She'd resented me for that, even if she never outwardly showed it. But we'd truly fought in the trenches right alongside each other. I had her back. I knew she had mine. When it came to it, I trusted this woman with my life. With my son's life. There had been times when that had been put to the test. I would follow her into hell if I had to. She knew it.

But now? Kenya Spaulding looked tired. I knew she felt like everything she had worked for was about to evaporate.

"There's more," Mercy said. She put another piece of paper in front of Kenya. "CJP isn't just funding Merkle's defense. I tracked down the names of some of the out-of-town protestors we've seen at every press conference since the indictment. The ones wearing those Pull the Weeds tee shirts. CJP foot the bill for their hotel stays and transportation down here. They're pouring a ton of money into a bunch of local races around here, including Skip Fletcher's."

"Kenya," I said. "I think we should ask for a continuance."

"What?"

"Push the trial back until after the election. Take that component out of it. If Skip Fletcher is planning to use this as a way to put this office on trial, we don't let him."

"On what grounds?" Mercy asked. "The continuance, I mean. Alexander Nash has gone on record saying he's ready to go."

"Mara," Kenya said. "You're ready too. I just got done saying, this is a ground ball. It's like the heavens opened up and handed you a perfect case. The evidence is overwhelmingly in our favor."

"It's not the evidence I'm worried about," I muttered.

"Then what?" Kenya asked.

"I don't know. It's a gut feeling. Something we're missing. I'd feel a lot better if I understood why Austin Merkle did what he did."

"You don't have to prove motive," Mercy said. "Don't we just have to make sure the jury understands that?"

"Yes," Kenya answered. "And you drew the golden ticket when Judge Saul was assigned to the trial. She's not going to let Nash get away with grandstanding or games. She'll keep this trial on track."

"Maybe ..."

"Unless ..." Kenya paused. "Mercy? Do you mind giving us the room?"

Mercy opened her mouth, then promptly clamped it shut. "Of course," she said. She gathered her files and excused herself, closing the door behind her.

"Mara," Kenya said. "What's going on? Really."

"I've got a bad feeling," I said. "It's not about the trial prep. I do feel the case is solid against Austin Merkle. More solid than most. You're right about that. But I also know Alexander Nash. He's working a bigger angle. I don't think he cares one bit about whether Austin Merkle gets convicted."

"You said yourself he wants to beat you. Of course he cares."

"Yeah," I said. "So why does he take a case even though he knows he'll likely lose on the merits?"

"Come on," Kenya said. "You're paranoid. I get it. The last year's been rough. You've had a figurative house fall on your head with Jason's trial. You're catastrophizing. I get that. But this? This case? This is not that. This is just you going in there, presenting the evidence. The *substantial* evidence. And getting justice for Bill Clancy. You let me worry about Skip Fletcher. Let the people of this town ... the voters ... see why you're in this job. I don't care about Fletcher. I don't care about Alexander Nash or the Legacy Foundation or CJP or anything else. I'd rather lose this election a thousand times than see Bill Clancy's killer go free. I trust you."

"Thanks," I said. "And I know."

"Mercy didn't really tell us anything we didn't already suspect. You knew Nash was up to something the second he filed an appearance."

"I just wish ..."

"What?"

"I just wish we had more."

"More what? More evidence? Mara, other than someone coming forward with an actual recording of the murder, there isn't any more you could ask for."

"Except there is. We don't know where Bill was murdered. We only know it wasn't in his car. Merkle drove him there. From where? How did he lure Bill out of the house?"

"It doesn't matter," Kenya said. "When Nash tries to raise those questions, you shut him down. The jury doesn't need to know what Merkle said on that phone call. It's enough you can prove he's the one who made it. And you have video evidence that Bill left the house at 3:00 a.m. right after he received it. Merkle's the only one who can answer that and he won't. Nash would never be foolish enough to put him on the stand."

She was right. Everyone was right. And yet ... I couldn't shake the feeling that another figurative house was about to fall on my head.

17

"Members of the jury," I said, stepping up to the lectern. I had said these words thousands of times. Faced twelve pairs of eyes, trained on me, judging me. My clothes. My hair. My tone of voice. My gestures. Even the breaths I took as I spaced my words. All of it, open to interpretation. Did I truly believe the defendant was guilty? Was I likable enough? Could I be trusted? Sometimes, just the slightest flutter of my eye could send the wrong message to someone looking for it.

Juries are fickle beasts. We do our best to ensure those seated can judge a case impartially. No. That's not really true. We do our best to try to ensure whatever hidden biases people have, weigh in our favor. We're often wrong. The most rock-solid evidence sometimes makes no difference. It's the story we have to sell.

"Sheriff Bill Clancy wasn't finished. He had good work to do for the people of this county. For you. For his family. And quite frankly, for me. But he won't get that chance. Something moved him to leave his home in the middle of the night on

April 15th. Something alarming enough, he said goodbye to his loving wife of ten years, got into his car, and drove off to meet his killer.

"His killer, ladies and gentlemen, is sitting right here in front of you. Austin Merkle. The evidence will show how Mr. Merkle made a fateful phone call to Bill Clancy and lured him out of bed. We don't know why and probably never will. The defense might want you to care about that. It's an interesting question, to be sure. A critical one. But in the end, it's immaterial.

"What we do know is shocking enough. The evidence will show that this man, Austin Merkle, shot Bill Clancy two times. Once through the shoulder. Then, the fatal shot through the temple. Mr. Merkle then stuffed Bill Clancy in the trunk of his own car and drove him to the Dollar Kart parking lot. Staging him behind the steering wheel, then leaving him there to be found.

"The physical evidence in this case is overwhelming. And all of it will point directly to Austin Merkle. Remember that. Don't lose sight of it, as the defendant's lawyer will want you to. He will want you to discount what you see with your own eyes. Hear with your own ears.

"What happened to Bill Clancy was senseless. Heartless. Horrific. There is one small mercy in it though. We have the only answer that matters. We know who committed this crime. Over the course of the next few days, you'll get to see and hear the overwhelming evidence pointing to Austin Merkle's guilt. In the simplest, most undeniable terms, I'm confident that you'll be able to return a just verdict for Bill Clancy. "You'll be able to deliver justice for his grieving wife and for the people of this town who loved him. In that way, you'll be able to finish some of the good work that Sheriff Bill Clancy himself cared so much about. So for now, I'll sit down and allow the facts to speak for themselves. I assure you. They are loud. Deafening. And will allow you to render a guilty verdict without any reasonable doubt. Thank you."

Sam sat in the back of the courtroom, flanked by several deputies. Shanna Clancy sat out in the hallway. Until she'd been called to testify, it was better if she stayed out of the courtroom. I didn't want to risk the accusation that I'd polluted anything she had to say.

Alexander Nash leaned over and whispered something in Austin Merkle's ear. Merkle's mother sat behind him. In all the months since Austin's arrest, she hadn't come forward. She'd refused every attempt my office had made to reach out to her. She wore a new, freshly pressed navy-blue suit. Her hair and makeup looked expensive.

Then there was Merkle. He looked a bit like Jean-Claude Van Damme in his prime. Handsome, yes. Big blue eyes but bugged out a bit more than normal. Broad through the shoulders. He wore a shiny blue suit that hugged his well-developed muscles. He was the kind of guy, the moment you saw him, you knew he was on steroids.

Anger. Rage. Side effects of those powerful drugs. It clawed at me, wondering why Nash had never once pursued a plea deal. Never asked me to entertain the possibility that his client had acted out of some fury he couldn't control. Something that could have made an argument for second-degree murder plausible. It felt like an irresponsible roll of the dice and out of character for someone as smart as Nash was.

Merkle's mother wiped away a tear she didn't appear to have cried. An act. A bad performance. Every intel I had on her told me she and Austin had been estranged since she threw him out of the house at sixteen. Yet here she was. Bought and paid for. Just like Nash.

I sat down at the prosecution's table. Beside me, Mercy Gale scribbled something on a notepad. She tilted it toward me. An arrow pointing to Merkle's mother. Next to it, a dollar sign.

I gave Mercy a silent nod and straightened my jacket.

"Mr. Nash?" Judge Saul said.

Nash cleared his throat and stepped up to the lectern. He smiled at the judge. He smiled at me. Then he turned to the jury and I watched his smile fade.

"Members of the jury," he said. "If Bill Clancy could speak. If he could walk straight into this courtroom with that trademark swagger he had, I think he would look you all right in the eye and tell you something you might find shocking. But by the end of this trial, that thing will seem like the only reasonable thing anybody could say to you. You see, if Bill Clancy could address you himself, I think he'd tell you Mara Brent is the last person he'd want prosecuting this case."

My blood ran cold. I felt Mercy stiffen beside me. Behind me, far in the back, I could even sense Sam's tension. I tried to keep my face neutral for a moment, tilting only enough to see Sam from the corner of my eye.

"I may not win any kind of popularity contest by saying that," Nash continued. "I get that. I'm not from around here. How dare I waltz up here and say that stuff about Mrs. Brent? Well, in the interests of justice, somebody has to. Today, that somebody is me."

"What is he doing?" Mercy wrote on the pad. I put my hand over it, willing myself to keep an even breath.

"There's the central tragedy in this case, to be sure," Nash said. "Bill Clancy seemed like a good guy. A noble and humble public servant. He was killed. That we know. That's all we know. That's all the evidence is going to show. But it's not the full story. Mrs. Brent raises a good question. The only one that really matters. And the only one you're gonna see she can't answer."

He left the lectern and started to pace. Nash stopped right in front of the defense table, putting Austin Merkle directly in the line of sight of every member of the jury.

Merkle sat up straighter. His face flushed. I had the sense that this moment had been choreographed. Merkle had been warned. At this moment in Nash's opening, he'd been told to expect all eyes on him. Sit up straight. Look at them. Show no fear. Behind him, Austin's mother started to make crying noises.

"Why?" Nash said. "Austin's nobody. Nothing. A former troubled kid, sure. He's made some bad choices in his life. Hung around with the wrong crowd. Broke his mother's heart. Mrs. Brent's going to parade a bunch of witnesses who will probably tell you all of that. He might not be easy to like. Then there's Bill Clancy. The victim. The hero. A solid, sure presence. The very emblem of law and order in this town. Mrs. Brent's going to work real hard to try to paint that picture for you. If Bill Clancy is your hometown version of a JFK, then Austin Merkle's a perfect Oswald. A loser whose only brush with greatness and history came from how he defiled it."

Nash walked away from the defense table on his way back to the lectern. As he did, he paused, stopped in his tracks as if something had just occurred to him. A revelation that had only just popped into his brain. I knew better. Alexander Nash always knew exactly what he was doing.

"That's an interesting analogy," he said. "Austin Merkle as Oswald. Hmm. One thing I know for certain, there's a lot more to that story than what we were told. You know what? That's true here too."

He tapped the lectern. "Why did Bill Clancy leave his wife's side in the middle of the night? We'll hear from her, I hope. That's the question. He got out of his warm bed for some reason and went out into the cold, dark night. For what? Mrs. Brent can't answer that so she wants you to think it doesn't matter. That, ladies and gentlemen, is what you have to pay attention to. What does Mara Brent want to hide? What motivation might she have for keeping certain answers from you?"

"Mara," Mercy whispered beside me.

"Open your eyes," Nash said. "Ask yourselves, with every piece of evidence Mrs. Brent tries to introduce, what isn't she telling you? What has she hidden?"

"Your Honor," I said, reluctantly rising.

"Counsel," Judge Saul said, sounding weary already. "Approach."

I couldn't believe I had to do this. Nash was obviously trying to make this trial about me. Trying to rattle me. By objecting during his opening and drawing focus, I knew I might be playing right into his hands. At the same time, he'd crossed about a dozen boundaries for appropriate opening statement territory. Judge Saul needed the opportunity to rein him in now.

"Your Honor," I said. "To the extent Mr. Nash is using his opportunity to attack my character, we've veered far afield of a proper opening statement."

"I agree," Judge Saul said, covering her microphone with her hand. "Knock it off, Mr. Nash."

"Your Honor, the entire investigation of my client is at issue. Top to bottom. I'm allowed to question whether there was a rush to judgment in this case. From all factions, including Mrs. Brent."

"Mr. Nash" Judge Saul said. "I know what you're up to with that. I've had enough of it. You'll have ample opportunity to cross-examine law enforcement during the prosecution's case in chief. You wanna raise the argument that this investigation should have been handled differently, you'll get your chance. But rein in your opening statement, Mr. Nash. Don't make me have to intervene again."

He didn't wait for her to excuse us. He simply turned on his heel and walked back to the lectern. I drew a sharp breath, fighting to keep my cool. I knew that's exactly what Nash hoped for. I went back to my table and took my seat.

"Sorry for that," Nash said. "Where was I before Mrs. Brent's objection?"

He turned to the court reporter. "What isn't she telling you? What has she hidden?" the reporter answered.

Nash looked down at his notes for the very first time. I knew he didn't really need them.

"Questions," Nash said. "Keep those in mind. Write them down. Add them up. I have absolute confidence that at the end of Mrs. Brent's case in chief, you'll have far more questions than you have answers. And if you have questions, you should also have doubts. You'll be asked to weigh that. That's your central role in this entire process. Has Mrs. Brent proved her case beyond a reasonable doubt? Add up your questions, ladies and gentlemen. Tally them against the so-called answers she's given you."

He raised his hands, palms toward the ceiling, mimicking a scale. He tipped himself far to the left. "I'm confident you'll see Mrs. Brent's case for what it is. A sham. A rush to judgment. And you'll have far more questions than reasonable answers. Thank you. From the bottom of my heart. I know you'll all do the right thing."

Nash took his seat. He let his gaze flick to me. Then, the bastard actually winked at me.

"Ms. Brent," Judge Saul said. "You may call your first witness."

18

"The State calls Special Agent Andrea Patel to the stand."

Patel walked in straight-backed, wearing a smart black suit, her hair pulled back. Her badge swung from a chain around her neck as she raised her right hand and swore her oath to tell the truth.

"Good morning, Agent Patel," I said. "Will you tell the jury what your job is?"

"Of course," she began. "I am an agent with the Bowling Green field office of the Ohio Bureau of Criminal Investigations. I'm called in to process crime scenes and provide investigative support, specifically with homicides."

"And what is your involvement with the Bill Clancy case?"

Patel cleared her throat and pulled the microphone closer to her face. "My office was contacted the morning of April 15th after Sheriff Clancy's body was found behind the wheel of a car in the Dollar Kart parking lot on Warren Road in Waynetown."

She handled her introduction to the crime scene smoothly, carefully detailing who was present at the scene, how it was secured. She had arrived roughly an hour after Gus was first called out, just after Sam and I left to go talk to Shanna Clancy.

"What did you find at the scene?" I asked.

"A white male, approximately mid to late fifties, was slumped over the steering wheel in the driver's seat. There was a gunshot wound clearly present through his right temple. It went through and through, the exit wound visible through the left temple. Later, once the body was examined, we discovered he had a second bullet wound in his right shoulder. The bullet was retrieved from that wound."

One by one, I introduced the crime scene photographs. From a distance, Bill Clancy could have looked like he was sleeping. Or passed out. But the close-up shots showed the gaping wound on the left side of his head. The thick dried blood and gray matter spilling out and running down his left ear. The tip of that ear had actually been blown off by the force of the bullet.

"Agent Patel, were you able to draw any conclusions about the nature of Sheriff Clancy's death?"

"Yes." She looked straight at the jury. "Sheriff Clancy's death was clearly a homicide."

"Clearly," I repeated. "How did you arrive at that conclusion?"

"The main interior of the car was essentially clean. All of the blood was found on the body itself. There was no spatter pattern or gray matter on the driver's side window or any other portion of the left side of the vehicle. The fatal wound through his left temple was delivered at close range by a nine-millimeter bullet. The force of the blast propelled the bullet through both sides of the sheriff's skull. In layman's terms, it blew out the side of his head. I don't mean to be indelicate. But ... with a penetration of that velocity positioned in the front seat, there would most certainly have been a spatter pattern on the driver's side window. There wasn't. That would indicate the body was placed in the car sometime after he was killed. In addition, we found blood and gray matter in the trunk of Sheriff Clancy's vehicle."

I introduced the photographs taken inside the trunk. Agent Patel went through them, identifying the large pool of blood in the far-right corner of the trunk, just over the spare tire.

"And here," she said, pointing to a bloody smudge on the top of the trunk.

"He was moved," I said.

"He was moved. In addition to the physical evidence I've described, we have security footage from the Dollar Kart showing the window of time in which Sheriff Clancy's Dodge Durango was driven into the lot."

We showed the enhanced photographs of the corner of Clancy's bumper and cross-referenced it with the time stamps.

This portion of her testimony took close to an hour. Nash raised no objections. Not one. He simply sat beside his client, nodding and whispering whenever Austin leaned in to make some inaudible comment.

"The vehicle came into the lot between 6:22 a.m. and 6:28 a.m. You can see the tip of the front bumper. Unfortunately, the majority of the car is off screen. But we had enough here to conclusively identify it. There's a distinct dent in the right front bumper of Sheriff Clancy's vehicle there. We were fortunate, actually, that the killer parked where he did. If the car had been just a few inches further back, none of this would have been picked up by the cameras."

"Objection," Nash said. I'd almost forgotten he was there. "The witness is assuming facts not in evidence. The State has so far failed to establish who drove that vehicle into that lot."

"Sustained," Judge Saul said. I couldn't fault her. It was a valid objection. Even Agent Patel looked chagrined. She shot me an apologetic glance. It was a rare, sloppy mistake on her part. One I knew she wouldn't make again.

"Agent Patel," I picked up. "What other reasons did you draw on to conclude Sheriff Clancy's death was a homicide?"

"Well, he never fired his own weapon. It was actually still holstered on his right hip. Still clipped. And as I indicated from the timing of when the vehicle was parked, Sheriff Clancy was already dead when he was brought there. The physical evidence indicates his body was inside the trunk. He was dragged out of it and positioned in the driver's seat. Then, at 6:58, the surveillance footage showed a second vehicle coming into the lot and pulling up near the sheriff's. At that point, two individuals were seen driving out of the lot together. Sheriff Clancy's body was discovered three hours later by a store employee."

Patel carefully took the jury through her next investigative steps. How she determined the owner of the second vehicle based on the partial license plate. Her interrogation of Ricky Wahl and his identification of Austin Merkle. I would call Ricky tomorrow or the next day.

"Agent Patel, what did you do next?"

"Mr. Wahl provided information that upon dropping the defendant off at home, he saw him dispose of a plastic bag in a garbage can at the side of his house. I sought and secured a search warrant for Mr. Merkle's home.

"We found Mr. Merkle at home, standing in the driveway at 5242 Canning Street in the south end of Waynetown. On approach to the house, I observed a blue garbage can with white paint stains on the side, as Mr. Wahl described."

For each fact Agent Patel recited, I moved to admit the photographic evidence corroborating it. I put the blue garbage can up on screen.

"The can was in the exact position and condition as you see in this photograph," she said. "There was a white garbage bag sitting on top and as I approached, I could see red stains on something inside the bag."

Patel had taken a video of her approach to the garbage can. I played it for the jury. Patel had walked right up to the can and pointed her camera, showing the contents. The white bag hadn't been completely closed. Two blue latex gloves could be seen turned inside out in the bag. They were covered in what looked like blood.

"What did you do next, Agent Patel?"

"At this point, I was concerned I was actually standing in another crime scene. I took steps to secure the scene. Coordinated with Detective Gus Ritter of the Maumee County Sheriff's. We cordoned off Mr. Merkle's property and I had the contents of and the actual garbage can tagged and sent into my lab for processing."

"What was Mr. Merkle doing at this point?"

"He was cuffed and seated in the back of Detective Ritter's vehicle. Detective Ritter administered the defendant's Miranda warning and the suspect immediately indicated he wished to speak to a lawyer. He was not questioned beyond that."

"Did you find any other evidence at the scene?"

"Yes. We searched Mr. Merkle's home and confiscated his cell phone, laptop computer, gaming device, and two tablets. While I was inside overseeing the collection of that evidence, I heard a shout from another room in the house. One of my agents, uh, Special Agent Martinez. He called out that he had a gun. I ran to the suspect's bedroom. A Glock 19 was found in the bottom of the suspect's laundry basket under a pile of dirty laundry."

I played the video. After that, a series of photographs of the gun.

"Agent Patel, what if anything were you able to determine after analysis of that gun?"

"Well, we had a positive match once ballistics came back. The bullet that penetrated Sheriff Clancy's shoulder was fired from that weapon. The gun itself was registered to Mr. Merkle and his fingerprints were found on it. Additionally, blood particles were found on the gun itself. We had a DNA match to Sheriff Clancy. His blood was on the gun. Which was consistent with him being shot from it at close range. Finally, the blue latex gloves found in the trash bag came back positive for DNA belonging to Bill Clancy."

Early the next morning, I would call the ballistics expert from BCI. He would give detailed testimony about how the barrel of every gun leaves identifying marks on a bullet akin to fingerprints. The bullet taken from Bill Clancy's shoulder could not have come from any other weapon than the Glock 19 registered to Austin Merkle and found in his possession.

"Did you find anything else in that trash can?"

"We absolutely did. We found bloodstained clothing. A tee shirt, pair of jeans, boxer briefs, and white tube socks. The blood on them matched Bill Clancy's. Then there were the shoes Austin Merkle was wearing the day he was arrested. We had those sent to the lab as well. They showed signs of having been cleaned with a chemical solution, bleach. But there was still blood embedded in the shoelaces that matched Bill Clancy's. I theorized that Austin Merkle had been wearing the shoes and those bloody clothes when he shot Bill Clancy. He tried to throw the clothes away but he kept the shoes, thinking he could clean them. And there was one more thing. At the parking lot, just behind the trunk of Bill Clancy's car. We had found a partial footprint made from blood. The tread was a positive match to Austin Merkle's right shoe."

"The one he was wearing when you arrested him?"

"Yes."

"What conclusion did you draw from those pieces of potential evidence?"

She let out a sigh. "Well, Austin Merkle fired the gun that killed Bill Clancy. Then he put Clancy's body in the trunk of his own car. The tee shirt, the jeans, the blood transfer likely happened when Merkle stuffed Clancy in that trunk. Then, for some reason, he drove Clancy out to the Dollar Kart parking lot, dragged him back out of the trunk. In doing so, he left a bloody footprint on the pavement. Then, he positioned Clancy behind the steering wheel and called for his friend Ricky Wahl to pick him up."

I paused at the lectern. "Agent Patel. You said you confiscated and got warrants to search Mr. Merkle's phone. What did that reveal?"

"We found two cell phones at Mr. Merkle's residence. One on his person in his back pocket. The other in a drawer in his bedroom. That second one was what we call a burner phone. Probably purchased at a convenience store or a grocery store. Not associated with a cell phone plan. It had prepaid minutes on it. At any rate, the cell phone number associated with that phone was used to call Bill Clancy's cell phone at 2:42 a.m. on the morning of April 15th. The call lasted approximately three minutes. It was the last incoming call Bill Clancy received on his phone."

"I see," I said. "Were there any other calls made from that burner phone?"

"There were. Three calls. All made to a number we couldn't trace. These too were made to another burner phone. Those went out at 7:48 a.m., 8:14 a.m., and the final one at 8:52 a.m."

"What did you conclude from that, if anything?"

"The defendant was the last one to speak with Bill Clancy on the phone the night he was murdered. Though we don't know what was said, it prompted Bill Clancy to leave his home and meet up with the defendant. Some point after that, the defendant shot and killed him, then planted the body as I've already testified."

I looked over my shoulder. Austin Merkle sat stone-faced. Alexander Nash scribbled something on a pad of paper. I looked back at Agent Patel.

"Thank you," I said. "I have no more questions for this witness." The urge came to me. At that moment, I could almost have rested my case. Later, I would wonder if things might have turned out far differently if only I had.

19

"Special Agent Patel," Nash said, shouting it out before he even made it to the lectern. He left his notes behind.

"Isn't it true it's not normal for you to take over as the lead investigator in a Maumee County murder case, right?"

"Normal? I would say it's absolutely within the normal parameters of my job."

"But primarily, your job is to offer investigative support to various local jurisdictions within the State of Ohio, isn't that right?"

"That is part of my job, yes."

"But this case was special. Unusual. Wouldn't you say?"

"No, I wouldn't say that."

"Well, let me come at this another way. Maumee County, while it may be a smaller jurisdiction, compared to say, Toledo, Cincinnati, Columbus ... it has its own homicide squad, doesn't it?"

"The Maumee County Sheriff's Department has a detective unit assigned to crimes against persons. I think that's what you're getting at."

"It is," Nash said, smiling. "It is indeed. And isn't it true that Detective Gus Ritter was actually appointed to investigate Bill Clancy's death at first?"

"I can't speak to that. I'm not privy to the inner workings of the department in that way."

Mercy slid her notepad in front of me. She'd written "she's good" in a diagonal. I underlined it. But I knew where Nash was headed with this. I casually looked behind me, hoping Sam had kept Gus out of the courtroom. I'd warned him to. This would get ugly, exactly as I'd predicted.

"Ricky Wahl," Nash continued. "You indicated in your direct testimony that you believed he was the individual who allegedly drove to the Dollar Kart parking lot to pick up the defendant. Isn't that right?"

"Yes."

"So you interviewed Ricky Wahl?"

"I did."

"But you weren't the first person to interview Ricky, were you? The first cop."

"No," she said. "I would like to clarify. My interaction with Mr. Wahl is what I would characterize as more of an interrogation, not an interview."

"The difference being?" Nash asked.

"The difference being, an interrogation is more focused. Mr. Wahl was a person of interest at the time we spoke. He waived his Miranda rights in writing and verbally."

"Okay." Nash walked back to his table and grabbed his notepad. He took a moment to scribble something. "But Detective Gus Ritter actually interviewed Ricky Wahl prior to your encounter with him, correct?"

"That's my understanding, yes."

"There was a recording of that prior interview, wasn't there?"

"Yes."

"One that you saw. In fact, you saw it prior to your ever having met Ricky Wahl, isn't that right?"

"I saw the interview recording, yes."

"Isn't it true that Detective Gus Ritter assaulted Ricky Wahl during the course of that interview?"

"Objection," I said. "Counsel is grandstanding and assuming facts not in evidence."

"Your Honor," Nash said. "I am establishing the character of this prior interview. I believe it has direct bearing on this witness's later dealings with the witness. Which are, of course, highly relevant to the information gleaned from Mr. Wahl and the basis for Special Agent Patel's investigation."

"Overruled," Judge Saul said. "You may ask the question."

"Agent Patel," Nash said. "Once again, did you have occasion to view the recording of Detective Ritter's interview with Ricky Wahl?"

"I did."

"Tell me, who appeared on that tape, if you recall?"

She straightened her jacket. "Mr. Wahl, Detective Ritter, then later in the interview, Lieutenant Sam Cruz and Ms. Brent."

"Ms. Brent," he repeated. "Mara Brent. The prosecutor in this case. She was present during the first interview with Ricky Wahl?"

"At the end of the tape. I was made to understand she observed the entire interview though. That particular interview room has one-way glass and there is an observation room next to it."

"Objection," I said. "Relevance for one. For another, Mr. Nash is violating the best evidence rule. And to the extent he begins asking about what was said at this interview, this witness wasn't present. Her testimony would be hearsay at best."

"Sustained," Judge Saul said. "Let's stick with information this witness has firsthand knowledge of, Mr. Nash."

"Fine," Nash said, his tone harsh enough to shock me. "Agent Patel, you took over this investigation from Detective Ritter, didn't you?"

"Detective Ritter and I have worked in collaboration."

"But it was his case. He was lead investigator. He was responsible for controlling the scene where Clancy's body was found, wasn't he?"

"Initially, yes. But my office was called by Detective Ritter within an hour of the discovery of Sheriff Clancy's remains."

"An hour," Nash said. "BCI arrived on scene at 11:39 a.m. on the morning of April 15th. Isn't that true?"

"That's correct."

"But the body was discovered just after 10:00 a.m. And Detective Ritter arrived on scene just after eleven, isn't that right?"

"I can't testify to Detective Ritter's comings and goings."

"Got it," Nash said. "But by your own admission, BCI didn't get to the scene until 11:39. So we're talking at least forty minutes where Detective Ritter had control of the scene before you had any involvement at the Dollar Kart parking lot."

"I'm based out of Bowling Green. I had to drive to get here."

"Sure." Nash paused. He rifled through his notes. "Agent, at the time you arrived on scene, you were providing investigative support only. Is that correct?"

"That's correct."

"But after Gus Ritter interviewed Ricky Wahl, you were made the lead investigator on the Clancy case, isn't that true?"

"Again, Detective Ritter and I have collaborated on this investigation. But yes."

Nash let out an audible sigh, signaling his frustration with Agent Patel. I knew he had to feel she was slipperier than an eel. If he was trying to get her to say a single negative thing about Gus Ritter, he was wasting his and the jury's time. I got the sense they felt the same way. Several members of the jury started looking around the room, losing interest or patience in Nash's line of questioning.

"You collaborated," Nash said. "Gus Ritter was at the scene when you served your search warrants on Austin Merkle's home, correct?"

"Yes."

"And he was there when you interrogated Ricky Wahl, correct?"

"Yes."

"Interesting," Nash said. "All right. Let's talk about some of the digital forensic evidence you collected. Specifically, you did a phone dump on Sheriff Clancy's cell phone, didn't you?"

"Not me personally," Patel answered. "Our forensics team prepared a report at my request."

"You don't know who Sheriff Clancy spoke to in the early morning of April 15th, do you?"

"As I testified on direct, the number, the incoming call to Sheriff Clancy's phone came from a burner phone found in the defendant's possession."

"In his possession. You mean it was in his house, according to you?"

"Yes."

"But you don't know if he's the one who made that call, do you? In fact, that's impossible to know from the phone records you have."

"Once again, the number came from a phone in the defendant's possession, with the defendant's fingerprints on it. No one else's."

"You don't have a transcript of the call made from that phone on April 15th to the sheriff's number, do you?"

"No. That doesn't exist. Only the log showing that incoming call and its duration. Two minutes and fifty-two seconds. Additionally, we know the call was placed within the service area of the Canning Road cell phone tower. That also happens to be the closest tower to the defendant's residence."

"But the phone itself, it's not registered to the defendant, correct?"

"Correct. It's not registered to anyone. It's a burner."

"Anyone could have made that call, isn't that right?"

"I'm sorry?"

"The simple fact is, you have zero proof that the defendant is the one who actually made that call to Sheriff Clancy. You also don't have the first clue as to what was said on that call."

"Objection," I said. "Counsel is making speeches, not asking questions."

"Sustained." Judge Saul gave a pointed stare at Alexander Nash.

"You cannot tell this jury with absolute certainty that Austin Merkle made that April 15th phone call to the sheriff, can you?"

"No. I can't. But I can infer from the position of the phone the fact that only the defendant's fingerprints were present on it, and the fact that it was found in his home, tucked away in a drawer."

Nash gripped the side of the lectern. He looked over at me and smiled. He actually smiled.

"Thank you. I have no more questions for this witness."

"Ms. Brent? Any redirect?"

I started to rise. Nash hadn't done real damage. Certainly, he'd opened the door to Gus's conduct. But I'd always known that would be a hurdle I'd have to clear. In my opinion, Andrea Patel had kept her cool, come off professional, authoritative, and respectful of every one of Nash's questions. Also, Nash was acting. His seeming frustration with Patel's answers wasn't what it seemed. I felt that in my gut. He was up to something. So I did the thing I thought he wouldn't expect.

"No, Your Honor. I have no further questions for this witness."

"All right," Judge Saul said. "Due to the lateness of the day, let's stop here. The jury is dismissed with the admonishment not to discuss this case with anyone. We'll reconvene tomorrow morning at eight thirty."

She banged her gavel. I stayed on my feet as the jury filed out and Judge Saul left the bench.

She waited until Nash and Merkle were out of earshot, then Mercy turned to me.

"What if you don't put Gus Ritter on the stand?"

The girl was quick. The same thought had swirled in my brain. There was only one problem.

"If I don't," I said, "it might look to the jury like I'm trying to hide him or protect him. The bottom line is, he didn't do anything wrong."

Sam came toward me. I saw the rage in his eyes. Of course, he understood exactly what Alexander Nash was trying to do.

"Mara, you can't let the jury see that interview tape. He's making it sound like Gus beat some sort of confession out of Ricky Wahl. That's not what happened."

"I know," I said. "But I don't see a clear path to keeping that tape out. So let's get in front of it. Is Gus ready?"

I got my answer in the form of the man himself. He strode down the aisle toward me, fire practically shooting from his eyes. My stomach flipped. That was exactly the demeanor that could sink this whole case.

20

"There are no real legal grounds to keep that video from coming in," I said. We sat around the conference room table. I picked at the remains of my shrimp fried rice from the paper takeout box. "Your one job, Gus, is to keep your temper on the stand. Nash is going to try to make the jury think you're unhinged. That everything you did in this case was aimed at vengeance for Bill Clancy."

"I stand by everything I did," Gus said, tightlipped. Kenya and Sam sat opposite me. Mercy started collecting all the empty food containers, stacking them together.

"What if you don't put him on the stand?" Sam suggested.

"That was Patel's suggestion months ago. Um. Mine too."

Next to me, Gus gripped his chopsticks, hard enough to crack one of them. He set them down and leveled a stare at me.

"If the best that pinhead can do is try to scapegoat me, the jury ought to take about two minutes to see through that."

"They will," I assured him. "Andrea Patel is competent and credible. Nash failed to make any dents in her testimony or raise doubt about the evidence we introduced. We just need to stay on course. Let Nash ask all the ridiculous questions he wants. He's going to be smarmy. He's going to try to grandstand. Try to rattle you. Don't fall for it. You let me deal with making any objections I see fit. But for the most part, it's better if I let him at you. Do you understand?"

He stabbed his broken chopstick into the container Mercy held out for him.

"I get it. I'm supposed to prove to those people what a calm and reasonable guy I am. Be a robot."

"No," I said. "You're a human being. There's no point in hiding that Bill Clancy was your friend or that you cared about him. The jury saw the most gruesome crime scene photos too yesterday. They'll understand the stress you've been operating under. That doesn't have to be a negative."

Gus's cell phone vibrated. He pursed his lips as he read it. "I've gotta go. Phone forensics came back on another case I'm working on."

"Go," I said. "Get a good night's sleep if you can. I'll put you on right after the ballistics expert tomorrow morning. Then probably Ricky Wahl right after you. He'll be able to dispel any notion that you influenced his statement at all. It's going to be fine."

Gus stuffed his phone back into his jacket, grumbled at Sam, then left the conference room.

Kenya waited until we heard Gus leave the lobby. Then she turned to Sam. "He won't be fine, will he?"

Sam wouldn't meet my eyes. He tapped his fingers on the rim of his coffee cup. Since the trial started, he'd been drinking it late into the evening. I worried he was running on fumes.

"He had one brief lapse," Sam said. "He blew a fuse in that interview room. It was minor. It was handled. And it was provoked. You need to make sure the jury understands that."

He rose then. I could tell he wanted to say more, but opted not to. Instead, he followed Gus out the door, taking the garbage Mercy had collected from her.

"I don't like it," Kenya said. "Sam seems like he's holding everyone in that department together with his bare hands. And barely at that."

I hesitated. It was on the tip of my tongue to voice the same concerns I'd had since Austin Merkle's indictment. Nash had a bigger agenda than just Merkle's defense. I knew Gus would be his entry point to it. I could only hope that Sam was right and that Gus could hold it together.

AFTER THE ROCK-SOLID BALLISTIC EVIDENCE, GUS GOT through the meat of his testimony the next morning with very little pushback from Alexander Nash. He'd only made one hearsay objection, but otherwise let Gus get his story out unbroken.

He was the first detective on scene at the Dollar Kart. He'd followed all protocols about securing the area, made logical decisions about canvassing. He reached out to BCI immediately. It had been a textbook investigation. Then, I asked the question.

"Detective, can you tell me what happened when you first interviewed Ricky Wahl?"

"He was evasive. Said he didn't want to be there. Cocky. Arrogant. Uncooperative."

"What did you do?"

"I explained to Wahl how serious this situation was. Then I tried to leverage what I knew about his living situation. I knew he lived with his father and received financial support from him. I knew that Ricky had run-ins with him. When canvassing, a couple of his neighbors said that in the past, they had a rocky relationship. So, I told Ricky that I was going to speak to his dad and see if Steven Wahl had any information about his whereabouts. Ricky got angry. He grabbed my cell phone out of my hand and threw it against the wall. He barely missed hitting me in the head with it. And he shoved me."

"What did you do?"

"I reacted."

I went through my authenticating questions regarding the video interview. Then, I played it for the jury.

I kept my eyes on them as it came to the part where Ricky launched himself across the table at Ritter. A few of the jurors winced as Ritter grabbed Ricky and pushed him against the wall. The audio was loud, grating, as Ricky kicked over a chair. I wished the quality of the video was better. It was hard to see where Ricky's hands were and where Gus's were. Then the door flew open and Sam burst in, pulling Gus off Ricky Wahl and putting the kid in cuffs.

Through all of it, Gus bore up. He was genuinely humble when talking about what happened in that interview room.

He wasn't remorseful and I was glad about it. The jury would have seen through it. The simple fact was, Ricky Wahl had escalated the situation first. Some of the jurors would have felt Gus was justified. I gave Gus a small smile as I made my way back to the table and turned cross-examination over to Nash.

"Detective Ritter," he started. "You were given a verbal warning regarding your conduct in the interview with Ricky Wahl, isn't that right?"

"I don't know if I'd call it a warning. There was nothing formal. That kid shoved me and destroyed my phone. I was justified in getting control of the situation."

"Getting control. He walked out of that room with a black eye, didn't he?"

Nash displayed the photo Sam took of Ricky just after the altercation. That was standard protocol, too.

"I wouldn't call that a black eye," Gus said. "He had a red mark on his cheek. When he was interviewed again a couple of days later by Agent Patel, there was no evidence of a black eye as you've described it. The kid didn't have a scratch on him."

"So you were in a position to get a good look at him a few days later when Mr. Wahl was brought in to be interrogated, is that right?"

"I saw him, yes."

"You saw him. And he saw you. You made sure of that."

"Objection," I said. "Asked and answered."

"I'll move on," Nash said. "Detective, isn't it true that during your tenure with the Maumee County Sheriff's Department, you've been accused of using excessive force more than twenty-two times?"

"I have never been disciplined for using excessive force," he said.

"I didn't ask if you'd been disciplined, though that brings up another interesting point. We'll get to that. I asked you if you'd been accused."

"I have no idea," Gus said.

"So you've lost count?"

"Objection!"

"Sustained, Mr. Nash," Judge Saul said.

"Detective Ritter, you were angry when you brought Ricky Wahl in for questioning, weren't you?"

"Angry? No. I wouldn't say that I was angry."

"You became enraged when Mr. Wahl took your phone, didn't you?"

"He didn't take my phone. He threw my phone at me and broke it against the wall. He acted violently toward me. I met force with appropriate force. Mr. Wahl wasn't hurt. He wasn't scared of me. He was not intimidated. And I didn't do anything wrong."

I gripped my pen and tried to transmit a warning to Gus with my eyes. Keep it under control. Let him ask you questions. Then answer them. Nothing more. Nothing less.

"Bill Clancy was your friend, wasn't he?" Nash said.

"He was a friend. Yes. We'd worked together for over twenty years. He was a good boss."

"You cared a lot about Bill Clancy?"

"Yes."

"It had to have been awful for you seeing what happened to him. Seeing his dead body. It had to have affected you deeply, didn't it?"

"Did I like seeing Bill Clancy shot to death? Is that what you're asking me? No. No, I didn't like that. But if you're trying to suggest that it rendered me unable to do my job objectively, you're wrong."

"I don't believe I've suggested any such thing, Detective. But since you mention it ... other people did, didn't they?"

"What?"

"You were pulled off as lead investigator on this case after your violent outburst with a principal witness, weren't you?"

"No. That's not what happened."

"Special Agent Patel was called in within hours of your altercation with Ricky Wahl, wasn't she?"

"I can't give you an exact timeline. BCI was always involved in this investigation. From the very beginning."

"Well," Nash said. "Not until almost an hour after you personally took control of the scene at the Dollar Kart, isn't that right?"

"Every single thing in this case was done according to proper protocol."

"You personally spoke to every witness in this case before Agent Patel had a chance to, didn't you? Ricky Wahl, the victim's widow, the Dollar Kart employees, including the individual who found Bill Clancy's body, isn't that right?"

Gus folded his arms in front of him.

"Isn't that right, Detective?"

"I spoke to witnesses in this case," he finally said. "Yes."

"There isn't a single witness in your report that you didn't get to first, is there?"

"I was conducting a homicide investigation. The first forty-eight hours are the most critical in that type of investigation. But if you're suggesting I was working alone, that's not true. Lieutenant Cruz was also involved from the outset—"

"Sam Cruz," Nash said. "Your former partner, right?"

"We worked crimes against persons together before he moved over into command, yes."

"Lieutenant Cruz was also a close personal friend of Bill Clancy, wasn't he?"

"I believe so, but you'd have to ask him about that."

"Detective, you have no idea why Bill Clancy was killed, do you?"

"No."

"You have no idea who really called Clancy the night he was killed, do you?"

"I know he was called from a burner phone found in your client's possession and covered with his fingerprints."

"You don't know if he spoke to Austin Merkle or someone else, do you?"

"I've answered your question."

"You want him to pay, don't you?"

"Excuse me?"

"You want to make sure whoever killed Bill Clancy fries for it, don't you?"

"Objection!" I stood up.

"I want justice to be served for my friend, yes. For this town, yes. I want to make sure whoever did it never walks the streets again, yes. But if you're trying to convince these people that I was personally out to get your client or anyone else, that is false."

Gus was red-faced, sweating. He jabbed a finger in the air, pointing at Merkle while he spoke. His anger and vitriol, written in every line of his face.

It was cheap. Ridiculous even. But I watched as two jurors in the front looked at Gus Ritter with new disdain. As Nash finished and Gus left the stand, I had no real clue how much damage had been done.

21

Dr. David Pham had an infectious smile and an easy way in front of the jury. "Warm and fuzzy." That's how past jurors had described him after being polled. It was a good thing. And also entirely unexpected, considering what he did for a living.

"I serve as the Chief Medical Examiner for Maumee County. I'm the county coroner," Pham said in answer to my initial question.

"Doctor, will you explain to the jury what your principal findings were after your post-mortem examination of Bill Clancy?"

Pham sat tall in the witness chair. He made a point of looking at each of the jurors in turn. If he had a superpower, it was the innate ability to deliver credible testimony.

"The most remarkable wound Sheriff Clancy suffered was a through and through gunshot wound to the head. It entered just above his right ear, cut a path through the midbrain, severing the basilar artery, then exiting through the left neocortex, the left side of his head above the left ear. The bullet actually took off the upper portion of his left ear upon exiting. This was the fatal wound."

"The fatal wound," I repeated. "Were there other wounds?"

"Sheriff Clancy was hit with another bullet as well. It penetrated his right shoulder, causing superficial damage to the tissue ... what you'd call the meat of his shoulder, lodging in his right deltoid muscle."

As he said it, Pham placed his palm over his own right shoulder, gripping the muscle to illustrate where the deltoid muscle was.

"Were you able to determine when that second bullet wound was made?"

"Likely no more than a few minutes before he received the fatal gunshot wound to the head. Sheriff Clancy would not have remained standing or upright after the shot to the head. It would have been almost instantly fatal. Due to the angle of the bullet through the shoulder, the sheriff was standing with the shooter at or near his same height. But that first wound in the shoulder would not have been fatal by itself. The wound through the skull ... death would have been essentially instantaneous, as I've said."

"Were you able to estimate how far away the shooter would have been from Sheriff Clancy?"

"Based on the size and density of the pattern of residue, the smoke, soot, and other particulates present on Sheriff Clancy's skin and skull ... the shot was made at close range. No more than two feet away."

"What other findings did you make during your post-mortem, Dr. Pham?"

I introduced the doctor's full autopsy report, including the photos. It was difficult, I knew, for the jury to see Bill Clancy in that way. Bloodless. Vacant eyes staring up at the fluorescent lights in the examination room. Pham had taken several close-up shots of Clancy's head wound. In grisly, full color, they saw the massive damage done by the path of Austin Merkle's bullet.

"There were several areas of marked lividity on Sheriff Clancy's back, buttocks, and in the area of his hamstrings."

Pham scrolled to the photographs of the back of Clancy's body. Large, black blotches covered the skin.

"What does that mean?" I asked.

"When a body dies, obviously the blood stops circulating. The heart isn't functioning to pump it through the body. So gravity takes over. Blood will begin to pool based on the body's position. It looks like bruising as you can see here. This means that Sheriff Clancy's body was likely lying flat in a supine position for a while after he died."

"Why is that significant?" I asked.

"Well, it means his body was moved from its original position after death. Sheriff Clancy was found sitting upright behind the wheel of his own car. That isn't where he was shot."

"You're sure of that?"

"Completely. Had he been shot there, sitting in that position, the blood in his body would have pooled primarily under his buttocks and legs due to gravity. I wouldn't expect to see lividity in his back like it was. He wasn't sitting upright when he died. He was shot, then likely fell and lay on his back for some time before he was moved."

"I see. Did you note any other wounds on the body?"

"I did." Pham scrolled through the photographs, landing on one showing a close-up of Bill Clancy's wrists.

"I found bruising and abrasions around the sheriff's wrists, indicating they were bound. I found fibers in the wound. He was tied with rope. There was also a sizable hematoma on the back of his head that showed signs of healing. This was indicative of blunt force trauma."

"Were you able to draw any conclusions from that?"

"I was," he said. "The victim was struck by something heavy. There were splinters of wood in the wound and it had a sharp, straight edge to it. My best guess, he was struck by a plank or a board. A two-by-four perhaps."

"How severe was this injury?" I asked.

"It was a heavy blow," Pham said. "He was struck from behind. In all likelihood, the blow would have rendered him unconscious, or at least momentarily stunned. There were no other signs of what we would call defensive wounds. Such as bruising or scraping to his knuckles, skin tissue under his nails. The man was hit in the head and tied up before he could recover from the blow."

"Objection," Nash said. "Calls for speculation."

"Which is exactly within this expert witness's purview, Your Honor. Dr. Pham's entire job is to make conclusions on a victim's cause of death and injuries within a reasonable degree of medical certainty."

"Overruled," Judge Saul said.

"Dr. Pham," I continued. "Did you find any evidence in your examination that Sheriff Clancy had fired his or any gun immediately before he died?"

"No. I'm aware he was found with his service weapon. It was clipped and holstered on his belt. But there was no evidence that he had recently fired it. No gun residue or powder on his hands. And as I indicated, there was evidence that the sheriff's hands were bound. It would have been impossible for him to draw his weapon if ..."

"Objection!" Nash shouted. "This type of speculation is nowhere near this witness's area of expertise."

"Sustained," Judge Saul said.

I paused. Though I hated to end on a sustained objection, Pham had said everything I needed him to say and then some.

"Thank you, Dr. Pham," I said. "I have no further questions."

Nash passed me on the way to the lectern.

"Dr. Pham," he started. "Sheriff Clancy's hands weren't bound when he was found, isn't that right?"

"That's correct."

"I mean ... you saw him. You were out at the Dollar Kart parking lot, right?"

"That's correct. My office was called and I personally went to the scene to oversee the removal of the body and transport it to my lab for the post-mortem examination."

"So with your own eyes, you saw. Bill Clancy's hands were not tied up."

"By the time the body was found, that's correct."

"So you don't know whether his hands were bound when he was shot or when he died."

"I can't say for sure, no."

"You've testified you found no evidence that Clancy fired his weapon that day. But you cannot say whether he drew his weapon that day, can you?"

"No. I can't say that."

"You have no idea whether he drew that weapon. Whether he pointed it at someone. Whether he threatened anyone with it."

"Well, other than the fact that I know his wrists were tied behind him at some point and that he was beaten unconscious ... no."

"At some point," Nash said, shaking his head. "At some point. You said there was bruising and abrasions on his wrists. But those showed signs of healing, didn't they?"

"Yes. That's why I concluded in my report that Sheriff Clancy was still alive when his hands were bound."

"A person wouldn't need to use their fists or their nails to fight back if they were holding a gun ... pointing a gun at another individual, would they?"

"Objection," I said. "Now Mr. Nash is calling for improper speculation."

"Well, I mean, this witness is an expert on how to identify defensive wounds on a body. I'm within my rights to explore the parameters of that expertise."

"I'll allow it," Judge Saul said.

"Can you repeat the question?" Pham asked.

"Let me ask it another way. There's more than one way to threaten someone, isn't there?"

"Are you asking me based on what I observed on Sheriff Clancy's body? Or are you asking me as a general point of discussion?"

"Dr. Pham, if Sheriff Clancy was pointing a gun at someone, he wouldn't have needed to scratch or punch that person, would he? I mean, it would make it kind of difficult."

"Objection," I said. "Counsel is making speeches at this point."

"Sustained, move on, Mr. Nash."

"Doctor, you have no idea whether Bill Clancy pointed his gun at anyone, do you?"

"No. But I know he was shot through his right shoulder. He was right-handed. I would think with that kind of wound, he would have had a hard time holding a pencil for any length of time, let alone his gun."

Nash walked away from the lectern. He sighed, rubbed his jaw. Made a show out of his frustration. Finally, he walked back to the lectern, legal guns blazing.

"Dr. Pham, isn't it true that you've been involved in a romantic relationship with Mara Brent, the prosecutor in this case?"

"What?" Pham said.

"Objection!" I rose.

"Your Honor, I'm allowed to explore any biases this witness may have. His personal relationship with the prosecutor in this case is directly relevant to his credibility."

"Are you serious?" Pham asked.

I could feel the blood rising to my cheeks. Mercy began scribbling furiously beside me.

"Overruled," Judge Saul said. "Everybody just calm down. I'm going to caution you to tread lightly, Mr. Nash. Keep your questions narrowly focused."

"Oh, they will be," Nash said. "Dr. Pham. Answer the question, please. You and Mara Brent have a romantic relationship, don't you?"

"No. That is not how I would describe it."

"Well, enlighten me. How would you describe it?"

I stayed on my feet. I could feel Sam's eyes boring into my back. Pham looked over my shoulder straight at him. God help us all. David looked scared.

"Our relationship is strictly professional," David said. "And I have to be honest, I take great issue with your attempt to characterize it otherwise."

"You dated Mara Brent last year, didn't you?"

"We went to dinner a couple of times."

"It was more than dinner though, wasn't it? You considered her your girlfriend."

Pham's eyes widened. He shook his head in confusion. I couldn't blame him.

"I don't know that I'd use that term. We went out to dinner a couple of times. Nothing more came of it."

"Isn't it true that you told several colleagues that you'd fallen in love with her?"

His face went white. My heart dropped to the floor. No. This could not be happening.

"I was very fond of Ms. Brent," Pham said. "But to insinuate that I'd ... that my testimony ..."

No. No. No.

"You texted a close friend about her, didn't you? You told that friend Mara is my dream girl. I can't get her out of my head. She's the total package. I'm ready to tell my mother about her, if that tells you how serious I am."

"Objection! Counsel is assuming facts not in evidence and testifying."

"Well, the witness can tell me whether he sent those texts or not."

"Mr. Nash," Judge Saul said. "You know better than this. Sustained."

"Dr. Pham," he said. "Did you or did you not send texts to a friend relating to your feelings about Ms. Brent?"

David squirmed in his chair. I had no doubt Nash had somehow gotten to one of David's so-called friends.

"I did text that, yes," David said. "But it was a long time ago. It has nothing to do with this case."

"She broke up with you, didn't she? If it were up to you, you'd still be romantically involved with her, wouldn't you?"

"Objection! Your Honor ..."

"Overruled, but get to it, Mr. Nash."

"Your answer, Dr. Pham?" Nash said.

"I wasn't ... what ... can you repeat the question?"

"The question is, you're still in love with Mara Brent, aren't you?"

"No."

"But if she hadn't broken things off, you'd still be dating, wouldn't you?"

"I can't answer that. I don't know."

"Really? Isn't it true that you texted your same friend just two days ago? When asked, are you excited to be in the same room with Mara again, what was your answer, Dr. Pham?"

He looked like he was about to be sick. So was I.

"I don't remember. I might have said ..."

"You might have said? Might you have said yes? Can't wait to see her. At least now she'll be legally required to pay attention to me."

"Unbelievable," I said. "Your Honor, I'd ask this entire line of questioning be stricken from the record. It's irrelevant and highly prejudicial to ..."

"I have no more questions for this witness," Nash said.

"Overruled, Ms. Brent," Judge Saul said, scowling at me.

I walked up to the lectern. All traces of charm and confidence had drained from David Pham's face.

"Doctor," I said. I realized I had absolutely no earthly clue how to rehabilitate him. If I asked him to reiterate his truthfulness, that would make it sound like I bought the premise he'd been lying. The jury was reading me as much as they were reading him. I wanted to kill Alexander Nash. And part of me wanted to kill David Pham as well.

I took two minutes to have Pham reiterate some of his key medical findings. Then, I put us both out of our misery and had him leave the stand.

22

After introducing all the cell phone data from Clancy's phone and Merkle's burner, Judge Saul called a recess for the rest of the day. I had seven text messages waiting for me from David Pham. Each one was a different version of "I'm sorry."

I poised my thumb over the keyboard, debating how I could answer. It came to me then. There really was only one way to respond. I typed simply, "I know."

When I came back to the office, Kenya and Hojo waited for me. Kenya wore a path through my carpet, pacing with her hands on her hips, steam practically coming out of her ears.

Hojo leaned toward me as I brushed past him. "She's been like this for three hours."

"This is unacceptable," Kenya said, pivoting on her heel. "Pham knows better."

I set my briefcase down and took a seat behind my desk. My feet hurt. I slipped off my heels and rubbed my arches.

"It's not as bad as you think, maybe," Hojo offered.

"He should have told me," Kenya said.

"Told you what?" I said as I slid out of my blazer and tossed it over the corner of my desk. "He was texting with a friend. Somebody he apparently trusted. What Nash did violated his privacy."

"Not if this so-called friend willingly showed those texts to him," Hojo said. "Do you know who it was?"

"I'm sure David does," I said. "We didn't have a chance to talk in person after he left the witness box. I spent the last two hours getting the rest of Clancy's cell phone records in and the ones from Merkle's burner phone."

"Great," Kenya said. "So maybe we bored the jury to death after Pham's screw-up."

There was a soft knock on the door. Mercy poked her head in.

"Come on in," I said. "You were in the courtroom, too. I'd like to hear your reading as well."

Mercy gave Kenya a sheepish look. I couldn't blame her. Kenya Spaulding on a tear could be a frightening sight to behold. I knew she felt the pressure of her situation. Three weeks from now, the voters of Maumee County would decide if she got to keep her job. I locked eyes with Hojo. I had a feeling he was thinking the same thing. In three weeks, we might *all* be out of a job if this verdict didn't go my way.

"What's your read, kid?" Hojo asked as Mercy took the chair next to him. "How bad did Mara get hurt today?"

I gave Hojo a wide-eyed stare. He shrugged at me.

"Well," Mercy started. "The jurors were definitely paying attention during Dr. Pham's testimony. I think the autopsy results were pretty definitive. That stuff about his feelings for you though ... I don't know. If Nash is going to suggest that Dr. Pham ... um ... doctored his results during the postmortem to impress you?"

"That's exactly the suggestion he'll make in closing. Maybe not that direct. But he's going to use that crap to call David's credibility into question. He's going to say that David interpreted every finding in a way that he thought would impress or please me."

"Bill Clancy died of a gunshot wound through the head. One that he clearly didn't inflict on himself," Kenya said. "You don't have to be a coroner to draw that conclusion."

"And that's the argument I'll make," I said.

"He's making this trial about you," Mercy said. "His whole strategy from the outset. The reason Nash was hired to defend Austin Merkle in the first place. That's what's been bothering me. That's what I've been trying to figure out."

It was then I noticed she had a file folder under her arm. Mercy took it out and placed it on the desk in front of me.

"It won't work," Kenya said. "This is about as open and shut as I've ever seen. We've said this from the beginning. Short of having video of Austin Merkle actually shooting Bill in the head, we've got all the evidence any prosecutor would want. And it's spotless. We've done this ... Mara ... you've done this by the absolute book. Andrea Patel was pure gold on the stand. We're fine. We're fine. I know we're fine. What's next?"

"Ricky Wahl is next," I said.

Kenya nodded but kept on pacing. "He's solid? I mean, you're sure he's solid? You've been in communication with him?"

"Yes."

Usually, it was Kenya's job to give me the pep talks. I tried not to take it personally.

"He's going to come at that kid, hard," she said. "You've anticipated that. What's he got? Wahl's immunity deal?"

"And Gus Ritter," Hojo said. "Nash is going to suggest that Wahl said what he did because he was intimidated by Gus and probably by his father, too."

"That doesn't explain all the physical evidence found at Austin Merkle's house. It's in. The jury knows it," I said. My head started to pound. I realized I hadn't eaten more than a bite of a donut this morning as I chugged down my coffee.

"If that kid goes south," Kenya said. She finally stopped pacing and plopped down on the couch against the wall. "I'll kill him. I mean ... I'll *kill* him. But you're sure he's solid."

"Yes!" Hojo and I answered in unison.

"Ricky Wahl doesn't want to go to jail," I said. "He knows he would have been charged with accessory after the fact. He understands the terms of his immunity deal. Full cooperation. If he tries to waffle now, he faces real prison time. I've made that clear. Plus, the evidence we have corroborates his story. It's the only reasonable interpretation for what happened."

Hojo turned to Mercy. "Kid, what would your dad do in this situation, do you think?"

Mercy looked stunned by the question. So was I ... at first. Then, I found myself deeply curious about her answer.

"Well," she said. "I think if my dad were defending Austin Merkle, he'd probably be doing exactly what Alexander Nash is. He'd try making the trial about anything other than what it really is."

"Smoke and mirrors," Kenya said.

"Yeah," Hojo said. "Only people tend to believe what they see. Or what they think they see. Smoke and mirrors work."

"We cannot lose this trial," Kenya said. "I am not going to have Bill Clancy's murder hung around my neck as a failure."

"While I appreciate the vote of confidence," I said, "I'd like to think we're all working together on this."

Kenya's face fell. She took a seat in the corner of the room. "I'm sorry. Mara. Dammit. I'm sorry. I'm not being fair to you."

"We're all under a lot of pressure. Never mind the political climate. Bill was our friend. Shanna is our friend."

"He supported me," Kenya whispered. "He didn't have to. The sheriff's command union was going to endorse Fletcher. But Bill came out and personally endorsed me, not caring what the union did. Whenever someone stuck a phone or a microphone in his face and asked him who he wanted heading this office, he never equivocated in his endorsement of me. All that stuff that happened with my predecessor. Phil Halsey hired me. Bill caught flak for that, too. He put his own re-election at risk four years ago when he stuck by me. And now ..."

"Now," I said. "I still like my side of this case better than I do Alexander Nash's. If his strategy rests on trying to rattle me, it won't work. He's got innuendo and obfuscation. I've got real evidence and facts."

The room fell silent for a few moments. Kenya's posture changed. She sat straighter. Though her timing wasn't ideal, I knew she needed the catharsis of her confession.

Hojo got up to go. Mercy leaned forward and laid a flat hand on the file she'd set on my desk.

"You asked me what you thought my dad would do if he were defending Austin Merkle? He started out his career as a prosecutor. I think I know what he would have done if he were in your shoes, Mara."

She picked up the file and handed it to me. I had the distinct feeling I wasn't going to like what was inside. I opened it.

It contained just a few sheets of paper. An invoice from some outfit called Taub Investigations. Several grainy photographs.

I snapped my head up and looked at Mercy. "Where did you get these?"

"I think my dad would have tried to beat Alexander Nash at his own game. If he's trying to make the trial about you, then he'd want to know everything he could about Nash himself."

Kenya came to my desk. She picked up the file and leafed through the photographs. "That's Nash," she said. "Is that the Milan prison?"

"You had him followed?" I asked Mercy. "I didn't authorize that. I didn't ask you to ..."

"Mara," Kenya said, handing the file to Hojo. "That last photograph shows Nash having lunch with Stoney Gregg. He's Jason's lawyer, isn't he? Then he's seen coming in and out of Milan prison. Mercy, do you know who Nash was meeting with? Was it Jason Brent?"

"I'm not sure yet," she answered. "I can find out if you want me to. But I thought ..."

"No," I said. "No. I'll take care of this." My head was spinning. My stomach twisted into a pretzel. This couldn't be happening.

"He can't be still pulling strings from prison, Mara," Kenya said. "What on earth would Jason have to gain by getting involved in this?"

"It's me. He's been asking me to bring Will to visit him. I've resisted. I don't think he's ready. And Will hasn't asked to see his dad yet. I'm following his lead."

"Because that's the right thing to do," Kenya said. "I can't even wrap my head around it. You think Jason is somehow meeting with Nash as a way to get back at you?"

"What if Jason is feeding information to Nash about you?" Mercy asked. "Look, I don't want to overstep my bounds any more than you clearly think I have. Maybe you're right. But this office? You're all very close to this case. Kenya, all the things you said ... your relationship with the victim. It's heart-wrenching. And I'm sorry you lost your friend. But maybe what you all need is someone who can look at what's happening with an objective eye. I can. I have been. And I think it's not a coincidence that Nash has potentially been meeting with your ex and his lawyer. I think what happened in court today could be the least of what Alexander Nash is capable of. Ask yourself, did your ex-husband know that you dated Dr. Pham? He could have been the one to tip him off."

"We cannot let this happen," Kenya said. "I should have seen it. I should have ..."

"Should have what?" I said. "Pulled me off the case?"

"No," she said, but her tone wasn't convincing. "But Mercy may be right. We're all so close to this. If we ..."

"I'll handle it," I said.

"How?" Hojo asked.

"The same way I always do. I just ... do."

"But how? Specifically how. Think, Mara. What kind of ammunition could Jason have given to Nash that could be used to blow up this case?" Kenya asked.

I squeezed the bridge of my nose. "I don't know."

"I do," Hojo said. "Mara, Nash has already hinted at it. He invoked Lee Harvey Oswald in his opening statement. Oswald went on camera the first chance he got and told everyone he was just a patsy. Bill Clancy was also a political figure. Jason's in prison for colluding with a crime ring that manipulated state and national politics. Murder was never off the table. If Clancy was mixed up in that somehow."

"He was no one," I said. "Bill was important to us, but his seat had no value for Jason or any of his cronies. I can't see it."

"Maybe that doesn't matter," Mercy said. "Maybe it only matters that Nash gets people to *think* that's what happened."

I clenched my jaw so hard I saw stars.

"What are you going to do?" Hojo said to me.

"I'm going to get ready to put Ricky Wahl on the stand tomorrow. And I'm going to go visit my ex-husband and see what he has to say."

"What can we do to help?" Kenya asked.

"Nothing," I said, rising. Suddenly, I wanted to be anywhere but in this office. I needed to think, to clear my head. And I needed to find the strength not to wring Jason's neck once and for all.

23

"My name is Richard Steven Wahl. I live at 424 Broad Street. I'm twenty-three years old."

That was the last statement Ricky Wahl made without having to fight the urge to bite off his own thumb. We'd talked about it in trial prep. I suggested he skip caffeine or any stimulants this morning. When he suggested the need to smoke a joint before coming to court, I emphatically told him not to. About halfway through his testimony, I started to regret my own advice.

"How are you acquainted with the defendant in this case, Austin Merkle?"

"We're friends," Ricky said. "I mean, we *were* friends. Before all of this started."

"How'd you meet?"

"I knew Austin from high school. He was a grade above me. We didn't really hang out then. He ran with a crowd I wasn't too friendly with."

"Why's that?"

"Well, they used to beat me up in middle school. Not Austin specifically, but some of his best friends. But I don't know, maybe two years ago, Austin started showing up in an online game I play. *Legends of Warfare*. He went by Turk online. We got to talking over a couple of weeks. I figured out he was Austin. We got close. You know, friends."

"Did you only interact online?"

"Mostly. For the first few months, anyway. Then we started hanging out. Meeting up at the Blue Pony sometimes with other friends. Playing pool, drinking. Just ... hanging out."

"How close did you become?" I asked.

Ricky shrugged. "I considered Austin to be one of my best friends. I'd say in the last year, I mean, before this whole thing with the sheriff, Austin was one of the people I talked to the most."

"Was it just talking? Hanging out at the bar? Was that the extent of your friendship?"

"Austin helped me get a side job at the Muscle Hustle. The gym over on Cleveland Street. He was a personal trainer there for a while. I was doing general maintenance. Custodial duties. It wasn't a full-time gig. Just a few hours here and there for extra cash when I was in between jobs."

"How frequently did you interact with Austin during the year leading up to what happened to the sheriff?"

"We talked at least a couple of times a day. When I was working at the gym, I saw him maybe twice a week. We'd also hang out after work at the Pony. For a while, Austin didn't have a car. Well, he had a car but it was always breaking down. Austin didn't have any family in Waynetown. His relationship with his mom was ... um ... pretty strained. Like, at one point he put me down as his emergency contact at the gym. When we had to all fill out some forms for H.R."

I walked around the lectern, standing at the end of the jury box. "Ricky, how often did you carpool with Austin Merkle?"

"I wouldn't say carpool. Because he never really offered me rides. Cuz like I said, his car wasn't reliable."

"So how regular of an occurrence was it for you to offer him rides?"

"Oh, every day he worked it started to be. Originally, I was just picking him up on days I had to work too. Then, he started asking me to take him every single day."

"Did you ever say no?"

Ricky shook his head. I reminded him he had to give me verbal answers.

"I didn't mind," he said. "Austin was always good about paying me for gas."

"Ricky, can you tell me about your day on April 15th? Do you remember what happened?"

Ricky's thumb went straight to his mouth. He began chewing on the cuticle. I made a small fist and held it in front of me. We'd worked out the signal in trial prep. Ricky pulled his thumb away from his mouth and folded his hands in his lap.

"I got a job at Braxton Windows last February. Afternoons. So I'd go in at noon and get home at eight or so unless I worked over. The 15th was a regular day. I came home, took a shower, then got online and started playing *Legends of Warfare*."

"Do you recall who was online with you?"

"Yeah, it was three other players from my platoon. Four of us total. So me, Yager124, Woodstock, and Gotcha_15. We waited for Turk but he didn't log on. I messaged him but he didn't answer. Then I kinda lost track of time. I usually log off by three in the morning. But I finally got a private message from Turk just after six in the morning. He asked me to come pick him up. Said he was at the Dollar Kart and that I should come right away."

I introduced screenshots and the transcript from Ricky's chat with Austin/Turk.

"What did you do next?"

Ricky took a big breath. "I logged off and went to go get him."

"Did you find that unusual? Him contacting you like that?"

"Not really. Sure, it was a little weird just because he seemed super hyped. Like it was some kind of an emergency. I thought maybe he'd gotten into trouble. Like with a dealer or something."

"A dealer? What kind of dealer?"

"Objection," Nash said. "Counsel is calling for speculation."

"Your Honor," I said. "This witness's perceptions, his prior dealings with the defendant aren't speculation. It's proper and relevant direct for him to be questioned about this event."

"I'll allow it," Saul said.

"What kind of dealer would Austin Merkle have run into trouble with, in your experience?"

Ricky squirmed a bit. "Austin was jacked. He'd always been heavy into personal fitness and weightlifting. But in the last year, he bulked up more than usual. I knew he was taking steroids and growth hormones because he told me. And because I saw him shooting up and saw some of the stuff in his fridge at his house."

"Do you know where Austin was getting these drugs?"

"Yeah," Ricky said. "He had a contact he called Bullitt. Two times, when I picked Austin up for various stuff, he had me take him over to this Bullitt guy's apartment and wait for him. Austin would come back out holding a brown paper bag. One of the times, he showed me what was in it."

"What was it?"

"Some kind of Arnolds."

"Arnolds?"

"You know. Steroids. Austin shot up in the front seat of my car. Asked me if I wanted to try it. I said no thanks. That just wasn't what I was into. Austin got kinda mad at me. Started calling me names."

"Do you recall when that was?"

"Yeah. It was Valentine's Day this last year. Austin was seeing some girl. That's actually what he called me to pick him up for. He wanted to go to the mall and try to get her some present."

"Did you ever meet this girl?"

"Nah. I gotta be honest. I wasn't sure she even existed. Austin liked to brag a lot. Always telling these wild stories about different women he bang ... um ... had intercourse with. Only I never met any of them. It got to be kind of a running joke with our platoon. Like we'd tease him. Doctor pictures of Austin with different celebrities. Models. One time, one of the guys posted a picture of Austin with the First Lady. He got really mad about that one. And he was always texting me these pictures of naked chicks he claimed he was sleeping with. It started getting old. And well ... weird."

"Weird how?"

"I didn't want to see that crap from him. Then he started getting really mad about us teasing him. So he started sending more and more pictures of these girls. And him *with* these girls. One time, he sent me a video of himself actually, um ... having sex with some girl. It was kind of obvious she didn't know he was recording her. He was ... um ... doing her from behind."

I cringed.

"Objection!" Nash asked. "I think we've moved far beyond relevance with this line of questioning."

"Sustained," Judge Saul said before I could respond.

"Mr. Wahl," I said. "Let's focus on the early morning of April 15th, shall we? You testified Austin contacted you, asking you to pick him up at the Dollar Kart. Tell the jury what happened."

"Oh. Right. Yeah. Well, I went to go get him. When I first pulled into the lot, I thought he wasn't there. I was ticked, you know? It was after six in the morning. I had to work later that day. It's when I would have been sleeping. Then, I saw Austin get out of this silver SUV and he waved me over."

"Then what did you do?"

"I pulled up alongside Austin's car ... er ... the car he got out of ... and rolled down the window. Austin came over. He was only wearing his underwear and carrying this white plastic garbage bag with all his clothes in it. I could see that dead guy in the front seat. I didn't know he was dead at first. Thought he was passed out. But then ... I mean, you could tell. He had a big hole in the side of his head and blood running down. It freaked me out. Austin got in and told me to just start driving. Told me to keep my mouth shut. I kept asking him, what the hell, man? You know? He said I should just shut up, drop him off at home, and to pretend I never saw anything."

"Where did you go?"

"I did what Austin said. I didn't know what to think. Thought maybe that guy was a new dealer or something. Austin was really keyed up and agitated. He's ... I don't really trust him when he gets like that."

"Like what?"

"He would go into these 'roid rages. Just all paranoid. I've seen him get violent when he's like that. Punching holes into walls and stuff. He did that at my house in the basement one time. Last December. My dad was home and it was a whole scene. My dad kicked him out of the house and told me he didn't want me hanging out with Austin."

"You took Austin home?" I asked. This was the problem with Ricky. He tended to go off on tangents.

"Yeah. I took him home. Told him to get out and not call me anymore. Whatever was going on, I didn't want to be involved. He was pissed. Told me he needed my help cleaning up. I said no way. Well, Austin told me I better keep my mouth shut if I knew what was good for me. He said I was part of this thing now so if he went down, I was gonna go down."

"What did you do then?"

"I went home. I was totally freaked out. I started packing some things. Figured it would be best if I just got out of town for a little while. My mom lives in Phoenix. She'd been bugging me to come visit. I had a few days of PTO coming to me at work so I thought maybe I'd just take them."

"Did you leave?" I asked.

Ricky shook his head. "No, ma'am. I didn't. I regret that. I regret everything about what happened in those next couple of days. I should have listened to my dad when he told me Austin Merkle was going to bring me nothing but trouble."

"Did you hear from Austin after that?"

"He texted me a few times but I didn't answer him. I didn't want anything to do with him."

I introduced the three texts Ricky received from Austin Merkle after he returned from the Dollar Kart. Austin had twice asked Ricky if he was "cool." His final text was that veiled threat warning Ricky not to ghost him.

"What happened next, Ricky?"

"A couple of days after that, the cops showed up at my work and brought me in for questioning."

"What did you tell them?"

"Nothing," Ricky said. "I was cocky. I didn't trust what Austin would do if he found out I was talking to the cops. I was ... well ... like I said. I was freaked out on the inside when they first called me in. That detective threatened to get my dad involved. They knew. They already knew I'd been at the Dollar Kart. I didn't know there were cameras. I ... I panicked. I'm not proud of what happened, but I grabbed that cop's phone and threw it against the wall when he said he was gonna call my dad with it. I'd ... I'd taken some edibles that day. They made me too jittery."

"Mr. Wahl," I said. "That's not the only time you spoke to law enforcement, is it?"

"No," he said. "After that first day at the station. When I got into it with that cop, I went home and told my dad everything. I told him I knew I was in trouble and I asked him for help. I didn't know what to do."

"What did you do?"

"We talked it over, my dad and me. He was actually a lot cooler about everything than I was giving him credit for. Anyway, he helped me see that the only thing I could do was tell the truth. By that point, we knew the dead guy in that car was actually Sheriff Clancy. When I found that out ... I knew. I didn't want to be a part of this. I knew whatever Austin had gotten himself into, it was bad. I wanted clear of it. So, my dad called the cops again and arranged it for me to come in."

Ricky spent the next hour recommitting to the statement he'd given to Agent Patel. With his cell phone records, the transcripts from his gaming chat, he never changed a single detail on the stand.

"Mr. Wahl, why did you agree to testify today?"

"Because I don't want any of this on my conscience. I don't think I did anything wrong. I had no idea what Austin had done when I picked him up that night. That's on him. Not me. So I said what I know. I don't want to be in trouble for what Austin did. I wasn't involved other than being dumb enough to go get him that night."

"Have you received anything in exchange for your testimony?"

"I have immunity," he said. "If I tell the truth about what happened, my part in it, then I won't get charged. And I swear, I had no idea Austin was going to do that with the sheriff. None. I didn't know what I would find when I pulled into that lot. I regret not driving him straight to the cops. I regret that I didn't say something right away. I was scared. I believed Austin that he'd drag me down with him. In a way, he has. I'm just ... sorry. I saw his wife on television. Mrs. Clancy. All those cops that showed up for the funeral. I don't know what happened between Austin and Sheriff Clancy, but the man didn't deserve to be shot. And I don't deserve to go to jail for being stupid. I've done the right thing now. I'm just ... so sorry. Tell his wife I'm so sorry."

"Thank you," I said. "I have no further questions."

Ricky's thumb went to his mouth again as Alexander Nash walked up to begin his cross-examination.

24

"You don't want to go to prison, do you, Ricky?"

Ricky Wahl shifted in his seat, looking straight at me. I kept my expression neutral.

"No," he said. "I don't want to go to prison."

"You'd do anything you have to to avoid it, wouldn't you?" Nash asked.

"Yes. I mean, no. I wouldn't lie if that's what you're saying. I'm telling the truth about what happened."

"The truth," Nash said. He looked down at his notes, up at Ricky, then leaned against the lectern.

"This game that you and Austin Merkle play, what's it called again?"

"We played lots of different ones."

"But the main one. The one where you claim Austin reached out to you the night of April 15th. What was the name of that game, again?"

"It's *Legends of Warfare*."

"*Legends of Warfare*. And the premise, if I'm understanding correctly, is you go around waging battles in different environments. In urban settings, am I right?"

"Sometimes."

"In fact, on the night of April 15th, you were engaged in a role-playing game where you and the other members of your platoon were shooting up a fictional version of Chicago, weren't you?"

"It's part of a post-apoc … um … post-apocalyptic campaign. Yes."

"Right. In that campaign, killing cops earns you extra points or rewards, isn't that right?"

"Objection," I said. "Relevance. Unless counsel has forgotten the line between fiction and reality."

"Oh, I think this witness's perception of reality is pretty relevant, Your Honor."

"Overruled for now," Judge Saul said. "But get to it, Mr. Nash."

"Ricky," Nash continued. "Isn't it true that in the week leading up to Sheriff Clancy's death, you personally earned two hundred bonus points for leading a campaign to kill the police chief in *Legends of Warfare*?"

"The zombie police chief," Ricky said. "It's not real."

"Ricky, you had direct messages with the rest of your online platoon members that night, didn't you?"

"Um ... sure ... we're always messaging back and forth. But mostly it's in real time. We talk through our headsets. When we're in the middle of a campaign, we don't stop to message each other a lot."

"But you did that night, didn't you? You messaged with an online player named Woodstock. You said, I've got to go straighten Turk out. Isn't that right?"

"Yeah. I was just letting him know I had to log off after Turk ... Austin asked me to come pick him up."

"Right. Straighten him out. Sure. Ricky, you weren't a fan of Sheriff Clancy, were you?"

"What? A fan? I didn't know the guy. I didn't even vote in the last election."

"You're not a fan of cops in general, are you?"

"I don't have an opinion. They do their job. I do mine. That doesn't mean I think Sheriff Clancy deserved what Austin did to him."

"You've said on multiple occasions, all pigs should die, didn't you? You messaged that to Gotcha_15 on February 18th of this year, didn't you?"

"It was in the game. I told you. Zombie cops."

"Are you telling me you've never had a personal beef with Sheriff Clancy?"

Ricky put his hands up in disbelief. "No. I told you. I didn't even know the guy."

"You were never told not to trust the cops?"

"I mean, sure. My dad always told me what to do if I ever got pulled over."

"And what was that? What did your father tell you?"

"Objection," I said. "Hearsay."

"Sustained."

"Ricky," Nash said. "I just want to clear something up. You're telling me that you had no family beef with Sheriff Clancy, to your knowledge?"

Beside me, Mercy wrote "family beef?" on her notepad. My fingers began to tingle. Nash was setting something up. I just had no idea what.

"My dad got arrested for a DUI a few years ago. I wouldn't say that it was a family beef. He's straightened himself up though. I don't know if that's what you're talking about."

"Ricky, in the month leading up to April 15th, you exchanged more than five hundred messages with the other players in your platoon, as you call it. Isn't that right?"

"I don't have a count. If you've pulled transcripts and you say that's what the number is, then that's what the number is."

"Would it surprise you to know that you mentioned killing cops forty-three times?"

"What? I don't know."

Nash moved to have Ricky's chat transcripts entered into evidence. We'd already stipulated to their admission, so I had no objections. In every instance Nash wanted to mischaracterize, I would argue it would be clear to any reasonable person, Ricky and his friends were talking within the context of their game. The jurors might not like it, but I felt confident they could differentiate between fact and fiction. If this was all the ammunition Nash had, Ricky's testimony should play very well for us.

"Ricky," Nash said. "One last thing I want to ask you about. Your car, the Uplander. It has manual transmission, doesn't it?"

"Yes. It's a stick shift."

"You offered to loan it to Austin Merkle, didn't you? When his own vehicle broke down."

"I think, yeah. Once or twice. I offered to let him drop me off at work and pick me up later so he could go to this job interview in Cleveland."

"But Austin didn't take you up on that offer, did he?"

"No."

"Why not?"

"Austin couldn't drive a stick. I offered to teach him once. But we never got to it."

"Right," Nash said. "Austin Merkle couldn't drive a stick. I have no further questions for this witness but reserve the right to recall him during the defense case in chief."

Once Ricky was excused from the witness stand, Judge Saul turned to me. "We've got time for another witness yet today, Ms. Brent."

"Your Honor," I said, rising. "The State calls Shanna Clancy to the stand."

25

She looked small on the stand. Childlike. Shanna had worn very little makeup and her hair pulled back into a ponytail. I had to have her remind the jury that she was Sheriff Clancy's widow, not his daughter. For the bulk of her testimony, Shanna managed to keep her tears at bay, but she blinked rapidly.

"Mrs. Clancy," I said. "Can you tell me what your day was like on April 14th of this year?"

"Normal. It was just normal. I volunteer at the Union Hall on Wednesdays. There was a retirement party for one of the deputies scheduled for that Saturday. I went in to help organize. You know. Put up decorations. Make sure we had all the serving spoons we'd need, outlets for hot plates, room in the fridge for desserts. Just all the little details that had to be done."

"Were you in communication with your husband during this?"

"Bill normally worked a day shift. Eight to four. Though most of the time, he'd end up working over. I could usually expect him home by six. He was really good about letting me know though. So yes. He'd texted me a couple of times that afternoon. There was a budget meeting the mayor wanted him to attend. He told me to expect him home by seven."

"Was he?"

She nodded, then leaned forward, speaking loudly into the microphone, causing feedback.

"Oh. I'm so sorry." She put her hand over the microphone and sat back. "Um. Yes. Bill was home just before seven. Things ran a little longer at the Union Hall than I anticipated, so I just picked up takeout for dinner. Bill likes ... liked ... Thai food. So I got some of his favorites. We had a nice dinner together."

"How was his mood?"

"Fine. Well, he was a little grumpy after the budget meeting. The mayor was talking about some cutbacks that Bill was worried about implementing. I don't know how people expect their streets to stay safe anymore. You can't hire good people, you can't retain the ones you've got. Those were things that Bill was always concerned about. It got harder and harder to run the department every year. It was a source of stress. Bill just cared so much about his men and women. He knew every deputy by name. He knew their families. Their kids. With this latest budget, it was really weighing on him how bad things could get. So we talked about that. He didn't eat very much. I remember that. He said his stomach just wasn't right. I knew it was the stress."

"What happened after dinner?"

"We watched television for a while. *Jeopardy*. A couple of World War II documentaries. I'm not much of a fan of those. But Bill liked them."

"What time did you turn in?"

"I'm more of a night owl than Bill. He was always pretty regimented. He would turn in no later than ten and be asleep in about thirty seconds. I've always envied that. Just hit the pillow and out like a light. I could never do that. And now ... well, I don't sleep much at all."

"So you went to bed after your husband on the night of the 14th?" I asked.

"That's right. I stayed up and watched a movie. Um ... *Pretty Woman* was on. I went to bed when it was over, a little after midnight. Bill was sound asleep and snoring. He could shake the whole house. I could usually get him to stop if I adjusted his pillow a little. Now ... it's so quiet. I almost miss it. I don't know what I'd do if I didn't have our little Frenchie. Daisy. Sometimes when she's sleeping, she makes noises like Bill used to. He never let her sleep on the bed. Now, I do."

I took a moment, letting Shanna collect herself. But she kept her head up.

"Mrs. Clancy, what happened next?"

"Bill got a phone call. His cell phone started ringing at like 2:40 in the morning. I had to nudge him to wake him up. I almost didn't. He never would hear it. He slept so soundly. And it would always be work if it was in the middle of the night. He'd been so stressed out at dinner, I'll admit. I thought about reaching over and just turning his phone off. And I keep thinking about what might have happened if I had. If I'd just turned off the ringer and let him sleep. I should have. I *should* have."

"Mrs. Clancy ..."

"I'm the one who woke him up. I nudged him and made him answer that phone. He got up. Walked in the other room so he wouldn't keep me awake. He was on the call for two minutes, I think. He came back in, kissed me, told me he had to go into work. And that was it. That's the last time I saw him. The last time I heard from him. I woke up around eight, had my coffee. Did some work on the computer. I run an online store selling dress patterns I design. Later, I had my workout. Then Sam ... um ... Lieutenant Cruz came to the door. You were there. That's when I found out what happened to Bill."

"Sheriff Clancy never told you who was on the phone that night?"

"No. He was just adamant that I should go back to sleep. It's happened before. More times than I can count. It wasn't at all unusual for Bill to have to go in like that. It was just a normal day. A normal night. And then ..."

It was then she started to cry. "It's been a nightmare. I keep thinking I'm going to wake up. If I just wake up, it'll all be over and Bill will be here. He'll tell me it was just a bad dream. I can't sleep anymore. I don't even go into our bedroom anymore. I sleep in the guest room down the hall. His pillow ... it's still got the dent from where he slept that last night. I don't want to lose that. When I go in there, I can convince myself that he's not really gone. Just for a second. But ... he is. He's not coming back. And for what? Why?"

She dabbed at her eyes. I couldn't dare to look at the jury. But I knew two members had lost their spouses. I could feel their eyes fixed on Shanna Clancy and her palpable pain.

"Thank you," I said. "I have no more questions."

"Mr. Nash?" Judge Saul said.

Nash was leaning over, listening to something Austin Merkle whispered. He put a hand up, reassuring Merkle, then he got up and took his place at the lectern.

"Thank you for being here, Mrs. Clancy. I know this is a tough time for you. I promise I'll be brief. Your husband would have had to run for re-election next year, isn't that right?"

"Yes."

"He was worried about that, wasn't he?"

"What do you mean? Worried about running or worried about winning?"

"Winning," Nash explained.

"Bill never took things for granted. He felt like we're in a climate where his office was being scapegoated for a lot of things. An easy target. So yes. He worried about whether he'd get to keep serving the people of Maumee County. He didn't feel like he had accomplished everything he wanted to. It was something we argued about ... well, not argued. But we disagreed."

"You didn't want him to run?"

"No. I disagreed that my husband had anything left to prove. But being the sheriff was his calling, he felt. It's what he loved. So I was going to support him no matter what."

"No matter what. Mrs. Clancy, have you ever heard of the Mechanics?"

"Have I heard of mechanics? You mean like someone who would fix my car? I don't understand what you're asking me."

"The Mechanics," Nash repeated. I gripped the pencil I was holding that much tighter.

"The Mechanics. The name given to a group of individuals recently convicted of various violations of the RICO statute. They had ties to unsavory tactics employed by the current mayor's political rival."

Shanna looked unsure. She met my eyes. I could do nothing but stay neutral. For a moment.

"Yes," she said. "Of course I read the news about all of that."

"You did more than read the news though, didn't you? You're saying it never came up in your dinner conversations with Bill?"

"I don't remember specifically."

"Mrs. Clancy, were you aware that Web Margolis was a major contributor to your husband's last election campaign?"

"No," she said. "I didn't keep track of who Bill's donors were."

"But you're personally acquainted with Web Margolis, aren't you?"

"I know Mr. Margolis. Part of being the sheriff's wife required me to attend different functions with him. So yes. I met Web Margolis once or twice."

"He had dinner at your home last year, didn't he?"

"He might have. We hosted fundraising dinners. If Mr. Margolis came over, it would have been with a group of people. You're making it sound like he was some personal friend. He wasn't."

Web Margolis had been a major political player in Maumee County up until a year ago. He'd been caught up in the corruption scandal that had landed Jason in prison. But hundreds of local politicians had meetings with the man. I personally knew that Bill couldn't stand him.

"And you have no idea where Bill went in the early morning of April 15th, do you?"

"He didn't tell me. No."

"And you didn't find it odd that he still wasn't home when you woke up?"

"No. He was almost always gone by the time I woke up. That wasn't unusual."

"No idea where he went. No idea how many times he'd met with or spoken with Web Margolis."

"No," she said. "I wasn't one of those wives who kept their husband on a short leash. Bill and I got married late. He was in his mid-forties. He'd been a bachelor for most of his adult life. And I had my life and interests too. I never henpecked him. I trusted him."

"Trusted him," Nash said. "Of course."

Nash turned and caught my eye. There was a smirk there I didn't like. Then, he abruptly pivoted and looked back at Shanna Clancy.

"Thank you, Mrs. Clancy. I have no further questions. No ... wait ... I have one. Mrs. Clancy? Have you ever driven your husband's Dodge Durango?"

"What? No. That was Bill's car, not mine."

"But you never borrowed it? Say, if your car was in the shop or something?"

"I can't drive the Durango. No."

"Can't. Why do you say can't?"

"Because the Durango is a stick shift. I don't know how to drive one of those."

"Ah," Nash said. "I have no further questions. Thank you, Mrs. Clancy. I am truly sorry for your loss."

Shanna started to get up, then stopped herself, looking at me for guidance. The bit about the stick shift was a cheap ploy. But one I should have seen coming. Nash had gotten Ricky Wahl to say Austin Merkle didn't know how to drive a stick. Later, I knew he would argue that Merkle therefore couldn't have been the one driving the Durango after he shot Bill. Only all the physical evidence pointed to the fact that he had. I was kicking myself. But there was no way I could fix it now. I could clean it up in closing if I had to.

"I have no more questions either," I said.

"You may step down, Mrs. Clancy."

"Thank you," she said. Then she turned to the jury. "Thank you."

She hustled her way down the aisle and disappeared out into the hall.

"Ms. Brent?" the judge addressed me.

I looked one last time at my notes. Then I rose and faced the judge.

"Your Honor, at this time, the prosecution rests."

26

Over the years, I'd learned to fear my own doorbell. No one ever used it unless they were delivering bad news. At 10:00 p.m., the night after I'd rested my case, that insistent ring came just after I'd gotten out of the shower.

Sam.

I pulled up the security camera live feed. He was still in uniform, standing with his back to the door.

God, I thought. Please don't let it be more bad news.

When I opened the door, Sam turned and gave me a smile that lifted my heart just a little. At the same time, he held the heavy weight of sadness in his eyes. It had settled over him the morning we got the call about Bill Clancy and hadn't let up.

"Come on in," I said.

"I'm sorry to bother you so late. Were you already in bed?"

I pulled my cotton cardigan tighter around me. He'd caught me with wet hair, wearing a tank top and a pair of lounge pants.

"No. I just got out of the shower."

"Is Will still awake? I wanted to wait until after he went to bed. Didn't want to disrupt his routine."

Smiling, I opened the door even wider. Sam hesitated. I realized it had been weeks since I'd seen him outside the office. Since he became acting sheriff, since the murder trial had started, neither of us had a chance for anything social.

"He's asleep," I told him. "And thank you."

"I know how agitated he gets when you're in trial. How's he handling all of this? Gosh. I haven't seen him since school started up again. Mara, I'm sorry. I'd promised him a weekly basketball game this summer."

"It's okay. Really. Will's doing fine."

"No," Sam said as he walked into my kitchen. He went for a stool at the island, then pivoted, going instead to the dining room table.

"No. It's not fine. It's on me. I'll make it up to him. Promise."

"He knows," I said. "How about a beer? Glass of wine?"

Sam shook his head. "I could actually go for a cup of coffee, if you don't mind."

I raised a brow. "Sam, how much sleep have you been getting?"

I went to the coffeemaker and pulled a pod out of the cupboard. He still hadn't answered me by the time I brought him his coffee.

"I'll sleep when this is over," he said.

I resisted the urge to lecture him. This was never going to be over. Bill Clancy would always be gone. I knew it hung over Sam. He was working ten times harder to do a job he'd convinced himself he was only half as good at as Bill Clancy. I knew different.

"I've got to ask," he said. "How do you feel like it's going?"

I got up and poured myself a glass of wine. "I don't know," I said as I sat back down. "It's hard for me to gauge from where I'm sitting. I got everything in that I needed to get in."

"Shanna's a wreck. I actually stopped at her place before I came here. She's got Dawn Melvin staying with her. Our records clerk. There's a woman from the Silver Angels who has popped in and out."

"It's good she's not alone. She did well today. Earnest. Sympathetic. Nash didn't come at her too hard."

"Smart man."

"Sam," I said, setting my wine down. "My concern ... Nash asked questions about the Mechanics. The corruption ring Jason was involved with. I think he's going to call a witness that's going to say Clancy had a meeting with Web Margolis. Do you know anything about that? Did it come up at all during the investigation?"

Sam's frown deepened. "Nash is making crap up. Bill Clancy was as straight-laced by the book as they come. I guarantee you, he had no involvement with the Mechanics other than doing everything he could to make sure their dealings came to light."

"That's what I believe too. But I can see where this is going. Nash is going to try to create some story that Bill was dirty."

Sam slammed a fist on the table. I quickly put my hand over his.

"I know he wasn't. I'm saying Nash is going to try to make the implication. It's a desperate tactic and he won't have proof. I'll cut him off at the knees."

"He's a snake. Nash is scum."

"He's doing a job. And ... he's made some mistakes. He went after Ricky Wahl in a way that made no sense. He went into a whole line of questioning about that *Legends of Warfare* game. Cop killing was a theme inside of it."

"He's trying to make the jury think Wahl was involved more than just as a getaway driver?"

"Maybe. But the point is, Merkle was deep into the same game. Nash might have just handed me an argument for motive. These kids were earning in-app coins and unlocking special quests for killing cops. I don't have direct proof that's what Merkle was thinking, but maybe I don't have to. The idea is out there. Thanks to Nash."

"I said he's scum," Sam said. "I didn't say he was stupid. Has it occurred to you that he wants you to take that bait for some reason?"

"It has. But I'm more concerned about what he's trying to do with this mention of the Mechanics. And ... I know Nash paid a visit to the prison in Milan. I need to know who he was there to see."

Sam gripped his coffee mug. "Jason."

"I'm not sure."

"That son of a ..."

"Sam ... it's bothered me from the outset. We still don't know what Austin Merkle did or said to lure Bill away from home in the middle of the night. That's the one great mystery. Nash is going to use it to try to raise reasonable doubt."

Sam got up. Tearing a hand through his hair, he walked into the living room. He stood at the sliding glass doors, staring out at the woods. I took my last sip of wine and went to join him.

"Where's the trap?" he said. "The land mine we're about to step in. You feel it too, don't you?"

I debated how to answer. Sam and I were in uncharted territory. There was the part of me that was his friend ... more than. This man had lost someone very important to him. He'd been thrust into a difficult job under nearly impossible circumstances. He could use a friend and some moral support. But I was also Mara Brent, assistant prosecutor. In the end, that's how I answered.

"Yes. I feel it too. Something's coming. I wish ... this trial ... We needed more time. We needed to be sure about whether Austin Merkle was acting alone."

Sam turned to me. "We've given you a solid piece of police work. Gus. Andrea Patel. They didn't make any big mistakes. The thing is tight."

"I know. And I'm not blaming you or anyone. This was Nash's strategy. I had no power to delay this trial. Merkle's got a constitutional right to a speedy trial. Nash knew what he was doing when he refused to waive it. We had to go with what we had. And what we have *is* rock solid. There is no doubt in my mind that Austin Merkle is the man who pulled that trigger and ended Bill Clancy's life. We just may never know why. But I've won murder convictions on less evidence and even muddier motives."

Sam smiled. "You don't have to handle me. And I'm the one who should be giving you a pep talk."

"Sorry. I'm just ... I worry about you. You're my friend."

His smile fell just a little at the word friend. At the same time, I think we both knew this wasn't the time to challenge the premise.

His face changed again. He cocked his head and scowled. "How did you find out Nash has been out to Milan? That didn't come from us."

"No. That came from my new intern. Mercedes Gale."

"Tom Gale's kid. How's she working out?"

"Pretty good, actually. She's hungry. Eager. Smart. Maybe too smart for her own good. She's been an asset in this case."

"Do I want to know how she got that intel on Nash?"

I went back to the kitchen and poured myself a second glass of wine. Sam waved me off when I offered him one. I rejoined him in the living room, sitting next to him on the couch.

"You didn't answer my question. Do I want to know how Tom Gale's kid got intel on Alex Nash's comings and goings?"

"I didn't ask. But I think she pulled some strings with one of her father's top P.I.s. She didn't give me a name."

"You're gonna want to be careful of that," Sam said. "Gale was a shark in his day. Do you think he'd have someone shady working for him? Someone who might bite you in the rear before this is all over?"

"So far no. I made it clear to Mercy we can't take any chances like that. Ever. And nothing she found out was illegal or even improper. It was just ... uncomfortable."

"He's trying to get under your skin," Sam said, his tone turning to simmering anger. "Has it occurred to you that Nash knew he had a tail? I wouldn't put it past him to just show up at the prison for no reason other than to make it look like he was visiting Jason or one of his cronies. So you'd sit here just like you are, wondering whether he'd pulled the pin out of some grenade that'll explode in the middle of this trial."

"Lord. That's a lot of ifs. And it's a lot of wasted time on his part. I can't imagine Nash would go to all that trouble just to ..."

"Mara," Sam said, turning so he faced me full on. "I've never known you to suffer from a lack of imagination. And this guy? Nash? You have a history with him. He knows you."

"He knew me fifteen years ago. Briefly. He doesn't *know* me, know me."

"But Jason does ..."

A thick, uncomfortable silence grew between us. I finished my wine, letting that floaty feeling settle my nerves.

"Nash is being bankrolled by people who are connected with the same people the Mechanics were trying to keep in power, Mara. Candidates the Legacy Foundation wanted elected. You told me the Legacy Foundation is behind the Cerberus Justice Project. And you got that information from the same source, didn't you?"

The warm feeling from the wine turned into a cold chill. I met Sam's eyes.

"Mercy Gale. Sam."

"I'm going to check into her."

My head spun. It was almost too much to process.

"Sam, wait a minute. Mercy came to work for our office *before* Bill Clancy's murder. It makes no sense that she'd somehow be involved in trying to undermine my case or working as some kind of double agent."

"Maybe it's more a case of being in the right place at the right time for her. I don't know. And it's probably nothing. Me just being paranoid and cynical. It just strikes me that this girl seems to have ready access to information that we didn't."

"Right."

"So, I'll do a little sniffing around."

I nodded. "So will I. Starting with Jason. I'm going to see him tomorrow morning."

Sam went stiff. I knew he'd be happier if I never had contact with my ex again. Sometimes, I felt the same way.

"Do you think he'll be honest with you?"

I smiled. "Not one bit."

"Just be careful," Sam said. "I know you have to do it. But it doesn't mean I have to like it."

"I know. So we'll circle back Sunday night. That's a promise."

I rose with Sam and walked him to the door. He hesitated for a moment before grabbing the knob. Then, he leaned in and gave me a kiss on the cheek.

"Watch your back, Mara." Then he walked out into the night.

27

Six months. It was the longest I'd ever gone without seeing this man in the eighteen years since we first met. Jason Brent, former rising star of his political party. Freshman congressman and future presidential hopeful. I'd seen him as a young man. Handsome. Hungry. Filled with ideas, plans, and the singular drive to make them happen. Now, he sat across from me, haggard lines through his face and new gray in his hair. He had lost weight. He wore his hair longer, brushing his collar. Though it gave him a new, rugged appeal, this didn't look like the man I knew, except for one thing. That same naked hunger filled his eyes as he looked at me.

"What do you want from me, Mara?" he said.

I nearly told him straight out. But something stopped me. Even now, from inside these prison walls, I knew Jason was strategizing. Moving chess pieces in his head. Looking for ways to leverage what he could. Perhaps the most dangerous thing of all? He knew me. Sam's last words to me echoed in my mind.

Watch your back, Mara. Be very careful indeed.

"Do you have what you need in here? Are you …"

He smiled. "What I need? I'm curious. What is it that you think I need?"

I knew what this was. In the first few weeks since his incarceration began, Jason could easily deny the gravity of it. It was a mistake. Something that could be quickly rectified with the power and money he was so used to wielding. But as the weeks and months dragged on, his new reality had finally set in. The friends who'd promised to stand by him were suddenly unreachable. He was trapped by the slow wheels of the appellate process that I knew were unlikely to save him in the end anyway. Maybe now he was beginning to realize that, too.

"Will," he said. "I want to see him. I at least want to talk to him. You can arrange that."

"We've talked about this. You've spoken with Will's therapist. You've read Will's letters. He's read yours. We've agreed to let Will take the lead."

"How do I know what you've been telling him? Did you tell him I'm guilty? That you're some justice warrior looking out for the common man?"

"Stop it. I didn't come here to argue. I came to see how you are. Will is concerned about that too."

"He's a creature of habit. If I'm not part of his routine anymore, he's never going to ask to see me or talk to me. We have to make it happen."

I didn't answer. He was right. But he was also very wrong.

"I need the truth," I said. "I know you met with Alex Nash. Tell me why."

Jason's brow went up. I got the first genuine smile out of him but his eyes stayed dead. It sent a chill of fear through me. And now I'd stepped into the breach.

"Your case not going well? It's not so easy for you without me, is it?"

"Stop."

He leaned forward and put his hands over mine. His were rough in a way they hadn't been before, not since he was a kid. He'd been working with them. Hard.

"We were a good team, remember? You needed me to see ten steps ahead. We were brilliant together. Remember the Lathrop trial? Your first capital murder case? I was the one who helped you see how your star witness was going to turn on you. I was the one who helped you cut him off before he could."

"Tell me what you talked to Nash about," I said, sliding my hands away from his.

"Are you scared?"

"Yes," I said. "I'm always scared. Bill Clancy had a family. A wife. He was a good man who didn't deserve what happened to him. Nash is up to something. He's trying to make this personal and I need to know if you're helping him."

"You sure it's Nash you're afraid of?"

I shook my head. "Jason. Look at me. Were you involved in this? Am I wrong about Bill Clancy? Was he involved with the Mechanics too? Or was it that someone tried to get to him and he refused? Was this a hit?"

Jason's eyes darkened. It was a small tell, but he straightened his shoulders and looked around the room. I realized then what he was afraid of. He thought I might be wearing a wire.

"This is me," I said. "Just me. If you know something about what happened to Bill, tell me."

Nothing. Just those cold eyes staring right through me. I couldn't read him. God. I realized I never could. He played me just like everyone else.

"You know," he said. "Alex Nash had a thing for you back in law school. Did he tell you that?"

"That's not interesting to me."

Jason barked out a bitter laugh. "It was interesting to me. Still is."

"So that's what this was? He came here to gloat or something? Come on. It's always a game with you. Every single thing. You think I'm going to willingly bring my son around that?"

He struck with the speed of a rattlesnake. Launching himself forward, he grabbed my hands. "You're not going to use my kid as leverage over me, Mara."

"Brent! Hands off!"

Behind us, one of the guards came off the wall and took two steps closer. Tight-lipped, Jason abruptly let go of me and sat back in his chair.

My heart jack-hammered in my chest. I folded my hands in front of me so he wouldn't see them shaking. I had wondered how far Jason would be willing to go to get what he wanted from me. The answer was written in his eyes. He would do anything.

"If you want my help, you're going to have to do something for me," he said.

I stayed stone still.

"Was Bill Clancy dirty?" I whispered.

No answer.

"Tell me what Nash wanted. You didn't ask to see him. It was the other way around. I know that much."

Still, no answer.

"Dammit, Jason. Bill's dead. You're in here. If you know something, you're asking for the wrong thing."

His brow went up. A little of the old Jason came back. "You think you can get me some kind of deal in here?"

"Absolutely not. You know I don't have that kind of power as a county prosecutor. But if you do know something about the assassination of a county sheriff, then, yes. I can at least arrange a meeting with the U.S. Attorney's office. If you tell me what you know."

"So what, I can get a few extra minutes of yard time? Ding Dong at the commissary?"

"Jason, please ..."

"Time's up, Mara," he said.

"There's a bomb about to go off," I said. "You're right. I can't see it. I do need you. I need your brain. Your analytical mind.

Nash is playing me. He knew I'd find out he came here. And he knew I'd ask you about it. Was that it? It was for show? To rattle me into having this exact conversation with you? You're no fan of Nash's. You hated each other in law school. It almost came to blows. So why do anything to help him? Wouldn't it be more satisfying for you to help me beat him?"

"I don't know," he said. "What I do know is the two of you are the ones coming to me."

I wanted to be the one to launch across that table and wring his neck. He was enjoying this far too much.

"I'll help you," he said abruptly. "You're right. Alexander Nash is playing you. I don't know what he has on Bill Clancy and that's the truth. But I know it's something. I can help you find out."

And now we were coming to it. Jason's price.

"Will is off the table," I said. "I'd rather lose this case than leverage my kid's well-being."

"Could you have stopped this?" he said. It wasn't a question I expected.

"What?"

"Nash said he thinks you had a heads-up about the evidence they used to charge me. That you could have quashed it but you didn't."

I tried to keep my breath steady. How could Nash have known that? To my knowledge, the only people who did were Sam Cruz and ... Bill Clancy. Every warning bell in me clanged loudly. I started to sweat.

"I asked you for the truth," I said. "So I'll give it to you. Yes. I had a heads-up. But that doesn't mean I could have stopped it. It was bigger than me, Jason. Bigger than both of us."

He became a statue. Only the slightest tension in his jaw belied the storm raging behind his eyes.

"Time's up, Brent," the guard said. Jason straightened. Going silent, he rose and turned his back on me. I thought he would leave without saying another word. But just as he was about to walk through the door, he looked at me over his shoulder, paused, and said, "Answer the phone next time I call. Then we'll talk terms."

Then the door slammed shut behind him.

28

"The defense calls Cameron Whittaker to the stand."

Alexander Nash stood at the lectern, facing the jury. Austin Merkle fidgeted in his seat. I didn't see how it was possible, but the kid looked strung out. He was sweating, picking at his skin. I made a note to have Sam do some checking to see who Merkle had been in contact with in jail this week

Cameron Whittaker weighed about ninety pounds. She had long red hair and big blue eyes. She wore a pair of jeans and a pink sweater today. Her parents sat in the gallery looking as nervous as Austin Merkle did. "Miss Whittaker," Nash started. "Do you know Austin Merkle?"

She nodded.

"You're going to have to verbalize your answers, Miss Whittaker. This lady in the corner is typing out everything we say."

"Got it," Cameron said. "Sorry. Um. Yes. I know Austin."

"How?"

"I mean, from around. From school. From town."

"Were you friends?"

"No. Not really."

"How else did you know him? Other than just around."

There were the first signs of frustration in Nash's tone. Some witnesses are like drawing blood from a stone when you put them on the stand. A lot of times it's just nerves. Other times, they want to do everything they can not to cooperate for whatever reason. I knew Nash got her here by subpoena. At the same time, he was smart enough not to put a witness on the stand that wasn't going to help him.

"I don't know, I just knew him," Cameron said, defiant.

"Miss Whittaker, how did you know Ricky Wahl?"

"Ricky was my boyfriend. We dated a little in high school. Then we got back together."

"He's not your boyfriend now?"

She shook her head. After another admonishment from the judge, she sat straighter and practically shouted her answer into the microphone. "Ricky isn't my boyfriend anymore. I broke up with him over the summer."

"Was Ricky friends with Austin?" Nash asked.

"Yeah. They hung out."

"How did you feel about that?"

She shrugged, then shouted into the mic again. "Never much liked Austin."

"Why not?"

"He's a ... um ... can I say a bad word?"

Judge Saul, not looking up from her notes, answered, "I'd really rather you didn't."

"Oh. Okay. Well, Austin was what we call an um ... F-word Boy. You know. Rhymes with luck."

Whatever answer Alexander Nash was expecting, I don't think it was that. Though I knew he had to ask the follow-up question. From my angle, I could see him wincing, anticipating the answer.

"Can you explain what you mean by that?"

"Sure. Austin's like a man whore. Thinks he's God's gift to women. Struts around bragging about all the girls he's been with. The kind of guy that when you find out your friend wants to hook up with him, you try to stop it. So, no. I don't like Austin Merkle."

"Is that why you and Ricky broke up? Over his friendship with Austin?"

"Objection," I said. "Counsel is leading the witness."

"Sustained, Mr. Nash," Judge Saul said.

"Why did you and Ricky break up?"

"Because I was done waiting for Ricky to grow up. He spent all of his time gaming. He was working a dead-end job. And he seemed to care more about impressing Austin than me. I was just done."

"How did he try to impress Austin?"

"It was just always Austin this. Austin that. I got sick of it. Austin's a poser. All talk. Even Ricky was getting sick of it but he wouldn't ever call him on it."

"What do you mean?"

"Austin bragged all the time. Always had to one-up Ricky. I don't care what it was. If Ricky said he made so many bucks an hour, Austin would tell him he was a slave. Austin always had some scheme going. Said he was gonna get rich and Ricky would always just be working some hourly wage job like that was a bad thing. And Ricky would fall for it. He quit his last two jobs after Austin hassled him, wanting him to invest in these muscle-building shakes he was gonna sell, or a club he wanted to open. It went on and on. Austin was just a liar."

Why is he putting her on the stand? Mercy slid her note to me. I didn't have an answer for her, just an uneasy feeling. Alexander Nash wasn't stupid. And he wasn't about to get outsmarted by this girl.

Her testimony went on in the same vein for almost an hour. She expounded on her disdain for Austin Merkle and painted him in the worst light possible. Then, Nash finally got to the heart of her testimony.

"Miss Whittaker. Did you see Ricky Wahl on April 15th of this year?"

"No. I saw him the next day though. It was our anniversary and we were going to go to dinner. He asked me to pick him up."

"Was that usual? That you would pick him up?"

"No. Ricky was kind of backwards about that. He never liked me driving. But he told me his car was on the fritz. So I picked him up."

"What happened when you got to his house?"

"He wasn't ready. I was ticked because we had reservations at my favorite restaurant. Giorgio's. They don't hold your table if you're more than five minutes late. And Ricky was nowhere near ready. He hadn't showered. Hadn't shaved. Nothing."

"What did you do?"

"I laid into him. When I got there, he was on his gaming system playing *Legends of Warfare*. It was like he forgot I was coming. I lost my shi— um ... I lost my cool. There was dirty laundry all over the basement. I picked some up and threw it at him. That's when I saw the shirt."

"What shirt?"

Mercy wrote the same two words just as Alexander Nash asked the question.

"It was a gray tee shirt with SpongeBob on it. I got it for him as a joke the previous Christmas. When I picked it up, it stank. And it had blood all over it."

"Blood?"

"Objection," I said. "This witness is assuming facts not in evidence."

Nash gave me a sly smile. "This witness is testifying to her observations. If there was no evidence on this, whose fault is that?"

"Enough," Judge Saul said. "Keep the snide remarks out of this, Mr. Nash. The objection is overruled. You may continue."

"Blood," Nash repeated. "You're saying this shirt was covered with blood? How much?"

"Well ... covered. Just like you said. All over the front of it. I asked Ricky what happened. Like I was worried he'd hurt himself. He said ..."

"Objection," I said. "Calls for hearsay."

"Sustained."

"Miss Whittaker, what was Ricky wearing at the time of this altercation?"

"He was shirtless. Wearing sweatpants."

"Did you observe any injuries on him?"

"No."

"And you said he hadn't shaved?"

"Nope. He was scruffy. That's why I was so mad."

"Got it," Nash said. He stepped back from the lectern and shifted his weight from one foot to the other.

"Miss Whittaker, how well did you know Ricky's father?"

"His dad? Yeah. I knew him. We didn't talk a lot."

"Would you say you had a good relationship with Steven Wahl while you were dating his son?"

"No. I wouldn't say that. No."

"Why not?"

"Because I didn't like how he treated Ricky. I didn't like what Ricky told me about things Mr. Wahl had done to him when he was a little kid. He used to beat him up."

"Objection," I said. "To the extent this witness's testimony relies on alleged statements made to her by Ricky Wahl, it's hearsay."

"Miss Wahl, did you ever personally witness Steven Wahl physically abuse his son?"

"Mr. Nash," Judge Saul said. "There's an objection outstanding. One I'm going to sustain. I'd advise you to follow proper courtroom procedure and wait for my ruling before proceeding. Now, the witness may answer to the extent she has personally observed something."

"What?" Cameron said.

"You can answer my last question," Nash clarified.

"Oh. Yes I've seen Mr. Wahl punch Ricky. More than once. It's been a long time, but back in high school after a basketball game. Ricky came home drunk. His dad threw him into a wall and slapped him. And I've seen bruises on Ricky's body after he and his dad have gotten into fights."

"I see. Do you know whether Ricky ever reported this to the police?"

"No. He never called the cops," she said.

There was nothing. No reports of domestic violence at the Wahl household. Nothing of the kind. Behind me, I heard a rumble of activity. When I turned to look, Sam was leaving the courtroom.

"Do you know why?"

"Ricky didn't like the cops," she said. "Like, he hated them. He marched against them a few times. Donated money to different protest groups. I asked him one time why he was so mad about it. He told me ..."

"Objection," I said. "Once again, hearsay."

"Miss Whittaker, you cannot repeat things other people have told you. Do you understand that?" Judge Saul said. "You can testify about what you personally observed."

"Well," she said. "I personally *observed* Ricky peeing on one of Sheriff Clancy's yard signs."

"Miss Whittaker," Nash said. "Do you know why Ricky urinated on Clancy's yard sign specifically?"

"Ricky didn't like the cops. They never did anything to protect him when Ricky's dad used to wail on him. He told me Sheriff Bill Clancy was the reason his mom ran out on him."

"Objection!"

"Your Honor," Nash said. "This isn't being offered for the truth of the matter asserted. It goes to Ricky Wahl's state of mind."

"I'll allow it," Judge Saul said. "The answer may stand."

"Why did Ricky think that?"

"Objection! This doesn't go to state of mind. Mr. Nash is asking Miss Whittaker to repeat things she claims she was told. It's improper hearsay."

Judge Saul frowned at Nash. For a split second, I thought she was going to overrule me again. Instead, she barked out, "Sustained."

Nash paused, standing with his hands on his hips. He was flustered. But I knew he'd already inflicted the worst damage he could with this witness. "I have no further questions for this witness," he said.

"Ms. Brent?" Judge Saul said.

Fuming, but trying not to look like it, I went to the lectern.

"Miss Whittaker, you were interviewed by the police twice during this investigation. Isn't that true?"

"I talked to the cops, yes."

"And yet you've never mentioned this claim about Ricky's mistrust of the police. You've never mentioned this so-called incident with a yard sign. And you never brought up any stained tee shirts. Isn't that right?"

"They didn't ask," she said.

"Didn't ask? You knew Ricky was asked to pick up Austin Merkle the morning after Sheriff Clancy was murdered, didn't you?"

"I saw that on the news, yes," she said.

"And yet you're only just now bringing these concerns to light. Interesting. Isn't it true that Ricky Wahl was the one who broke up with you last summer?"

"What? No way. Is that what he's saying? He's a liar. I was the best thing that ever happened to that loser. I was done with him. Told him not to call me anymore."

"I see," I said. Anticipating my next question, Mercy handed me the transcript I had of Ricky Wahl's cell phone records.

"And yet, in August of this year, you texted him no less than a dozen times, isn't that right?"

"I don't know."

"You texted him on July 28th asking him if he wanted to hang out. Didn't you?"

"I don't remember."

I handed her the transcript and had her read it.

"Does that refresh your recollection?" I asked.

"I don't remember sending that. I don't know."

"You don't know. He didn't respond, did he?"

She shrugged.

"And you texted him ten more times. No response. Miss Whittaker, Ricky Wahl ghosted you, didn't he?"

No answer. Just a shrug.

"Miss Whittaker?" the judge said.

"I broke up with Ricky. That's the truth."

"Fine," I said. "I have no further questions."

Which was true for Cameron Whittaker. For Ricky and Steven Wahl, I had a million.

29

"The defense calls Nolan Bellamy to the stand."

At just seventy, Mr. Bellamy walked bent over with a cane. The bailiff held on to his elbow as the man climbed into the witness box. He had clear, green eyes and focused them straight at Austin Merkle as he was sworn in.

"Mr. Bellamy," Nash started. "Where do you currently reside?"

"I live in Palm Springs, Florida. Retired down there five years ago with my wife, Flo."

"Where did you retire from?"

"Victory Spark Plugs. I was ... am ... a tool and die maker."

"So you lived here in Waynetown?"

"Born and raised. Yes, sir."

"Mr. Bellamy, what was your last address in Waynetown, before you retired to Florida, that is?"

"Had a house I built on Broad Street. 427."

"427 Broad Street. And who lived across the street from you, at 424?"

"Ed and Charlene Holt built that house in the seventies. They lived there for maybe twenty-five years. But they sold it to Stevie and Margie Wahl in the early aughts. Margie took off a couple of years after that. But Stevie and his boy Ricky lived there up until the day I moved. I think they still do."

"So how long in total did you live next door to Steven and Ricky Wahl?"

"A little over ten years."

"Were you friendly with them?"

"Oh, sure. I helped Stevie get a job at Victory. Took him under my wing. He was a fair bit younger than me. But he kinda reminded me of myself at first. Hard worker."

"So you were close?"

"I'd say, yes, sir."

"Are you still close with Steven Wahl or his son?"

"No. I wouldn't say that. Haven't talked to him in probably seven years."

"Seven years. You said you moved to Florida five years ago. What caused you to not be close with Steven Wahl in the two years before you moved?"

"Stevie had his demons. Ones I understand. But I watched him piss away most of the good stuff he had in his life. He was a drinker."

"How do you know that?"

"Cuz I saw it. He'd show up to work smelling like bourbon. Got worse and worse until finally he lost his job. Lost his wife over it too before that. It was a sad story to me. Then ... there was what he done to that boy. To Ricky."

"Objection," I said. "I fail to see anything relevant to this line of questioning."

"Counsel, approach," Judge Saul said. Nash and I joined her for a sidebar.

"Mr. Nash," she said. "I tend to agree with Ms. Brent."

"Steven Wahl isn't a witness in this case," I said. "This man admitted he hasn't even lived in Waynetown in over five years."

"Your Honor," Nash said. "I'm begging for a bit of leeway here. The State has put forth Ricky Wahl as their star witness. I have every right to question Ricky's credibility and motives for saying what he said. The prosecution has admitted that it was Steven Wahl who convinced his son to come forward. The dynamic between Steven and his son is relevant. Mr. Bellamy is uniquely qualified to speak to that. I promise I'll get there in just a handful of questions."

"Your Honor," I said.

Judge Saul put a hand up. "Your objection is overruled for the time being." She said it again for the record as I walked back to the table.

"Mr. Bellamy," Nash said as he resumed his position behind the lectern. "What did you observe about the relationship between Ricky Wahl and his father?"

"It was a rough one. Stevie was strict. It was fine when he was sober. But when he got to drinking ... well ... he hit that boy more than what I felt was proper."

"You personally observed this abuse?"

"Yes, sir. Now listen. I was raised at a different time. So was Stevie. My own father wasn't afraid to give me a swat here and there when I mouthed off or to set me straight. But this was a little different. I saw Stevie push Ricky down in the driveway. I saw him punch him once or twice when the boy was a teenager. Couple of times it got so I felt I had to step in. Towards the end, before Stevie sobered up, the wife and me, we had Ricky stay over with us. This was after his mom walked out. That was a really dark time."

"Mr. Bellamy, you said you were close with Stevie. You were neighbors. Coworkers. Did you socialize with Steven Wahl?"

"I did. Invited him to a poker game. And we'd hang out at Rusty's Bar. That was three blocks over on Turner Street. The place burned down a few years ago but that was our local haunt for a good while."

"You were drinking buddies, you and Steven Wahl."

"Yep. Yes. We were. Like I said, until it became obvious to me Stevie's drinking went far beyond just blowing off steam after work. He got banned from Rusty's."

"Can you explain what happened?"

"Objection," I said. "Your Honor, once again, Steven Wahl isn't on trial. We've ..."

"Stevie took a swing at Bill Clancy!" Nolan Bellamy said over my objection.

Judge Saul banged her gavel as murmurs rose in the gallery. Nash threw his hands up.

"Mr. Bellamy, please refrain from answering anything while there's an objection pending. For now, I'm going to overrule that objection. The witness may answer."

I stayed on my feet.

"Mr. Bellamy, can you repeat your answer to my question? What happened to get Steven Wahl banned from Rusty's Bar?"

"One night, we were there after work. I had just one Jack and Coke. That was my drink at the time. Stevie ordered a straight shot. But he already reeked of whiskey. Bartender at the time told Stevie he wouldn't serve him. He was already slurring his words and couldn't sit on a stool. Stevie got pretty irate pretty fast. Rusty told him to leave. Asked me to get him out. Stevie got a little physical. Started making a scene. This was I think seven years ago. It was during one of the sheriff's re-election years. The one where that lady from the FBI tried to run against him. Anyway, Clancy overheard what was going on and came over. He and Rusty were friends. Rusty had Clancy campaign signs all over the bar and out in the parking lot. Well, when Bill Clancy tried to step in and help get Stevie out of the bar and squared away, Stevie punched him in the face. Knocked him over."

"What happened next?"

"Oh, Clancy rounded pretty quick. He bum rushed Stevie right out the bar. I went out there and Clancy and I tried to get him in my car so I could take him home. Stevie went crazy. He wouldn't go. Saying all kinds of things about how he'd kill Clancy. How Clancy was the reason his wife left him."

"Did he say why?" Nash said.

"Objection! This is improper hearsay."

"Sustained. Move on, Mr. Nash."

"All right, Mr. Bellamy, what happened next?"

"I promised Clancy that I'd get Stevie home safe. Since he wouldn't get in my car, I had Rusty give Ricky a call. Ricky could drive by that point. I wanna say he was sixteen. So Ricky got there in maybe five minutes. When he pulled up, Stevie sure didn't calm down. He took a swing at both Clancy and Ricky. It was Ricky who convinced Clancy not to call for backup or arrest his dad. See, Clancy was off duty at the time. Ricky and I both vouched for Stevie. Promised to get him home and that we'd make sure he slept it off."

"What happened next?"

"It must have bothered Clancy. Cuz next day, he come out to the house to check on Stevie. I always thought that was real good of him. I went downtown and put a couple of his yard signs out after that. What he did for Stevie? Clancy didn't have to do that."

"You witnessed this?"

"Sure did. Saw Clancy's car pull up. It was in the morning. I was getting ready for work and I walked out to get the paper. Clancy pulled into the driveway and walked up to Stevie's front door. I went over there."

"Why did you do that?"

"I was worried Stevie might do something else stupid. He didn't disappoint. Ricky came to the door. He and Clancy had some words on the porch. Don't know what they said, but I saw Ricky get pretty upset. Clancy kept on shaking his head no. Then Ricky got *really* upset. Swearing. Crying. That's when Stevie came into it. There was a lot of yelling and screaming. I thought for sure Stevie was gonna take another swing at Clancy. So I came running. Clancy was getting back in his car. Ricky was throwing dirt at it. They had a garden in front and this was fall. Stevie had his boy turning it. So there was dirt dug up. Ricky started picking up clumps of it and throwing it right at Clancy's car. I stepped in front of him, told him to go on back in the house. Stevie too."

"Did they?"

"Eventually, yeah. I went back to Clancy. Like I said, he wasn't in uniform or anything. He told me he pulled a few strings and got a bed for Stevie at a rehab place if he wanted it. I think he was just trying to do a good deed, you know? And you know what they say about those things."

"Sure," Nash said. "What did Clancy do then?"

"Well, he just looked kind of sad for the boy, you know? And I could tell he regretted even bothering. He gave me his card and told me to call him if I ever saw anything that worried me over there."

"I see. What did you do next? Did you ever call Sheriff Clancy?"

"I didn't. No. And I regret that. I truly do. But see ... back in my younger days, I had some issues with booze, too. I got a hold of it. I was never like Stevie Wahl. But my wife was worried what would happen ... if Stevie would drag me down. You can only extend a hand to help someone so many times and get bit. When I went to go talk to Stevie, he threw me off his porch. A week or two after that was when he got canned at Victory. Then the yard sign thing was the last straw, really."

"The yard sign thing? What was that?"

"I put a Clancy campaign sign in my front yard. It went missing a few days later. I found it crumpled up and soiled on the side of Stevie's house."

"Soiled in what way?"

"It was wet. And it smelled like ... sorry to be indelicate, but ... feces. Either Stevie or Ricky wiped dog doo on it. Ricky saw me. He didn't say a word. But the next day, that sign was back in my yard, still crumpled and soiled, but right back in the middle of the yard."

"Thank you," Nash said. "I have no further questions."

Clenching my fist around a pencil, I took my place at the lectern. "Mr. Bellamy, when did you find out Sheriff Clancy had been murdered?"

"I couldn't tell you the exact day. But my wife said she saw it on Facebook. She still follows a lot of the news from up here even though we're down in Florida. But she's the one who told me. It was before his funeral. So I wanna say it was no more than a day or two after it happened."

"So you followed the news of the sheriff's murder, isn't that right?"

"I read the articles, sure. I took an interest in it."

"Did you speak to anyone about your interest in it?"

"Well, my wife. Sure. And I still keep in contact with a couple of the old retired farts from Victory. Lot of them come down to Florida for the winter. So I'll see them in a few months. But I got a few phone calls."

"From whom?"

"Just a couple of the guys I worked with back in the day. Burt Meese. Gary Pritchett. Maybe some others."

I took a chance. "You never mentioned to Meese or Pritchett the story you just told here in court today, did you?"

"I don't think I did. Didn't see the point of it. Stevie'd turned his life around. And I didn't know Ricky was gonna be involved in this case then."

"But you found out Ricky was involved later, didn't you? You found out Ricky was in fact a material witness in this case, didn't you? It was in the news."

"Yeah," he said, dropping his head. "I heard that."

"Months ago. You admit you continued to follow the news of this story, right?"

"I sure did."

"You were fond of Bill Clancy, weren't you? I mean, that's what you just testified."

"I thought he was a stand-up guy. Yes."

"A stand-up guy. Did you ever tell Bill Clancy about what you believe happened to his campaign sign?"

"No."

"Did you confront the Wahls about it?"

"No."

"Did you ever report your concerns about Ricky Wahl's safety to Clancy?"

"No. Other than what he saw that night at the bar. I didn't file a report or anything."

"And in all these months, you never saw fit to come forward and tell the police this story, did you?"

"They didn't ask."

"But you were aware there was a tip hotline in this case, weren't you?"

"I think so, yeah."

"Mr. Bellamy, how did you get here today?"

"What do you mean?"

"Well, I mean, you said you live in Florida full time. Did you drive here?"

"No. Flew."

"Who paid for your flight?"

"Mr. Nash is taking care of that."

"He is. I see. Are you staying with friends? Family?"

"No, ma'am. I'm staying at the Allegra Inn off I-75."

"The Allegra? That's a nice hotel. Is Mr. Nash also paying for that?"

"Yes."

"And your meals? Mr. Nash is paying for those too, isn't he?"

Bellamy looked to Nash for help. Nash kept his face in his notes.

"He's paying me a witness fee."

"How much is he paying you:?"

"Objection," Nash said. "If the prosecution wants to accuse me of something, I'd like her to do it to my face."

"I believe I am!"

"Enough," Judge Saul said. "You can spar amongst yourselves later. Ask your questions of the witness, Ms. Brent."

"How much are you being paid to be here, Mr. Bellamy?"

"He's not paying me off, if that's what you're suggesting, lady. But I'm on a fixed income. I can't afford to just fly up here on a moment's notice. Mr. Nash is paying my expenses to be here and to get me back home. That's it."

"Thank you," I said. "I have nothing further."

With that, Judge Saul put us in recess.

"It's nothing," Mercy whispered when I came back to the table. "We're winning if that's all Nash has."

I gathered my files and stuffed them into my briefcase. "I need you to find Ricky and Steven Wahl. Tell them both to meet me in my office within the hour."

Fuming and with all eyes on me, I marched out of the courtroom.

30

"He can't be in here."

"Mara," Sam said. "This is his case. If we have a problem ..."

"He can't be in here, Sam. Nash isn't done. He's still calling witnesses. If he puts either one of those two knuckleheads on the stand and finds out Gus was in a room with them ..."

"Mara?" Mercy poked her head in. "I'm sorry to interrupt. But the Wahls are ready for you in the conference room."

I leaned against my desk, fingertips planted on my desk blotter. Breathe in. Breathe out. "Come on," I said to Sam. "You can go in there with me if you promise to let me do the talking."

Sam frowned, but gave me a nod. As we walked down the hall, I realized Gus's temper might not be the problem. Mine was.

Sam filed in silently behind me. Ricky Wahl sat at the end of the table, still in his overalls from work. Steven hadn't yet taken a seat. He stood in the back of the room, looking worried. Small town as it was, someone had clearly already filled them in on what happened in the courtroom today.

"It's not what you think," Steven started. Sam closed the door behind him and took a seat at the far end of the table.

"What I think," I started, "is that you withheld a critical piece of information from me."

"We came here of our own free will," Steven said. "Didn't bring a lawyer. My boy is trying to do the right thing. He's got immunity so ..."

"His immunity deal was contingent on him telling the truth, Mr. Wahl. All of it. He hasn't. And neither have you."

"I haven't told you a single lie," Ricky said. "Not one."

"Really?" I slid into a chair opposite him. "Let me lay this out for you. For both of you. As it stands right now, Austin Merkle's lawyer is laying the groundwork for a couple of pretty dark scenarios. One, you've harbored a secret hatred for Bill Clancy that you weren't forthright about. So, why should the jury believe your testimony? If you lied about one thing, why wouldn't you lie about everything?"

"I didn't lie!"

"Two, Austin's lawyer will argue that his client had zero motive for killing Sheriff Clancy. But you did."

Ricky Wahl's face changed. Big red blotches sprouted on his cheeks. His eyes went glassy and he started to sweat. Sam silently watched from the corner as if he were a human lie detector test.

"No," Ricky said. "No way. I'm not lying. I had nothing to do with what Austin did. Only the part I told you about after the fact."

"My boy came to you right away," Steven interjected. "We didn't have to. He could have ..."

"Your boy," Sam said, "only came forward when we had him dead to rights driving the getaway car. He's not exactly a Good Samaritan. And apparently neither are you."

"It's not like that," Steven said. He took the seat next to his son and put a fatherly hand on his back.

"Is Nolan Bellamy lying?" I asked. "You got in a bar fight with Bill Clancy. You threw him off your property. Nash has produced two witnesses who both testified that you smeared urine and feces all over Bill Clancy's yard sign."

"That was a long time ago," the elder Wahl said. "A long time ago. I'm not the same person I was then. I let my drinking get the better of me. Me and Bill? We made amends after that. I owe him. That day? When he came to the house? He told me I could lose everything. That he'd make sure of it if I didn't go get some help. It was a wake-up call. I started going to meetings after that. I changed. Bill Clancy was part of that."

"That's not the story Bellamy told," I said. "Bellamy said your relationship with him ended after that. That Ricky smeared urine and feces on one of the yard signs he had in his front yard after that confrontation. That doesn't sound to me like you were grateful for his help."

"I wasn't at first," Steven said. "And Ricky? He was scared. That's my fault. It's me he was scared of. He was trying to protect me."

"I was a kid," Ricky said. I didn't like his posture. The louder his father got, the more Ricky seemed to withdraw into himself. His father's anger was clearly triggering him and bringing up old trauma. That was probably exactly what had happened with the yard sign, too. To avoid a beating or blame, Ricky had likely made the gesture to prove to his father how loyal he was. This was bad. Awful.

"Why didn't you tell us any of this?" Sam asked.

"Didn't think it mattered," Steven said. "Didn't see how it could have. This stuff Bellamy brought up? It happened years ago. Sheriff Clancy and I were on friendly terms nowadays. Ask anyone."

"I'm asking you," I said.

"I never lied to you people," Steven said, shaking a finger at me. "I trusted you. I trusted my boy's future with you. Same as I'm doing now. He's held up his end. I expect you to hold up yours."

"Mr. Wahl," I said. "I think we need to talk to Ricky alone."

"He's my son!"

"He's over twenty-one," I said. "And I need you out of this room. Right now. Step outside. Mercy will show you to the waiting room."

"I ain't leaving!"

"Dad," Ricky said. "Just go. Let me talk to Ms. Brent alone."

Ricky was clearly terrified.

"There's something you should know," Steven said. He pulled a crumpled piece of paper out of his pocket and handed it to me. It was a subpoena. Alexander Nash intended to call him first thing in the morning.

"I never got a copy of this," I said. "Mercy, can you track that down?"

"Of course," she said. "I'll check with Caro."

"I cannot show up," Steven said.

"You will absolutely show up," I said. "This is a court order."

"Can you object since he didn't serve you with this subpoena?" Sam asked.

"No. The man's on my witness list as well. Mr. Wahl. Do I know everything you do?"

He frowned. "Yes. I'm not a liar." Steven exchanged a look with his son. For a moment, I thought he'd put up more of a fight. But Steven put a firm hand on his son's shoulder, then left the room as I asked.

I waited a moment, making sure Steven was well out of earshot. Then I looked at Ricky.

"Are you afraid of your father, Ricky?"

He reared back. "What?"

"Your neighbor and your ex-girlfriend both testified that your dad lays hands on you," Sam said.

Ricky shook his head. "No. My dad was telling the truth. He's changed. It's been a long time since those days. He used to smack me around some when I was a kid. Even he'll admit to that. But things are better now since he quit drinking. I swear to God."

"But you hated Bill Clancy. I need to know why."

Ricky laid his hands flat on the table. I didn't like that he was still sweating.

"Ricky … you need to understand what's at stake here. That immunity deal we signed is null and void if you've withheld the facts from me. You'd still be facing charges for murder as an accessory after the fact. I know you understand what that means."

He took in a breath and shuddered on the exhale.

"I didn't kill Sheriff Clancy. I had nothing to do with that. This was all Austin."

"Austin's lawyer is going to say that you were the one who wanted him dead. For what? You were angry with the sheriff because he didn't help you all those years ago, weren't you?" Sam said. "You were scared of your father. He had to have been pretty angry when Clancy showed up, threatening to have you removed from his home. That's what happened, isn't it?"

Ricky didn't speak, but his lips went white. "That's why you destroyed the yard sign," I said. "To placate your father? To get back at Nolan Bellamy?"

"You told Austin all of this, didn't you?" Sam said. "He knows about your family's history with Clancy."

Ricky's eyes snapped wide. He shook his head. "He's lying. Austin's lying. If he's trying to make it sound like I'm the one who wanted to hurt the sheriff, it's not true. I swear. I've told you the truth."

"But not all of it," I said. "You put me in a terrible position in court today, Ricky."

Ricky pulled his phone out of his pocket. He unlocked it and started swiping.

"Austin's lying," he insisted. "It's like I told you before. He was always working some angle. Some scheme."

Ricky turned his phone screen toward me and started scrolling through his texts from Austin Merkle. I'd seen them all before. He'd turned his phone over to Agent Patel. Half of what he showed me now, the jury had already seen.

"Look at that," Ricky said. "Austin got scared because I stopped answering his texts. He was worried I was gonna go to the police which is exactly what I did. Now why would he have texted me asking me if we were cool and warning me not to ghost him if I was the one who planned this whole thing? He was always doing this kind of crap. Trying to rope me in. Trying to impress me."

Ricky kept scrolling. His texts from Austin prior to the murder were hard to stomach.

"Every time he banged some chick, he tried to one up me. Bragging about it. He's a pig. Show the jury this crap and see what they think of Austin."

Ricky showed me the series of photographs Austin had sent him displaying various women in compromising positions. One girl barely looked eighteen. She posed in the nude for him. Gus had tried to track her down, but had no luck. One of the more disturbing videos to me was of the woman with the white lotus tattoo. Austin had her positioned with her back turned to the camera, her buttocks visible as Austin had intercourse with her. The text after he sent the video read, "This one can't get enough."

Bile rising in my throat, I slid Ricky's phone back across the table. "None of that matters," I said. "Austin's sex life isn't the issue at the moment. Your failure to tell me your history with Bill Clancy is what matters."

"I didn't lie. I shared all my texts with Austin with you. They prove I'm not lying. So put me back on the stand," he said. "I'll tell the jury everything I just told you. How can they think something I did or said when I was sixteen years old has anything to do with this?"

"Because it does," Sam said.

"Because if I'd known about it, I would have had you be honest about it right up front. Now, it looks like you were trying to hide it. Because you were."

Ricky had tears in his eyes. "I didn't do it. I didn't kill Bill Clancy. I didn't know Austin was going to or I would have stopped him."

Sam leaned forward. "Ricky, do you know why Austin killed Bill Clancy?"

"I told you. No. He didn't tell me anything. Not before or after."

"But you lied," I said. "You told me you didn't know it was the sheriff dead in that car. But you did. You had a history with him. You knew exactly who it was in that car."

Ricky bit his lip.

"Did your father tell you to lie to me? Did he tell you not to mention what happened all those years ago when your neighbor and Bill Clancy confronted him?"

"Son," Sam said. "You've gotta decide what's best for you. You're a grown man now. Austin's not here to tell you what to do, and neither is your old man."

"Yeah," he said. "My dad said none of that should matter. He said it would be okay."

I wanted to punch a wall. I wanted to punch Steven Wahl. I would get no such luxury. "Go home, Ricky," I said.

"Am I going to jail?"

"Just go home." I couldn't stand being in the room with him a second longer.

Ricky got up and left. As angry as I was, I felt Sam's quiet, bubbling rage as well.

"Do you think he played us?" I asked Sam.

No answer. New dread flooded my heart.

"Sam," I said. "For six months, we've been trying to figure out what Austin Merkle could have said to Bill to lure him out of bed in the middle of the night. What if it was Ricky? If he called Bill and told him he was afraid of his dad again, do you think Bill would have gone to get him?"

Sam was stone-faced. But the flicker in his eye gave me a window to his mind. Ricky Wahl's call for help, if that's what it was, would have been the exact thing Bill Clancy would have left home to answer.

31

Just after lunch the following day, Alexander Nash stood at his table, buttoning his jacket as he called his next witness. I felt the air rush out of the room. I had a bad feeling as if everything had slammed into slow motion as I watched Steven Wahl slouch his way toward the witness box.

I could bob and weave, but there'd be no stopping the punch Nash was about to land.

"Can you object?" Mercy asked.

I shook my head. "To him testifying?" I murmured the same point I'd made to Sam yesterday. "He's on our witness list, too. If I fight too hard to keep him out, the jury will wonder why."

"But ..."

Mercy let her voice fall as Wahl began his testimony. For the first half hour, Nash covered everything I already knew.

He was Ricky's dad. He'd been concerned about his son's friendship with Austin Merkle. He got to the night in question, bolstering Ricky's own testimony about when he arrived home from work. And that's when things began to turn.

"Mr. Wahl," Nash said. "So I'm clear. You work midnights. That's your testimony? Midnight to seven?"

"That's right."

"And when you got home on the morning of April 15th, you're saying your son was already home?"

"He's usually asleep when I get home. And I'm usually asleep when he leaves for work."

"But you got home after seven."

"Something like that. Yeah."

"You spoke to him?"

"I don't remember that. I go to sleep when I get home and he's usually asleep then too. Like I said."

"That bothers you, doesn't it?"

"What do you mean?"

"What I mean is ... you often argued with Ricky about his sleeping habits, didn't you?"

"I was on his rear end a lot. Yeah. I don't think it's good for a kid to sleep all the time and spend all their time in front of a screen."

"These arguments you and your son had. They got pretty intense, didn't they?"

"Objection," I said. "Counsel is leading the witness."

"Your Honor," Nash said. "I'd like permission to treat this witness as hostile. His son has testified for the prosecution."

"The defense has called this witness," I said. "I haven't. My office was not served with copies of any subpoenas compelling Mr. Wahl's testimony. Which means either Mr. Nash never bothered to give me a copy, or Mr. Wahl has appeared in court today voluntarily on behalf of the defense."

"I'm going to deny your motion, Mr. Nash. Ms. Brent's point is well taken. You may conduct your questioning as a direct examination. Proceed."

For the first time, Nash looked slightly flustered. He went back to the lectern.

"Mr. Wahl, how would you describe your relationship with your son?"

"I'm his father."

This got a snicker from members of the jury. Nash frowned.

"Do you get along with your son?"

"We get on."

"Do you ever get angry with Ricky?"

"What? Sure."

"Have you ever hit your son, Mr. Wahl?"

Steven Wahl straightened his back. "I have disciplined my son the way I've seen fit. I'm not proud of some of the things I've done in the past when my drinking was out of control. But we've moved past that."

"Moved past it. Which part? Drinking or domestic violence?"

"Objection! Your Honor ..."

Judge Saul put a hand up. "The objection is sustained. Mr. Nash, you know better."

"Mr. Wahl," Nash picked up. "Are you an alcoholic?"

"Objection. Relevance."

"Your Honor, the prosecution's case rests largely on the testimony of Ricky Wahl. Evidence has been presented that Ricky's father strongly influenced the son's decision to come forward. As such, the dynamic of their relationship is relevant."

"I agree," Judge Saul said. "To a point. Please make sure your questions are narrowly focused. The witness may answer."

"Mr. Wahl, are you an alcoholic?"

"I was," he said.

"You're of the opinion that's a disease you can be cured of?" Nash said.

"Objection."

"Sustained."

Nash crossed his arms in front of him. "Mr. Wahl, when was the last time you were physically violent with your son, Ricky?"

"I don't know."

"Within the last year?"

"I don't know."

"You might have gotten physical with him in the last year? You're saying that's a possibility?"

"I expect him to pull his weight around the house. Clean up after himself. Replace the food and beverages he drinks."

"Beverages. Do you mean beer?"

"I mean in general."

"Has Ricky not pulled his weight in the last year as far as you're concerned?"

"Listen," Steven said. "Ricky's a good kid. He's a hard worker. But he lacks motivation. If I'm not up his ass ... he'd lie around the house all day playing video games."

"Mr. Wahl, I'm going to ask you again as clearly as I can. Have you hit your son at any point in the last twelve months?"

Wahl gave me a helpless look as if to apologize. I couldn't believe what I was hearing. He'd lied to my face last night. Withheld facts that would now be used to stab me in the back.

"I might have," he said. "Not hit him like with a fist, if that's what you mean. I might have pushed him. I don't know. I can't remember."

"Is it worse when you drink, would you say?"

"I've got a handle on it," Wahl answered. It was then I saw the blow coming. But there was no way to duck in time.

"A handle on it," Nash said. "Mr. Wahl, you still drink regularly, don't you?"

"I've got it under control."

"Your Honor," I said. "I need to renew my objection. Mr. Wahl's sobriety is not an issue in this case."

"It is if he hits his kid when he's drunk, Your Honor. Ricky Wahl testified to as much. Nolan Bellamy testified to as much."

"Sustained this time, Mr. Nash. Confine your questions to the events relative to the charges against your client. That is all."

"Fine," Nash said. "I'll do just that. Mr. Wahl, how would you describe your relationship with Sheriff Clancy?"

"He was an acquaintance."

"You're aware of the testimony provided by your former neighbor, Nolan Bellamy, aren't you?"

"I am. But that was one-sided."

"Right. So let's hear your side. You admit that you and Bill Clancy once got into a bar fight?"

"It wasn't a bar fight. I had too much to drink. I apologized for all of that. It was water under the bridge."

That's when Nash pounced. He moved around the lectern, closing the space between him and Steven Wahl. It was a breach of courtroom protocol but Judge Saul didn't stop him.

"When was the last time you spoke to Bill Clancy, Mr. Wahl?"

"I don't remember the date," Steven said, but his gaze had dropped to the floor.

"He already knows," Mercy whispered.

I poised my pen over the notepad between us, debating which four-letter word I wanted to write.

"Do you remember where you last saw Sheriff Clancy in person?"

Wahl took a breath. "The Blue Pony."

"Inside the bar?"

Wahl shock his head.

"Out in the parking lot?"

"Yeah. Okay? Yeah."

"What happened in the parking lot of the Blue Pony, Mr. Wahl?"

"He got in my face, okay?"

"Did you leave the Pony on your own?"

"No," he said. "The owner took my keys and I was trying to get home. The sheriff came out and we had words, maybe."

"Maybe? Don't you remember?"

"No," he said. "Not all of it. No. I wasn't ... Look. I'm not proud of it. I got tipsy. Bill offered to drive me home and I got angry."

"Angry. Did you take a swing at him?"

"I don't know. Maybe."

"If someone saw you try to punch Bill Clancy in the parking lot of the Blue Pony, would they be lying?"

Wahl shook his head.

"Please answer, Mr. Wahl," Nash said.

"No," he said. "They wouldn't be lying."

I saw white spots in front of my eyes. The bastard set me up.

"You do remember when this happened, don't you, Mr. Wahl?"

"It was snowing," he said.

"Snowing. So it was this past winter? The winter before? Ten years ago? Help me out."

"This past winter," he said. "Just after Christmas. I got laid off for a while and it was unexpected. I took it harder than I should have and was just trying to blow off some steam."

"Your Honor," I said. "May I please approach the bench?"

Judge Saul waved Nash and me over. I caught Shanna Clancy's eye as she sat on the bench directly behind Mercy. She trusted me. Found a smile for me. I turned to the judge.

"Your Honor," I said. "This has gone on long enough. If we ..."

"This witness has been lying to everyone he's talked to," Nash said. "The cops. To his kid. To Ms. Brent. Everyone. As I've said and the Court has acknowledged ... Ricky Wahl's motivation to testify is highly relevant. That kid was abused by his father. Abused by the cops. At a minimum, I should be permitted to present evidence and make the argument that his testimony was coerced. But more than that, it is absolutely permissible defense strategy to pursue testimony from other witnesses who had a motive to do Bill Clancy harm. If the cops had done their jobs and not been in such a rush to bring someone to trial ..."

"You've been the one wanting to rush this to trial," I said. "You could have waived your client's right to a speedy trial. You didn't. It's not my problem if your strategy backfired."

"Enough." Judge Saul said.

"Your Honor, if Steven Wahl had previously testified that he was sober that would be one thing. But he didn't. He's been forthright about it. So I fail to see why defense counsel should be permitted to ... I don't even know ... impeach a witness for something he never actually lied under oath about. Not to mention the fact that this entire line of questioning has no bearing on the events of April 15."

"Mara," Judge Saul said. It was the first sign I knew I was in trouble. She rarely used my first name and never while we were in her court. "As much as I hate the circus atmosphere this is starting to take on ... and I'll address that with you in a minute, Mr. Nash ... Ricky Wahl is your star witness. The defense has a right to raise questions about his motivation and credibility. Having said all of that, Mr. Nash, you're coming close to grandstanding with this witness. Wrap it up."

"I was about to, Your Honor," Nash said.

She waved us away again. I tried to keep the fury out of my expression as I made my way back to my table.

Nash looked flustered as he took his place behind the lectern. I knew then that was the closest I'd get to neutralizing him. There was very little I'd be able to do with Steven Wahl on cross-examination at this point.

"Mr. Wahl," Nash continued. "The incident at the Blue Pony. That's not the last time you've gotten drunk, is it?"

He couldn't possibly be sure of Wahl's answer on that. Every instinct I had told me the man was on a fishing expedition. But Wahl's shrunken shoulders and newly red eyes indicated Nash had just hooked his catch.

"No," he said. "I had a rough patch last spring. I'm okay now. I haven't had a drop since ..."

"Since when, Mr. Wahl?"

"Since I heard what happened to Bill Clancy. He was a good guy, okay? He was trying to help me out and I know that. I just wish ..."

"What, Mr. Wahl?"

"I wish I'd had a chance to say thank you. That's all."

"Thank you," Nash repeated. Then he paused. "That's all I have as well."

"Ms. Brent?"

I rose. At that moment, I had no earthly clue what to do with Steven Wahl. Wringing his neck wasn't an option. His last answer was probably the best thing he could have said. I could only hope it was enough to stick in the jury's mind. My best strategy was to at least pretend Wahl's testimony was of little concern to me.

"I have no questions for this witness but reserve the right to call him on rebuttal."

"All right," Judge Saul said. "We stand in recess until tomorrow morning."

As I turned, Shanna Clancy and Sam stood white-faced in the back of the courtroom. Sam looked positively homicidal as Steven Wahl slunk his way past him and disappeared out into the hallway.

32

Kenya Spaulding stood in the middle of a small mob as I made my way to the side door of the office. Many of them carried picket signs that might as well have been pitchforks.

Justice for Sheriff Clancy

Pull the Weeds

"Mara!"

Sam's sharp shout stopped me. He rushed to my side and took my elbow. "This way," he said.

"We can't just leave Kenya in the middle of that."

"I've got a couple of crews on the way. They're not violent. They're just ..."

"Voters," I said.

"Right."

Kenya caught my eye over the crowd. She gave me a slight nod, indicating she had things under control. I doubted it, but Sam was right. Kenya could better control the narrative if I wasn't standing beside her.

"Just tell those crews to get here in a hurry," I said to him.

As we walked into the lobby, Detective Gus Ritter was already waiting for me, his face beet red.

"I'll kill him," Gus said.

"In my office. Everybody."

Sam and Gus fell into step behind me as I led them out of view. Caro gave me a sympathetic look that didn't do much to make me feel better. She thought I was losing.

So did I.

"I'll kill him," Gus repeated. "That lying son of a ..."

"How did this slip by?" I said. "Wahl was vetted."

"He's lying," Sam said.

"Which time?" I asked.

"Something doesn't smell right," Gus added. "His whole story today. It's too convenient. He's been interviewed multiple times. He's the one who encouraged his kid to come forward. Why serve him up on a platter like that? Why take the risk?"

"I need Ricky back here," I said. "I may have to put him back on the stand. But I want to talk to him again first."

"I'm one step ahead of you," Gus said. "I sent two deputies over to his job site to pick him up. I should be getting a call any minute."

"His immunity deal is off the table now," I said.

"Good," Sam said. "But I'm telling you, Steven Wahl is lying. That whole story about him with Bill at the Blue Pony last spring. Something doesn't sit right with me."

"Which part?" I asked.

"I don't know."

"To me it sounds exactly like Bill," I said. "If he had a history with Wahl like Bellamy testified. I think Bill absolutely would have talked to him out in that parking lot. And you see what Nash is teeing up. He's going to lay down this theory that it was Ricky who called Bill in the middle of the night on that burner phone. Who asked him to come over if Steven Wahl was out of control."

"No," Gus said. "I don't buy it. If Ricky was calling for help, why would he kill Bill? There is absolutely no physical evidence tying Ricky to any of this. That burner phone was at Austin Merkle's house. His were the only fingerprints on it."

"He wouldn't have gone there alone," Sam quietly said. He'd walked to the back of the room.

"Exactly," Gus agreed. "Bill would have called a crew if he thought there was a domestic violence situation over at Wahl's. And the cell phone tower hits don't line up. Wahl lived clear on the other side of town."

"No," Sam said. "I'm talking about the Blue Pony. Gus ... think about it. When's the last time Bill went and hung out in a bar? Ever since he became sheriff, he avoided places like that. He complained he could never eat a meal in peace out in public. There was always some yahoo in his face, wanting to talk. Wanting to complain."

"He's right," Gus said.

"Can you look into that more?" I asked Gus. "See if anyone remembers seeing him there or remembers Steven Wahl there drunk in that time frame. It just makes no sense though. Because Steven's testimony, if anything, is going to help Nash convince the jury that Ricky is lying and jeopardize his own son's immunity deal. I need to know everyone Steven and Ricky Wahl have been talking to."

There was a soft knock on the door. Caro poked her head in.

"I'm sorry to interrupt," she said. "But Shanna Clancy is here and she's pretty upset. She actually wants to speak with all of you."

"Hell," Gus said.

"Thanks, Caro. You can send her back."

"She's been through enough," Gus said. "We've promised her justice for Bill."

"We'll get it," I said. Though now, I wasn't sure it would take the form we all intended.

Caro reappeared and walked in with her arm around Shanna Clancy. Shanna dabbed her swollen eyes with a tissue and took a seat on the couch against the wall. Gus immediately went to her. She put her arms around him and hugged him. Gus stiffened, not knowing exactly what to do with her.

"I heard what happened," she said. "Was that other boy lying? Is he the one who killed Bill?"

"No," Gus said. "Austin Merkle killed Bill. There's no doubt in my mind."

"He can't get off," she said. "Mara, promise me that kid will go to jail for this."

I wanted to tell her what she needed to hear. I couldn't. I could make her no promises and it tore at my gut. I sank into the chair opposite her.

"Shanna," I said. "I need you to think. Steven Wahl testified today that he had a run-in with Bill at the Blue Pony a few weeks before his murder. Steven was drunk. He claims Bill confronted him in the parking lot. Did he mention any of it to you?"

She shook her head. Gus handed her another tissue from the box on the end table beside him.

"No. Bill never mentioned anything like that. But it would have been like him. If he thought he could help someone, he would have."

"He never went to places like the Blue Pony alone," Sam muttered. "I was just telling Mara that. We used to give him crap about that all the time. Why he didn't take you out for a proper dinner?"

Shanna smiled through her tears. "I didn't mind so much. It was difficult when we went out. Bill had a point."

"Steven Wahl claims he met Bill alone in the parking lot of the Blue Pony," I said.

Shanna shook her head. "Sam's right. That part doesn't sound like Bill at all. Did he say who else might have seen him there?"

"I'm going to check into it," Gus said. "Find out if there's anyone out there who might have seen him there that night."

291

"It won't help as much as you want it to," I said. "Wahl didn't testify to a specific date. He gave a vague time period."

"What about Bill's credit card statements?" Sam said. "I'm telling you. Shanna ... you know. If Bill was at the Pony by himself, it would have been a rare event. We ought to be able to look at his billing statements and see."

"He could have paid cash," I said. "I can't prove something in the negative like that."

"I'll give you anything you need," Shanna said. "Just tell me what I can do."

"I'll talk to Paula Dudley," Gus said. "See if she remembers seeing Bill there." It was a good start. Gus and Paula Dudley had a slow-burn mutual attraction going on.

"Guys," I said. "I think we're doing exactly what Alexander Nash wanted us to do. We're spinning our wheels on something that may not really matter in the long run. It's going to be virtually impossible to disprove Steven Wahl's testimony this way. And we're going to waste precious time on a dead end. That's playing right into Nash's hands. Shanna, you're sure. Bill told you he was heading into the office that night?"

"I'm sure," she said.

"It's what he would have told you to keep you from worrying," Sam said, his tone still grim.

"What?" she said.

"Face it. If Bill was headed somewhere he didn't want you to know about ... or didn't want you to worry about ... he would have just told you he was heading into the office. He did it hundreds of times, right? It's what I would have said."

"Are you saying Bill was lying to me?"

"We know he was lying to you," I said. "Because he didn't go to the office."

"I just don't get it," Gus said. "Let's say Austin Merkle wanted to lure Bill away from the house. Or let's say it was Ricky Wahl this whole time. We know those two punks were working together for at least part of it. If Ricky was more involved than he let on, why wouldn't Austin have turned on him sooner? It's a hell of a risky strategy on Nash's part to let it go this far if Austin told him all this from the beginning."

We were running in circles. I left the three of them to talk. I needed air. I needed a minute to think without the barrage of questions being thrown at me. As I walked out into the hall, Kenya was waiting.

We exchanged a glance. I could read the tension in her face. For the first time in weeks, I really looked at her. She'd lost weight. Her usual impeccably tailored suit hung loose.

"Tell me it's going to be okay," she said, smiling.

"Ha. I was going to say the same thing to you."

"How's Shanna holding up?"

I looked over my shoulder. "She's a mess. They're all a mess. This thing has spiraled and I'm not sure how I'm going to get it back, Kenya."

Inexplicably, the tension drained from her face at my response. I think it was because I gave her an unfiltered answer. We'd danced around the reality of it for so long, it actually felt good to speak the hard truth.

"Whose fault is it?" she asked. "I mean, really."

I thought for a moment. "All of us. I should have found a way to keep Gus away from this at the beginning. It's not that his detective work wasn't solid. But he was always going to get scapegoated by even a half-good defense attorney. And the Wahls are a problem Gus should have foreseen. And I should have foreseen it too. I lost control in that courtroom today. I'm sorry."

Kenya smiled. "You can say it, Mara. I know my part in this too. I put pressure on you to get this thing to trial before the election."

I read something else in her eyes. "You've had new polling data come in, haven't you?"

She gave me an unconvincing smile. "Don't worry about that."

I hung my head. "Well, the bright side. It's looking like after this trial, we're both gonna get some extended time off. Maybe we should start planning a trip."

She laughed.

"Hey," I said. "This isn't over yet. I still like the physical evidence I have."

"Nash is good. Maybe one of the best defense attorneys there is. But ... you're one of the best closers I've ever seen. So focus on that. Let the circus play out, then go in there and make that jury believe what they can see with their own eyes."

The door to the lobby opened behind Kenya. Deputy Al Trembly walked in red-faced. The little boost I felt from

Kenya's very effective pep talk evaporated. Gus and Sam walked out of my office.

"What?" I said. "Please don't tell me it's more bad news."

"Trembly?" Gus said. "What have you got?"

Trembly swallowed. "He's gone, Detective Ritter. Ricky Wahl never showed up for work today. Nobody can get a hold of him. His car's not at his house. I'm afraid he's in the wind."

Shanna Clancy stepped into the hallway just in time to hear it.

33

In thirty seconds on Friday morning, Alexander Nash's endgame became clear.

"Your Honor, the defense calls Martin Hyden to the stand."

"Your Honor, this witness did not appear on Mr. Nash's list. We've had no discovery."

Judge Saul waved us both forward. I knew before I uttered another word that her ruling would go against me. But I had to preserve the issue for the record at least. If I pulled out a win, I could practically write Austin Merkle's appellate brief for him.

"What say you, Mr. Nash?" Judge Saul said.

"I think Ms. Brent knows exactly what Mr. Hyden is here to establish. He has relevant information about the whereabouts of Ricky Wahl, her star witness. Once again, her entire case rests on Ricky's credibility. His actions during the conduct of this trial are something the defense could not have predicted. I'm playing catch-up because of a lack of due diligence on the part of law enforcement and Ms. Brent's own office. Therefore, I should be allowed to call this witness and any lack of notice or preparation to the State is their own fault."

"Ms. Brent?"

"Ricky Wahl has already testified. I stand by my objection that Mr. Hyden's testimony on his whereabouts isn't relevant."

"It is if that kid has violated the terms of your office's proffer!" Nash shouted.

"Enough," the judge said. "I'm sorry, Ms. Brent. Mr. Nash's argument is well taken. I'll allow this witness to testify. Let's get on with it."

I went back to my table and braced for the blow.

"Mr. Hyden," Nash started. "Please tell us how you're acquainted with Ricky Wahl?"

"He works for me as a production assistant at Braxton Windows."

"How would you describe his work history with you? Is he punctual?"

"He's mostly on time, yes. I mean, before all this."

"What do you mean?"

"Ricky didn't show up for his shift yesterday or today."

"Do you know why?"

"I don't. I called him on his cell phone twice and he didn't answer. I've sent him a few texts and he hasn't answered those either. I went to his house this morning and he's not there."

"Was anyone at the house?"

"No, sir. Ricky usually parks in the driveway. The car wasn't there. He's gone."

"When was the last time you spoke with Ricky Wahl?"

"Three days ago during his shift. We had some words as he was clocking out."

"What was the nature of your conversation?"

"I asked him if he'd work a double shift. I had a couple of guys call in sick. He said he would, so I put him on the schedule."

"And you're saying he hasn't shown up?"

"No, sir. That's why I got concerned. It's not like Ricky to just go AWOL like that. It took him a while to find his groove at Braxton. But once that kid's dialed in, he's the most dependable worker I've got."

"Thank you, Mr. Hyden. I have no further questions."

I shot up and took my spot at the lectern. "Mr. Hyden, by your own admission, you haven't spoken to Ricky Wahl since the day before yesterday, correct?"

"That's what I said and that's correct. Yes."

"And that's all you know, isn't that right? Just that he hasn't come to work."

"What do you mean?"

"What I mean is that you have no information about what's going on in Ricky Wahl's personal life other than the fact that he's missed a work shift."

Hyden looked at Nash for guidance.

"Mr. Hyden," I said. "Please answer the question. You don't have any additional information about Ricky Wahl other than his work attendance, right?"

"Well. Yes. That's right."

"Thank you," I said. "I have no further questions."

Nash called two more witnesses. Luke Morgan and Spencer Betkey, otherwise known as Woodstock and Gotcha_15. Both members of Ricky Wahl and Austin Merkle's gaming circle. Each of them testified that Ricky hadn't logged on to the game in forty-eight hours. But Betkey's testimony caused the biggest stir.

"Mr. Betkey," Nash said. "Tell me again the type of game you and your group play the most?"

"We play *Legends of Warfare*. It's a first-person shooter game. We go on combat missions in different campaigns. There are ones based on historical battles. World War II, Vietnam, even the Civil War. And the newer version lets you create post-apoc worlds. Um. Post-apocalyptic."

"Mr. Betkey, do you ever kill members of law enforcement within the game?"

"Sure. Depending on what side you choose to be on."

"What side did Ricky Wahl choose to be on?"

"It depends."

"But cop killing is a feature of the game?"

"Objection," I said. "Relevance."

"I've already ruled on this when Mr. Wahl was on the stand," Judge Saul said. "Overruled. You may continue, Mr. Nash."

"Did Ricky Wahl kill police officers within the game, *Legends of Warfare?*"

"Sure."

"Did he ever brag about it?"

"All the time. Reb_413, that's Ricky's handle in the game. He'd get bonus points. We all did."

"Did Ricky ever brag about it?"

"Reb? No. I don't think so. Reb is ... sorry, man. Reb was always the weakest player out of the four of us. To be honest, we only let him in because Turk vouched for him. But he used to drag our averages down because he was always getting killed in the game. Turk was level 59. I'm at 50. Woodstock ... uh ... Luke's a 47. Reb was 32."

"What does that mean?"

"It means Reb was a weak link. We knew if we were heading into a tough campaign, we'd have to put him somewhere he'd do the least damage. He'd usually be in the rear with the gear, you know?"

"Sure. What can you tell me about Turk and Ricky's relationship outside the game? Did you ever interact in real life?"

"Not much. I know Reb and Turk did. They lived near each other. I'm from Milwaukee. Luke's from Grand Rapids, Michigan. We met up once, maybe two years ago. But these aren't my real friends. We're just gamers."

"But you were in a position to observe how Ricky ... er ... Reb and Turk interacted online, weren't you?"

"Yeah. There was always a lot of chatter between us."

"Verbal chatter? Or were you messaging each other?"

"Verbal mostly. Through our headsets. Turk was the biggest smack talker. He'd get pretty frustrated with Reb for slowing us down."

"How was their relationship in the spring of this year? The last time Turk participated in your campaigns?"

"Pretty bad. Luke and I talked to Turk about bouncing. Forming a new platoon. We wanted to keep Turk, of course. But I have another friend I met online who's a level 51. I wanted to bring him in."

"Was Turk receptive to that?"

"Not at first. He felt bad."

"Mr. Betkey," Nash said. "Did you and the others make a decision about whether to keep Ricky Wahl in your group?"

"We did," Betkey said. "We were going to vote Reb out and form a new group. Turk agreed he'd be the one to tell him."

"Did he? To your knowledge?"

"He said he tried to. I don't know how that went. The next thing I knew, this whole thing blew up. Reb came back online and told us Turk was in jail for killing this cop. I haven't spoken to Turk since. We've kept Reb around because we felt sorry for him. But like I said earlier, Reb hasn't been online in a couple of days."

"Is that normal?"

"No. Reb lives online pretty much when he's not at work."

"Thank you. I have no further questions."

I went to the lectern. "I just have a couple for you, Mr. Betkey. I'll ask you the same as I asked Mr. Morgan. You're saying Turk, Austin Merkle, has the highest averages of the four of you in terms of these bonus points for cop killing within the game?"

"He did. Yeah. Before he got arrested and put in jail."

"And you also indicated that you don't really know Ricky Wahl in real life, do you?"

"No."

"So you have no idea why he hasn't logged on. You have no personal knowledge of his whereabouts or habits."

"No. I don't know where he is."

"Thank you," I said. "I have no further questions." I couldn't get around it. If Ricky Wahl was in the wind, the jury would know. The best thing Luke Morgan and Spencer Betkey could do for me was go home.

"All right," Judge Saul said after Betkey left the stand. "We'll stand in recess for fifteen minutes. How many more witnesses do you have today, Mr. Nash?"

Nash was busy conferring with Austin Merkle. Merkle had a hold of Nash's sleeve and was whispering something intently into his ear.

"Mr. Nash?"

"Sorry, Your Honor. I anticipate calling one more witness. Two at the most."

"Fine. Then let's try to wrap that up by four o'clock. We're back here in fifteen."

She dismissed the jury and banged her gavel.

I turned. Shanna Clancy sat directly behind me, tears streaming down her face. She looked like she was about to be sick. I moved in front of her as quickly as I could. But not before a few members of the jury saw her and heard the five words she gasped to me.

"Are we going to lose?"

34

"Hang in there," I said to Shanna. "Let's go out and get you some air. Mercy, can you go see if you can scare up some bottled water for Mrs. Clancy?"

"On it," Mercy said. The courtroom had mostly cleared. Only Sam sat in the back. I knew Gus was busy trying to figure out what had really happened to Ricky Wahl. His father was no longer talking to us without a lawyer present.

There were a few reporters milling around in the hallway. They accosted Betkey and Morgan as they left. Fantastic, I thought. Who knew what damning sound bites those two would utter.

"Come on," I said. "I think I can get us permission to use Judge Saul's private bathroom. It'll be quiet in there."

Nodding, Shanna got up and followed me. A quick word with Judge Saul's clerk, and I had access to the bathroom. I ushered Shanna inside and made her sit on a small bench against the wall.

"He's going to win," she said. "I've been watching that jury. They believe Alexander Nash. This is all crumbling around me. I can't breathe. I can't ... I can't ..."

She started to hyperventilate. I knelt in front of her and put my hands on her shoulders.

"Shanna look at me. Take a deep breath. In through your nose, out through your mouth."

She went stiff, arching backward. Her mouth opened and closed like a fish but I didn't see her take an actual breath. The woman was in serious danger of passing out.

"Shanna. Shanna!"

I started to mimic the deep breathing I wanted her to do. Gradually, she locked eyes with me and started to breathe. After a minute or two, her color got better but she was still sweating. I left her for a moment and rummaged through the small supply closet the custodians kept for Judge Saul. I found a stack of brown paper bags on the shelf, likely the ones used to line the receptacle for feminine products in the stall. I shook one out and handed it to Shanna to breathe into.

She took it, put her head between her legs, and breathed into the bag. I sat beside her with my hand on her back.

"It's okay," I said. "This is almost over."

She pulled the bag away. "Is he going to jail? That kid shot my husband. He has to go to jail. It's sick. Those kids made jokes. Made a game out of killing cops. Bonus points? Is that what this was? Some twisted way for them to bring their violent game to life?"

"I don't know. It's hard right now because you're only hearing the story the defense lawyer wants to tell. Let me do my job in closing arguments."

"I can't take this. Then I have to wait for those people to decide whether the man who shot my husband in the head will get to go free? They can't let him. They can't!"

I wanted to promise her they wouldn't. We both knew that was the thing I couldn't do.

"Shanna, you shouldn't be alone. Have you reached out to the Silver Angels? They want to support you. They ..."

She waved me off. "I don't want to take up their time. There are so many other women who need them. I wasn't the victim here. I wasn't raped or assaulted. Bill's the victim. Not me."

"You're a victim too," I said. "Please let me call someone for you. They can help you through this, no matter the outcome. It's what they do."

She shook her head. "I can't stand another stranger in my kitchen, Mara. I know they all mean well. I just ... I haven't said anything to Gus or Sam. They've both been so wonderful. But I can't stay here in Waynetown after this. I can't live in that house without Bill. When his benefits come in, I'm going to sell everything and maybe move to Florida or somewhere warm. Somewhere ... different. I don't know."

"You'll have plenty of time to decide all of that later. I think you need to focus on just getting through the next couple of days. Or even the next hour. One thing at a time. You don't have to plan your whole life right now."

She put the bag down. "Oh Mara. I'm so sorry. I shouldn't be your problem. I know you're doing the best you can. You're working so hard and here I am unloading on you when you need to focus on the trial. I'm so so sorry."

She got up.

"It's okay. Really. I told you when this whole thing started that I would be here for anything you needed."

She went to the mirror, pulled a tissue from the box on the counter, and dabbed her face. "I look awful. Bill always hated to see me cry. It seems like that's all I've been doing lately. Oh. That can't be helping you either, can it? If the jury thinks I'm scared ... they might ..."

"Don't worry about that. You're a human being. You lost your husband. Of course you're upset."

"How much time do we have?" she asked.

I checked my watch. "Five minutes. I should start heading back in there."

"Okay. Just give me one second. I'm ready. I can do this. For Bill. He'd want me to be strong."

"You are."

She threw her tissue away and opened the stall door. "Will you hold this for me?"

She handed me her suit jacket. I took it from her and folded it on the vanity.

While Shanna did her business, I checked my own face in the mirror. It occurred to me then that Shanna and Kenya weren't the only ones wearing the stress of the last few weeks on their faces. I had dark circles beneath my eyes. My mascara was starting to smudge.

I took a tissue and dabbed it, then reapplied my lipstick. A few errant hairs had escaped from the bun I wore today. I pulled it out and re-twisted it, pinning it in place. Ever since I was in my twenties, I'd gone white-gray at one section of my hair at the very front. My skunk stripe, Jason used to call it. He'd said it with affection, though I'd been self-conscious about it at first. I would have dyed it, but then I got pregnant with Will and never got around to it. Now, I liked it. It was something people noticed about me. Though, as I leaned closer to the mirror, I realized I had new gray at my temples too.

Behind me, I heard the rustle of fabric as Shanna Clancy adjusted herself. It was only a moment. A second or two. But my gaze fell on the stall door reflected in the mirror.

There was perhaps a one-inch gap in the door. Shanna had her back to it, her foot propped up on the edge of the toilet seat. She was wearing T-strap heels and adjusted the buckle.

She had not buttoned her skirt yet. It hung loose, showing the small of her back and the beginning curve of her buttocks.

I froze. In that split second, I thought it might be a scar. I turned, looking at her through the gap instead of the reflection in the mirror.

Shanna Clancy had a tattoo just above her right buttocks. An intricate white lotus, the edges drawn in silver ink.

She pulled up her skirt. I straightened and quickly turned to face the mirror.

My throat went dry. Now I was the one who couldn't breathe.

Shanna came out, pasting on a smile. She went to the sink beside me and washed her hands. I watched as she dealt with the errant strands of her own hair.

"Ready?" I said, though my voice didn't sound like my own.

She nodded. Then she came to me and pulled me into an embrace. I hugged her back, hoping she couldn't feel my hammering heart. "Whatever happens," she said. "If I forget to tell you later. Thank you. You were a friend to Bill. And now you're my friend. The first new one I've made since Bill died."

I found a smile. Shanna picked up her purse. We walked back into Judge Saul's courtroom together just as she took the bench and called the jury back in.

I found my seat at the table. Mercy turned to say something to me but I kept my gaze laser-focused on the judge.

"Mr. Nash?" she said.

"Your Honor," Alexander Nash said. "At this time, the defense rests."

It felt as though the air had been sucked straight out of the room. I was underwater. Struggling to swim to the surface but I didn't know which way was up or down.

"Ms. Brent!" Judge Saul's voice finally broke through. "Have you any rebuttal witnesses you'd like to call?"

I looked at the jury. I looked at Alexander Nash.

"Mara?" Mercy said. "Are you okay?"

I turned to her. I tried to whisper but I wasn't even sure I could.

"Go back to the office. As fast as you can. Bring me the printout of every picture text BCI pulled from Ricky Wahl's phone. Now!"

"Ms. Brent?" Judge Saul said, her impatience evident.

I felt every pair of eyes in the courtroom boring into me. I found my breath and took a giant leap, praying the ground wasn't too far below me. Otherwise, I was about to crash and burn.

35

"The State recalls Shanna Clancy to the stand."

I waited, holding my breath. But Alexander Nash barely looked up from his notes as Shanna rose from the back of the courtroom and made her bewildered way to the witness box.

I was far more interested in gauging the reaction of Austin Merkle as Shanna walked past him. It was there. Barely perceptible, but I swore he sat straighter in his seat, puffing out his chest, flexing his biceps so they strained inside his suit jacket. I wished Mercy was still in the courtroom. I needed her eyes in the back of my head, observing Austin. At the same time, I knew my first order of business with Shanna was to stall.

I gave her a reassuring nod as she raised her right hand.

"Mrs. Clancy," Judge Saul said. "You're still under oath from your prior testimony."

Shanna sat.

"Thank you for agreeing to testify again," I said. "I know how difficult this process must be for you."

Shanna smiled. "I just want the truth to come out. To get justice for my husband. He dedicated his life to helping get that for other people."

"I understand." In my head, I tried to count the minutes it would take Mercy to run across the street, up the stairs, down the hall, and into the war room. Had we organized the files well enough? Would she be able to find what I wanted in due time?

"Mrs. Clancy," I said. "You were in the courtroom for Steven Wahl's testimony yesterday, weren't you?"

Shanna relaxed, confident now with where she thought I was headed. That made one of us.

"I was."

"You heard him recount an incident in the parking lot of the Blue Pony bar early last spring?"

"I did."

"To your knowledge, when was the last time your husband frequented the Blue Pony?"

"I don't know. I can't specifically remember."

"When was the last time you frequented the Blue Pony?"

"You mean with Bill? Or with other people?"

"Either, for now."

She pursed her lips and looked skyward, thinking. "It's been a while. I went to a birthday dinner there for a girlfriend of mine but that was last year. In the summer. As far as Bill? He never liked going to places like that."

"Why not?"

"Objection," Nash said. "Relevance."

"Your Honor, as the victim's wife of ten years, she's qualified to testify as to her husband's habits and whether he would have acted in conformity with them."

"Agreed," Judge Saul said. "Overruled."

"I can answer?" Shanna asked.

"You can," I said. "So why didn't your husband like to frequent places like the Blue Pony?"

"He didn't like being bothered. When Bill came home and took off that uniform, he didn't want to be the sheriff, if that makes sense. When we'd go out in public. To dinner, or to a bar like that. People were always coming up to him. Asking him questions. Airing their grievances. Asking him for favors. Just ... expecting him to be Sheriff Clancy twenty-four hours a day. He didn't like that. He valued his privacy and the time he needed to decompress every day. His was a very hard job."

"Of course," I said. "So, were you aware of an incident between Bill and Steven Wahl at the Blue Pony like Mr. Wahl described?"

She shook her head. "Bill never mentioned anything like that to me, no."

"Were you acquainted with Steven Wahl?"

"No. I don't think so."

"What about Austin Merkle? Prior to Bill's death, did you know Austin Merkle?"

I turned, staring straight at Merkle. He sat rod straight in his chair, focused on Shanna. I stole a glance at my table. Mercy wasn't back yet. If my guess on timing was accurate, she was probably just now reaching the war room. Sam caught my eye. He gave me a quizzical expression. I knew he had to wonder what the hell I was doing recalling Shanna. He had agreed with me that I would get very little mileage trying to prove something in the negative, like the incident at the Pony. The thing was though, if my hunch was right, I had no doubt it had happened exactly like Steven Wahl had described.

"I don't know that man," Shanna said. A muscle jumped in Austin's jaw, but he stayed otherwise still as granite.

I turned back to Shanna. "You don't know him. You never met him before?"

"No."

"You're sure?"

"Of course I'm sure." Shanna's tone took a slightly harder edge.

"What about Ricky Wahl? Do you recall ever meeting him?"

Shanna let out a haughty laugh. "No. Why would I ever have anything to do with either of them?"

"You work out, don't you, Mrs. Clancy?"

From the corner of my eye, I saw Nash lean over and question his client. He, too, was beginning to suspect something strange might be coming.

"Yes."

"Where do you work out?"

"Mostly in my home gym."

"Do you have a membership to any other gyms?"

"Objection," Nash said. "Once again, relevance."

"It is relevant for me to explore how this witness might have crossed paths with the defendant, Your Honor."

"I didn't," Shanna said. "Let her ask me. I'm telling you. I don't know that kid. I would have remembered. Do you think I would have kept something like that from you?"

"Mrs. Clancy," Judge Saul said. "You need to refrain from answering questions until I've made a ruling. For now, I'm overruling the objection."

"Do you have any gym memberships, Mrs. Clancy?"

"Not current ones, no," she said. "I got a six-month membership to the Muscle Hustle when they opened their newest location. Didn't much care for it there though. Too many men."

"Sure. Are you aware that Austin Merkle worked at Muscle Hustle?"

There. Just there. Her eyes left me and flicked to Merkle's. But she found a quick smile and recovered.

"Mrs. Clancy," I said. "I'd like to take you back to the night your husband was killed. Specifically, to the phone call he received just before he left the house."

"Objection," Nash said. "This has been asked and answered. This ground was already covered by Mrs. Clancy's direct examination."

"Ms. Brent?"

"If you'll allow me a bit of leeway," I said. "Some new information has come to light that makes my question imperative."

"What new information?" Nash said. "If the prosecution has new evidence, she has a duty to disclose it to me. Anything less than that is grounds for a mistrial."

"Your Honor," I said. "I said new information, not new evidence. I assure you, I have no intention of covering any ground that wasn't disclosed to the defense in this case."

"All right," Judge Saul said. "I'm going to take your word on that. But please don't make me regret it. You may proceed."

"Mrs. Clancy," I said. "Once again, you heard Steven Wahl's testimony the other day. Did your husband tell you he was going to the Wahls' house that night?"

"No."

"Did you hear him mention a name during the phone call he took?"

"I already told you all of this. No. I never heard him say a name. I only heard the phone ring. I nudged him to wake up and answer it. He did, then he took the call in the hallway. I went back to sleep, or tried to. He came back a minute or two later and told me he had to leave."

"He told you he had to leave or he told you he had to go into work?"

"Work," she barked. "He said work. That it was work-related. He was going into the office. He told me not to worry."

"Right. But if he was going to intervene in a domestic dispute between Steven Wahl and his son, don't you think he would have mentioned that to you?"

"Objection," Nash said. "Calls for speculation."

"Only speculation that Mr. Nash himself has raised when he called Steven Wahl. I believe I have the right to explore that alternate theory with the only eyewitness to that phone call."

Judge Saul frowned. "Are you trying to impeach your own witness, Ms. Brent?"

"Not exactly," I said.

"I'm going to sustain the defense counsel's objection. You're both free to make whatever arguments you'd like on this issue. Or if either of you have concrete proof regarding the substance of that phone call ... otherwise, we're not going to play guessing games over it."

Behind me, I heard the courtroom doors open and shut. I went stiff. Praying. I turned and exhaled as Mercy rushed to the table carrying an armful of files.

"Your Honor," I said. "If I could have just one minute to confer with my legal assistant."

"Why not?" Judge Saul said, clearly irritated. I just hoped my prior reputation in her courtroom would buy me enough grace for what I was about to do.

Heart pounding, I rifled through the cell phone reports. At the bottom of the stack, Agent Patel had printed off all the picture texts Ricky had from Austin Merkle. Lord. There were dozens and dozens. There was also a clear plastic bag taped to one flap of the file. That contained a flash drive with the video texts Merkle had sent. Thankfully, Agent Patel had been thorough. She'd taken screen grabs from those videos too.

"Ms. Brent?" Judge Saul said. "If you have no other questions for this witness, say so."

"Sorry, Your Honor," I said. I tore off one sheet from the printout and walked back to the lectern.

"Mrs. Clancy, just so I'm clear. You say you've never met Austin Merkle in your life. Is that right?"

"That's right. That's what I said."

I walked over to the judge's clerk and handed her a copy of a photograph, and asked her to mark it. I took a copy of it over to Nash's table and stuck it in front of him.

He frowned. Beside him, Austin Merkle leaned in to have a look. This was the closest I'd ever been to him. We were just inches away. I could actually feel his breath on my arm as I laid the photograph down. His eyes snapped up. It wasn't anger. It wasn't fear I saw. No. It was raw desperation.

"You can't do this," he said. Then to Nash. "She can't do this!"

"Austin," Nash said. "Don't say another word."

"She can't do this, Your Honor," Austin shouted. "I object. I object!"

Judge Saul banged her gavel.

"Mrs. Clancy," I said, barreling through. "I'd like to hand you what's been marked as State's exhibit ninety-one for identification. Would you please take a look at it?"

Behind me, Nash was furiously whispering to Merkle. The man had a hand clamped down on Merkle's shoulder, forcing him to stay seated. "Do you recognize this photo, Mrs. Clancy?"

She'd gone alabaster-white. Then, she looked up at me, rage filling her eyes. She shoved the photograph far away from herself on the shelf in front of her.

"Do you recognize it, Mrs. Clancy?"

"I don't know what that is?"

"Well, you can describe it."

"It's a picture, okay? It's vile. It's ... pornographic."

"What is it, Mrs. Clancy?"

"It's a woman, okay? A woman being ... in a compromising position. I wasn't ... I haven't ..."

"Your Honor, defense counsel and I have previously stipulated to the entry of the cell phone records from Ricky Wahl's phone. They are attached to a certified report from Special Agent Andrea Patel. They are self-authenticating. Mr. Nash was provided with copies. At this time, I'd like to move for entry of State's exhibit number ninety-one."

"Objection," Nash said. He didn't wait to be told. He charged up for the sidebar. I went to join him. Judge Saul had her copy of the exhibit.

"What are you doing?" she asked.

"Exactly what I said."

"She can't," Nash said.

"What are you objecting to?" I asked.

"That's my question," Judge Saul said. "This is part of Agent Patel's report. You've already stipulated to its entry."

"Not to every photograph on it. They're not all relevant. My stipulation was narrowly focused on those images that meet the probative value test under Rule 403. I submit that this particular photograph is highly prejudicial."

"To whom?" I practically shouted. "Nash, have you lost your mind? I'm potentially handing you a gift. Open your eyes."

He'd gone pale. Judge Saul studied the photograph, scowling. I knew how unsettling the image was. It was Austin Merkle's arms, gripping a woman's buttocks as he had intercourse with her from behind. Her back and buttocks were clearly visible. Her face was not, but her brown hair spilled down her back, just above her tattoo. Then, something came over Vivian Saul's face. Her jaw dropped. She looked at Shanna. For her part, she stared at a point on the far wall. Austin Merkle was looking straight at her. My God. He was mouthing something to her. Nash saw it at the same time I did.

"Christ," he muttered.

Judge Saul put her copy of the photo down. "The objection is overruled. We're not going to waste everyone's time by dragging Andrea Patel back in here to authenticate her own affidavit.

"The exhibit is admitted. You may proceed, Ms. Brent."

"I'd like to do so using the hostile witness rule."

Judge Saul rolled her eyes. "Obviously. Go ahead. I hope you know what you're doing."

I wanted to say, me too. I went back to the lectern and faced Shanna Clancy.

"Mrs. Clancy," I said. Mercy was one step ahead of me. She had her laptop open. Within five seconds, she had the image displayed on the overhead in front of the jury. There were a few gasps as they processed what they were looking at.

"Is that you, Mrs. Clancy? In this photograph?"

No answer.

"Mrs. Clancy, the tattoo on the woman in this photograph. It's a white lotus, isn't it?"

No answer.

"You have a tattoo on your lower back, just above your buttocks, don't you?"

No answer.

"Mrs. Clancy," Judge Saul said. "You need to answer the prosecution's questions."

"Yes," she hissed. "But that doesn't mean ..."

"Mrs. Clancy, is that you in this photograph?"

"Shanna, I'm sorry," Austin Merkle shouted. "I'm so sorry."

"Austin," Nash said. "For the love of God, be quiet."

"Mrs. Clancy, please identify the man in this photograph."

She crossed her arms and looked skyward.

"Mrs. Clancy, please answer the question. Who is with you in this photograph? It's a still from a video. We can play that if it will refresh your recollection."

"Don't you dare," she snapped.

"This video was sent to Ricky Wahl from his friend, Austin Merkle. I'll ask you one more time. Who are you having intercourse with in this video?"

"You don't understand," she said.

"It was Austin Merkle who called your husband the night he was murdered, wasn't it?" I asked.

"You knew. Did you tell him to call? You were sleeping with Austin Merkle, weren't you? That's you and Austin Merkle in that photograph, isn't it?"

"I never told him to do this!" she shouted. "He raped me. Okay? He raped me!"

"Shanna!" Austin was on his feet. Nash practically tackled him, trying to get him back into his chair. "That's a lie. Shanna, I love you. Tell them. Tell them! You love me. I know you love me!"

"Oh Lord." This from Judge Saul. She banged her gavel as the spectators in the gallery erupted. Behind me, I saw Gus and Sam get to their feet. I met Gus's eyes first. He looked at me with pure hatred.

"Clear the courtroom!" Judge Saul said. "We'll take a fifteen-minute recess. Mr. Nash, please control your client. Mrs. Clancy, you stay right where you are."

36

"What are you doing?"

I barely got into the courthouse library before Gus Ritter slammed the door after me. Sam stood at the window. Mercy had gotten in just before me.

"What the hell are you doing, Mara? To Shanna?"

"Gus," I said, keeping my voice even. I wouldn't tell him to calm down. It would only make him worse.

"She's a wreck. That son of a ... he knew. He put his hands on her. He ... My God. Bill went out there to murder him that night. That's what happened." There was a law book sitting on the table. A thick one. Blue and gold. The contracts volume of *Corpus Juris Secundum*. Gus picked it up and threw it against the wall.

"You gotta let me into a room with him."

"No." Sam and I said it together. Sam met my eyes. I knew at once he was ahead of Gus on the five stages of grief over this morning's bombshell. Gus was still in denial. Sam saw. He had accepted.

"Gus," I said. "You need to sit. You need to hear what I'm telling you. I don't think Austin Merkle raped Shanna. You saw that cell phone video the same as I did. The woman with the white lotus tattoo. She wasn't being forced. That looked like consensual sex. It was Shanna."

"How?" Sam asked. "How did you put it together?"

"When we were in the bathroom during the recess. She was in the stall. There was a gap in the door. It just caught my eye. I saw her back and ... um ... lower down. That's her tattoo."

"Maybe lots of women get those," Gus said, though I knew he didn't believe his own words.

"It's Shanna," I said.

"The Blue Pony," Mercy said, taking a seat beside me. "The fight between Steven Wahl and Clancy. Shanna was there. Maybe waiting in the car or something. But she saw them. You tried to get her to admit it. Clancy never went to that bar by himself. Detective Ritter, you said he only went when Shanna finally dragged him."

"Yes," I said. "I think she was there. I think she somehow fed that information to Nash or Austin."

"She was trying to help him," Sam said. "God. All this time. Shanna's been working against us. Trying to help her boyfriend."

"He's in love with her," I said. "Obsessed, maybe. I'm hoping Nash can talk some sense into that kid."

"No," Gus said. "I just can't believe it. Bill was crazy about her. He couldn't believe his luck when she agreed to go out with him. Agreed to marry him. He did everything for her. Worshiped her. He bent over backward trying to make sure she was happy."

"Maybe he couldn't," I said. "Maybe Shanna Clancy is the type of woman who's never happy. We'll probably never know."

"It doesn't mean she had anything to do with killing Bill," Gus said.

"Gus. Of course it does. She's been lying and withholding information from the very beginning. I know you know that. She's not the person you thought she was. Who any of us thought she was. Not even Austin Merkle."

"What does this mean?" Mercy asked. "For the trial? Will Nash ask for a mistrial?"

"If he does, I'll fight it. Austin Merkle killed Bill Clancy. None of that has changed. We know Shanna wasn't there when Merkle pulled the trigger. It's just ... now we have a motive. I want this jury to deliberate on the facts. We can deal with Shanna later."

Gus finally sat. He buried his head in his hands. "I couldn't see it. She's one of us, Mara. She's family."

"I know."

"How did Merkle get Clancy out of the house that night?" Mercy asked. "I don't get it. Do you think he knew Shanna was cheating on him? Do you think she knew Merkle was going to kill him?"

"She made a mistake. That's all this is. That's all this can be. She got mixed up with the wrong people. She wasn't ..." Gus muttered.

"Gus," I said. "Unless Austin Merkle decides to talk or Shanna decides to start telling the truth, those are answers we may never get."

There was a knock on the door. Mercy was the closest. She cracked it open. She whispered to whoever was behind it. Then she closed the door and turned to me.

"Mara. Alexander Nash wants to talk to you."

Gus and Sam started to move.

"No," I said. "You two stay here. I don't want you anywhere near this yet. Mercy, can you go find Kenya? I don't want her hearing about all of this on the internet."

"Absolutely," she said.

I closed the door behind us. Nash sat on a bench in the hallway. He ran his fingers through his now disheveled hair. I'd never seen him like this. Shocked. Confused. In disarray.

"Mara," he said. He didn't get up. I started to think maybe I'd need to go find another paper bag for him to breathe into. That gave me pause. Shanna's whole episode in the bathroom. Had she really panicked? Maybe. Only now I believed it was over the wrong thing.

I took a seat on the bench beside Nash.

"He didn't tell me," he said. "My client withheld information about ..."

"Nash, I don't care. All of that? It's not my problem."

"I'll move for a mistrial."

"You won't get it. You had access to all my discovery, including those texts from Austin's phone. If your client lied to you or withheld information, that's not grounds for a mistrial. I know Judge Saul. She'll never grant it."

"I can appeal."

"You can. Knock yourself out."

He hung his head. I couldn't figure out what was upsetting him the most. Was it the fact he didn't have control over his client? That he knew he was about to lose?

"Can you give me some time?"

"That's not up to me. That's up to Judge Saul. We've got a sequestered jury. I'm ready to deliver my closing arguments. Are you?"

He shook his head. "I have the right to recross Shanna Clancy?"

I raised a brow. "You think that's gonna help? Once again. Knock yourself out. Me? I told you. I'm ready to proceed." I stood up.

"If I can get him to talk to you?"

I froze. The elevator doors opened. Mercy walked out with Kenya. She must have already been on her way over to the courthouse.

"Fifteen minutes," I said. "That's about as much time as Saul gave us. Use it. I'll wait. But not a minute longer."

I turned my back on him and headed for the elevators to meet Kenya. I would need her to make my biggest play yet.

37

"You understand you're being recorded," I said. "Both from those video cameras above us, and this voice recorder in the center of the table. Make sure you speak loud enough for the microphone to pick up. And I need you to verbalize your answers. Nodding or shaking your head doesn't work."

Austin Merkle started to nod, then leaned forward. "I understand."

"And for the recording, you acknowledge that you've been read your rights. You have the right to have your attorney present. You've consulted with him and you've agreed to waive your right to be silent?"

"Yes," he said. "I'm here of my own free will. I want to talk. I want to get my story out."

"Okay," I said.

Nash and Austin sat at one end of the table. I sat across from Nash. Sam was on my right. Gus on my left. Kenya and

Mercy were in the next room, watching through the one-way mirror.

His voice shaking at first, Austin Merkle stated his name again. The date. He looked at Nash for guidance. Then he cleared his throat and leaned forward, keeping his cuffed wrists in his lap.

"I met Shanna about a year and a half ago. She started taking a Pilates class at the Muscle Hustle where I was working. I thought ... well ... she was just the hottest chick I'd ever seen. I couldn't stop looking at her. After a while, she noticed me looking and we started talking. After that, she hired me to coach her. You know. Be her personal trainer. That didn't last long. But ... we did. We started hooking up."

"What do you mean by that?" Gus said.

"I mean we started having intercourse. You know. Sex. A lot of it. Like ... a lot, a lot. She couldn't get enough. First time was in the club in the locker room. We'd meet in the parking lot. She liked the danger of that. You know. Getting caught. I was into it too."

"How long did this go on?"

"It never stopped. Up until you arrested me, it never stopped. And she promised. She said we'd be able to be together. That she'd stick by me. Until she said that thing about me raping her, I thought she would. That's a lie. You need to know that. I've never had sex with a woman who didn't want it. It's always consensual. I make sure."

"Like you make sure they know you're recording them?" Gus said.

I put a hand on his shoulder, trying to settle him.

"You're a real gentleman, Austin," he said. "Glad to know you draw the line at rape, not murder."

"Gus," I said.

"Sorry," he said. "Keep going, Mr. Merkle."

"When exactly did your relationship with Shanna Clancy start?" I asked.

"A little over a year ago. End of the summer. She loved me. She said it anyway. I did too. I swear, as soon as I got serious with Shanna, that was it for me. I stopped seeing every other girl I hooked up with."

"But you knew she was married," I said.

"Yeah. But she wasn't happy with him. He ... she asked me if she could confide something in me. First she told me he couldn't, you know, get it up. Then she said she was afraid of the guy. I swear. I didn't know he was the sheriff then. It probably wouldn't have made a difference. But she told me he was hurting her."

Gus made a noise similar to a growl. I shot him a look.

"I wanted to do something about it. You know. Protect her. Get her away from him. I told her I would. I told her I'd do anything for her. She made me promise to wait. She said she was gonna find a way to leave him for good, but that I had to be patient. It was killing me thinking that she was with him. What he might be doing to her."

"She told you Bill Clancy was beating her?" I asked. Sam shook his head.

"Did you ever see marks on her?" I asked Austin. "Bruises. Cuts? Anything? You were intimate with her and saw her naked. In the whole time you were sleeping with her and she was telling you these things about her husband, did you ever see any injuries on her?"

He shook his head. "No. And I asked her about that. Because once she told me he'd kicked her in the ribs but she wasn't bruised. I suppose I should have known she was lying then. I just ... she was so sad. Crying. She seemed so scared."

"What happened next?" I asked.

"I asked her to marry me on Christmas Day last year. She said yes. I couldn't believe it. She said yes. I bought her a ring and everything. She was wearing it in court today. That opal on her right hand. Did you see it?"

I had.

"Yeah. She promised me she was going to leave him for me. She said after the first of the year she was gonna tell him she wanted a divorce."

"Did she?" Gus asked.

Austin shook his head. "No, man. No. She was too scared. Then, on Valentine's Day, she finally did. It was her present to me, she said. Only, when I picked her up, she had a black eye. I wanted to kill him then. I would have. I was going to go right over there and kill him for her for laying hands on her."

"Valentine's Day," I said.

"She played you," Sam said. "I saw Shanna and Bill Clancy on Valentine's Day. We had an event at the Union Hall. She didn't have a black eye, Austin."

"I did think that was weird," Austin said. "Cuz like a couple of days later, it was all healed. Do you think she lied about that too? Used makeup or something. Because you're right. I never did see a bruise on her. I'm such a dumbass."

"Probably," Gus said bitterly.

"Well, that's the first time she mentioned it. Me killing her old man. I mean, I mentioned it first. Cuz I was angry and wanted to protect her. But after that, she kept dropping hints. Like, how much easier her life would be if he were out of the way. How she knew he was never gonna give her a divorce. And if he did, she'd lose her rights to his pension. And we're talking about a lot of money. She showed me bank statements once. And she said ... she said if he got killed that there'd be a lot more. A benefit from the feds. Like over a million bucks. And I looked that up online. She was right."

"Austin," Sam said. "Did Shanna tell you that particular death benefit is only payable if the sheriff was killed in the line of duty?"

His face fell. The litany of lies Shanna had fed this dumb kid seemed endless.

"We were gonna live off it," he said. "She was talking about Fiji. Tahiti. All these exotic places. I was gonna open a fitness studio. She was gonna help me finance it all with what she got from the old man."

"Austin," I said. "What about the night Bill Clancy was shot? What happened?"

He looked at Nash. Nash gave him a nod and reached out, pulling the tape recorder closer to him.

"She told me what to say," Austin said. "That's what you need to know. How the hell would I have known the sheriff's personal cell phone number otherwise, huh? Ask yourself that. Shanna gave it to me. It was her idea to go to the grocery store and buy a burner phone. She bought it for me. She told me to call the house. She told me when. She told me what to say."

"Which was?" Gus asked.

"She had it all planned out. She primed him for me. Told me she was gonna tell Bill this story about how I took advantage of her at the gym. That I had pictures and videos of her. Of us together. She was gonna tell him to do whatever I said to keep that stuff off the internet. See, it was Shanna's idea for me to take those pictures of the two of us. Of me ... screwing her. So you're wrong about that too. I didn't tape her without her knowing. It was part of how she wanted me to get him to agree to meet me. I called him just like she said. He answered. It was a short phone call. He was expecting it, just like Shanna said he would. I told him I knew some things about his wife. That if he didn't meet with me and bring me ten grand, I was gonna blast them all over the internet."

"Those pictures of Shanna weren't on Bill's phone," I said.

"I didn't send them. She was really specific. She didn't want me sending them to anybody. She didn't trust they wouldn't end up in the wrong hands. But I knew enough to get Bill Clancy's attention, you know? Like her birthmarks. Her tattoos. I told him I'd meet him in the parking lot behind the high school biology pond. You know. Over on Mill Pond Road?"

"I don't understand how you got him to agree to that," Sam said. "Bill wasn't stupid. He wouldn't have taken that meeting alone."

"I told you. That was all Shanna. He put me on speaker phone. Shanna admitted everything to him with me on the line. She put up a good show. Crying. Saying she was sorry. She begged him to do whatever I said so I wouldn't upload those pictures of her."

"He'd do anything for her," Gus whispered. "You son of a ... she knew. She knew if she asked Bill to meet with you, he would."

"Yeah. She's smart as hell, right? Anyway, Clancy came out there. He got out of his car and started walking toward me. I kinda panicked and shot at him. I had a lot of time to think. I started wondering if maybe Shanna might underestimate him. Like what if he brought his gun? So I shot first so he couldn't. It nicked his shoulder and he fell down. It went kinda sideways then. I had this two-by-four in my truck. I hit him with it. Shanna had this whole plan for me. She wanted me to just kill him right away. But I wanted him to suffer for what he did to Shanna. See how he liked being beat on. So I tied him up and waited for him to come to.

"When he did, I tried to get him to admit to what he did to Shanna. He wouldn't. That made me even angrier. Finally, I just got it over with. BOOM! One shot in the head. Lights out. I mean. Wow! I'd never done anything like that before. Killed a guy. Have you? It's ... well ... it's a rush. I didn't think I'd have the courage to do it. I took some X just before. It helped but I'll tell ya, the second I took that first shot, I sobered right up."

"Whose idea was it to move the body?" Gus asked, his distaste for the question evident in his tone.

"That was me. All me. I told you, Shanna had this plan but I got to thinking. The guy *did* have his gun on him. So I was smart to shoot first, it turns out. I started dragging him to the bog. I had weights. Shanna told me to tie them to his ankles and arms and sink him. She said nobody would ever find him and if they did, there wouldn't be enough left to prove anything. But ... I thought about it. I shot him right in the temple. Right close up. Just like you would if you were gonna off yourself, right? So wouldn't it just be better to make it look like he did it himself? So that's what I did. I put him in his car, drove out to that parking lot. I used to work there for a while. Collecting carts. I know where the cameras are. I got him out there, cut off all ropes around his wrists, and stuck him behind the wheel. Then I called Ricky to come get me and I thought that would be the end of it."

I saw the expression on Nash's face. I could swear I knew what he was thinking. If Austin Merkle had simply done what Shanna had told him to, we might not be sitting here today. He might have even got away with it.

"I kept my mouth shut. Shanna panicked. I told her everything was gonna be okay. I was never gonna turn her in. She promised me she was gonna get me a good lawyer and that he'd find a way to get me off. She told me I'd know she was still with me when I saw her wearing that ring."

"Why did she want him dead?" I asked.

Austin shook his head. "I've had a lot of time to think about that. Shanna's a princess, you know? That was one thing that she didn't like about her old man ... I mean ... other than the fact he wailed on her and his junk didn't work."

"Except he didn't," Gus said. "Wail on her."

"Yeah. See. I didn't know that. I believed her. But the other thing is. Shanna loves attention. She likes when people look at her. That's why she was into me. I treated that woman like a queen. I know her. At the funeral. All those people at her house making sure she's got food, doing her yard work. Now she's everybody's queen. She said that would happen. She talked about all these cop funerals the sheriff used to make her go to with him. All their wives were treated like saints. She wanted that. She figured she deserved it after everything he put her through."

Sam's jaw twitched with rage. This was a kind of blasphemy. Shanna Clancy had taken something sacred, the honor of a fallen officer, and perverted it.

"Why did you send those pictures to Ricky?" I asked. "If you did everything Shanna told you, why violate that one rule of hers?"

For the first time in the retelling of his story, Austin Merkle looked remorseful. "I don't know. Ricky was just always bragging about the girls he could get. We all knew he was lying. I got sick of it.. It was stupid. But Shanna was just so hot. I wanted him to see. You couldn't see her face though. I made sure."

"Big of you," Sam said.

"You have what you need," Nash said.

"What we have," Sam said, "is your word against Shanna Clancy's. She isn't going to admit to any of this. She's going to say you've made it all up, her involvement."

"I have the receipt for that ring," Austin said. "It's at my mom's house. In her safe. And I told you, Shanna showed me exactly where she wanted me to dump Bill's body. She took me out there. It was the last time we ... did it. She actually got a phone call from Bill when we were ... you know. She answered it. She thought that was really funny. She kept on talking to him right through it. We got a laugh out of that. It was three days before I shot Bill. Shanna's birthday. April 12th. Can't you check that? Like her phone? You did all that stuff with mine. Where it shows you where the phone is. I bet if you checked hers, you'd find a call from Bill right when I said. It was ten o'clock in the morning. Before I went to work. They talked for three or four minutes. Can't you track the GPS on it too? I'm telling you. We were right by the boggy part of Mill Pond."

"What about the Wahls?" I said.

"I complained to Shanna about the way Ricky treated me. I didn't think she cared. She always seemed annoyed by it. When things would get bad with Ricky's dad, I used to let him crash at my place. That's why I was pissed when he treated me like crap. I told her about that. And then she told me she knew Mr. Wahl was a mean drunk. She told me her husband had a run-in with him at the Blue Pony. They were getting takeout cuz he didn't want to eat in. Shanna waited in the car and she saw the sheriff and Mr. Wahl come out together and Wahl was staggering. They got into some argument and Wahl went off."

"You don't think Steven Wahl ever saw Shanna that night?"

"I don't know. Probably not. When he gets drunk like that, he doesn't remember too much the next day."

I stared hard at Nash. "You told your lawyer that?"

"Mara," Nash said. "You know that's privileged."

"Are you protecting your client or yourself?" I said. "If you knew ..."

"He didn't," Austin said. "I never told anyone about me and Shanna. I never told him how I knew about the sheriff and Wahl."

"That's good, Austin," Nash said. "There. You've got corroboration. Are we done here? Do you have a proffer?"

Kenya walked in carrying a thin file folder. She laid it in front of Austin Merkle. Nash opened it. "I've already signed it," she said. "We'll drop the death penalty in your case. You plead to first degree. Life without parole. It's the best deal you'll get. If your statement leads to a conviction against Shanna Clancy, I'll see what I can do about getting you incarcerated someplace close. Your mother will be able to visit you."

Austin picked up the pen as Nash read over the terms. He set them down in front of his client, his expression grim.

"She really screwed me, didn't she?" For some reason, Austin looked at me. "Do you think she was ever gonna marry me like she said?"

"No, Austin," I said. "I don't. I think she used you."

He nodded, then signed the paper, regret filling his eyes. But I knew it wasn't remorse for ending Bill Clancy's life. He only cared that Shanna didn't really love him.

"It was for nothing then," he said as he closed the file and handed the paperwork back to Kenya. "All of it. I did it for nothing."

Gus couldn't take it anymore. He stormed out of the room. His footsteps became a steady drumbeat. A funeral dirge as he walked by Bill Clancy's empty office.

38

T uesday Morning
November 2nd

Election Day

I stood outside room number 482. The closest thing the Waynetown Alegra Inn had to a Presidential Suite. Just two rooms and a kitchenette, but it had a nice view of the Maumee River.

I held a large, padded manila envelope in one hand as I raised the other to knock on the door. I almost didn't. But the decision was out of my hands as the door opened and Alexander Nash stood there in jeans and a tee shirt. It occurred to me it had been over fifteen years since I'd seen him wear anything other than a suit and tie.

We stood there for a moment. Staring at each other. Nash had the hint of a smile on his face. Enjoying my discomfort, maybe. Finally, I lifted the envelope and waved it at him.

"The final paperwork on your client's plea bargain," I said. "I figured you'd want a copy before you left town."

Peering over his shoulder, I saw bankers boxes stacked high against one wall of Nash's sitting room. Beside it, two suitcases.

"Come on in," he said. "I was just about to give you a call."

I hesitated. When Nash opened the door wider, I went in.

"I've got some coffee left," he said.

"From the pot in your room?" I said. "No, thanks. I'm friends with too many cops. You maybe don't want to know about the risk you're taking using those things."

Nash grimaced. "You're probably right. How about something stronger?"

"I'm good. Thank you. I won't take up too much of your time. I assume you've got a flight to catch."

"Rental car. I've got some business in Cleveland next."

I was still holding the envelope. I ran a finger along one edge. Nash moved a garment bag off the couch and offered me a seat. I took it.

"I thought you'd want to know. BCI has finished processing the scene out at Mill Pond. They found a shell casing matching Austin's gun. The one used to kill Clancy. Also, some bone fragments. It'll take a little while for them to see if there's any usable DNA, but the M.E.'s pretty confident he'll be able to match the fragments to Bill's skull. They expect a positive ID within the week. I appreciate your help getting the receipt for Shanna Clancy's ring. Shanna and Bill's cell phone records match up with what Austin said about the phone call he overheard between them on April 12th while she was with him out at the bog. Every single thing he told us checked out. I've put my sentencing recommendation in the report. The hearing's in six weeks but there shouldn't be any hiccups to what we agreed on. I made a copy of Andrea Patel's final report too. It's all in here."

"Thanks," he said. "I'll make sure to look it over before I head out. I've got a meeting scheduled with Austin on the way. This will be good news for him."

I nodded.

"You know," he said. "My one regret ... I would have liked to have gone to verdict on this one."

"Are you serious? You'd rather have gambled with your client's life?"

"Not because of Austin. But because of you. You're good, Mara. I still think I was better. I think the jury had doubts. If it weren't for Shanna Clancy, I would have had an acquittal. Ricky Wahl was a terrible star witness."

He'd taken a seat on the opposite end of the couch. Nash leaned back, casually draping one ankle over his knee. His usual arrogance dripped from every word.

"But your client was guilty," I said. "That doesn't bother you?"

He smiled. "You know better than that. It's never about whether they did it."

"Maybe it should be."

"Are you going to lecture me about whether I've sold my soul to the devil, Mara?"

"That depends. Are you going to lecture me about how the justice system works?"

"Why are you here? I mean, really. All this? Patel's updated report. The sentencing rec. You could have emailed it to me. Sent a courier. Or just called me on the phone."

I met his gaze. Something blazed behind his eyes. A secret, maybe. A hunger.

"Alex, I still have some questions. There are things about this case that still don't sit well."

"Like?"

"Like I think Shanna herself is the one who tipped you off."

Nash just stared at me with that glint in his eye.

"Did you know?"

"Know what?"

"Did you know that Shanna was behind all of this? And if you did, why did you let Austin twist in the wind as long as he did?"

Nash picked a piece of lint off his shoe.

"I didn't know," he said. "Not until the end. Just like you. And you know I can't divulge the communications I had with my client."

"I'm not asking you to. But there's something else that's been bothering me. Ricky Wahl. He's still in the wind. His father doesn't even know where he is. It occurred to me that Ricky didn't have the means to just disappear like that. So he probably had help. And it's also occurred to me that your biggest hook with the jury would have been Ricky's sudden flight. It went against his own interests and nullified his immunity deal."

He smiled. "Maybe you're giving me too much credit, Mara."

"I don't think I am. And I can't prove any of this."

"No. You can't. And I still liked my chances with the jury if Shanna Clancy hadn't broken."

"Right. With your guilty client and witness tampering, if that's what happened. You asked me why I came here in person. Nash, I know the Legacy Foundation funneled the money for your legal fees in this case. I also know the kind of people they've helped put in power."

"The Legacy Foundation was cleared of any wrongdoing or connection in Jason's case. Don't believe everything you read."

"You're good," I said. "The truth is, you might have gotten an acquittal if not for Shanna. I'll admit it. But I also think you're good enough to win honestly."

"You need to be careful what you accuse me of."

"I'm telling you that you need to be careful, Nash. The Legacy Foundation can be ruthless. They don't care who they destroy."

"Noted," he said. "If that's all you have to say, then maybe it's time for us to part ways."

"You wanted me to think Jason was somehow involved in all of this," I said, feeling my head start to pound. "You went to visit him because you knew I'd find out about it. If you couldn't win on the merits, you were going to try mind games with me. That's all that was, wasn't it? My God, Alex. All that stuff about the Mechanics. You knew Clancy had nothing to do with that. You were willing to tarnish the reputation of an honest man. A good man."

He got up from the couch and went to the window.

"I think you owe me the truth," I said. When Nash turned, his expression turned grave.

"Are you sure about that?"

"You tried to meddle in my personal life," I said. "And you did it in defense of a man I think you knew was guilty. You made this case personal. You're not the same guy I knew fifteen years ago, Alex. So I'm telling you, be careful. If you sell your soul to the devil, he's going to come collect."

"Mara, I think you're the one who needs to be careful. What I did? Visiting Jason? That was too easy. And he knows it. Don't underestimate Jason Brent's ambitions, even where he is right now."

"You're the last person I need to hear that from. I know who my ex is."

"I don't think you do. I don't think you have the first clue how much power he still has. He blames you for everything that's happened. And now, he's already faced the worst thing that could happen to him in his mind. He's got very little left to lose. So here's my warning. Give him what he wants before you're the one who gets destroyed. Don't underestimate him."

My blood turned to ice. I don't know what I expected to gain by coming here. The man I once knew in law school was long gone. If I thought my words might save him, I'd grossly misjudged.

"Take care of yourself, Alex," I said. "But don't ever come back here. You're right. I can't prove my suspicions about what you did with Ricky Wahl or any of the rest of it. But don't underestimate me if I set my mind to trying."

I didn't wait for his answer. I tossed the envelope on the coffee table and left the room. When I closed the door to room 482, I hoped I'd never see Alexander Nash again.

39

At four thirty, Kat and Bree brought Will home from robotics club. He was animated, talking about their latest build and how well he thought it would do at Districts in a couple of weeks.

"How do you feel about some spaghetti tonight?" Kat asked. She made herself at home in my kitchen, pulling out the pots and pans she'd need to whip up Will's favorite meal.

"Great!" Will said.

"How about you?" Kat asked me. Bree sat at the kitchen table, going over the schematics of what his team was calling The Bone Crusher.

"If you two don't mind hanging out here tonight, I'm thinking about heading over to the Blue Pony later. Kenya rented one of the back rooms to watch the returns come in."

"For her wake?" Bree teased. I caught Kat giving her a look and the kill gesture across her throat.

"Don't count her out just yet."

"I'm sorry," Bree said. "Bad joke."

"You won't get fired if Aunt Kenya loses, will you?" Will asked. "We've got savings to cover the mortgage and expenses for two years."

"You don't need to worry about that," I said. This was an ongoing battle between us. My son refused to cede concerns over my household finances to me, where they belonged. It was another thing I could lie at Jason's feet. Years ago, he thought it would be a good idea to teach Will about household budgets and 401k plans. It sounded good in theory, but I could never tell what Will would fixate on.

"I'm just saying," he said. "You've got some wiggle room if you need to look for a new job."

"Bree?" Kat said. "I could use your help with the sauce."

Bree gave Kat a quizzical look, but left the table to join her wife.

"Come on," I said to Will. "Come out in the living room with me and show me this monster robot you're building."

"If we make it to States, can we stay in Columbus for a whole week? I'd like to go to COSI. It's the Center of Science and Industry."

"I know what COSI is. I think I can arrange that," I said.

Will came to join me in the other room, but left the schematics on the table. He had a dark look on his face as he sat beside me and I knew there was something he'd been working up to tell me.

"You okay?" I asked. "Mrs. Pulaski said you haven't been wanting to participate in gym class this week. Is there something going on?"

"No. I just don't like dodgeball. She said I could sit it out."

"I never liked dodgeball, either."

"And I've been helping Mr. Winslow with his coding class. He's starting a club for that. I thought maybe I might try it."

"That sounds like a great idea."

"I'm not very good at it yet. But Mr. Winslow thinks I've got potential."

"I've always liked that guy."

"Mom," he said. "I've made my decision."

For a moment, I thought he was still talking about the coding club. My son often switched topics mid-sentence. I lovingly called it Will-ease. At times, I had to be his translator. It was the expression on his face that clued me in. He did all the things his therapist worked on with him. He turned to face me. He made sure to make eye contact. And then he reached out and put a hand on my knee.

"I don't want to see him."

I felt a whoosh go through me. My pulse skipped and I took a beat before I answered. "You mean your dad."

Will nodded quickly. "I'm not ready yet. Dr. Vera and I have talked it out. I don't want to go to that place. The prison. I don't want him to tell me lies."

His words hit me with the force of a two-by-four to the solar plexus. Pain. Guilt. Sadness. For months, I feared what would happen if I had to take Will to visit Jason. I hadn't realized how much it would hurt, knowing he saw his father for what he was.

A liar.

"Okay," I said, trying to remember all the things I was supposed to say when Will asked me questions. When he shared his feelings. I wanted to hug him and tell him everything would be all right. But my sweet, intelligent, sensitive, literal boy knew I couldn't deliver on that promise.

"Okay," I said again.

"Do I have to? Will the judge make me?"

"I think your dad will ask the judge to. But the judge has to rule based on what is in your best interests. You're almost thirteen years old. You have a say."

"Will I have to go to court?"

It was in me to soften this. But I knew that would not serve my son.

"Yes. Probably."

Will nodded. "Dr. Vera said that too. And she said she would write a letter for me."

"I think that will go a long way toward convincing the judge it's not the right time to take you to see your dad."

"Do you think he'll be mad?"

Again, the urge to say easy things filled me.

"Yes. He will probably be mad."

"Will he be mean to you? Because I'll say it. Dr. Vera will write it in her letter. This is my decision."

"Will, it's not your job to protect me. We've talked about this before. Whatever comes. I can handle it. You come first, remember? Always."

Will nodded. Then he leaped forward, throwing his arms around me. The hug was brief but intense. Then, just like that, it was over. He got up and went into the kitchen to help Bree and Kat with the spaghetti. I would have to break this news to Kat later. Jason was her brother. The last year had torn her in half as well.

For me? I felt as if I'd had the wind knocked out of me. In a good way. Relief flooded me. At the same time, dread. Alexander Nash's words came back. There would be a battle. Jason would blame me for this. And he would do everything in his power to try to destroy me over it.

As I looked over the couch and watched my son stir the sauce with his aunts, a smile came across his face. He was happy. I knew he'd been carrying the weight of this decision ever since Jason was arrested last year. I thought of Jason and what might come. And then, I thought ... bring it.

40

The second I walked into the Pony, I regretted it. Kenya's low-key get-together had turned into a full-on party ... or wake ... depending on the next hour or so. Paula Dudley, the owner, had all the big-screen televisions tuned to the two local news stations. My plan to slip in unseen into the private room in the back went to dust as Channel 8 reporter Dave Reese cornered me, holding his cell phone out, recording me.

"Mara," he said. "Would you care to comment on Shanna Clancy's formal arrest last night?"

"I have no comment on anything, David. I'm here to support my friend."

"Your friend? Kenya Spaulding was down five points according to the latest polls. Are you sure you want to go on record like that? There's a good chance you'll have a new boss by morning."

"No matter what happens," I said, "Kenya Spaulding is my friend and her current term doesn't end until January 1st. Now, I've said all I care to say. If you'll excuse me."

"Will you be assigned to prosecute Shanna Clancy's case if and when it goes to trial? Her lawyer put out a statement that she believes in her client's innocence."

"I have no comment on pending cases, Reese. You should know the words to that song by heart by now."

Shanna faced a laundry list of charges. Conspiracy to commit murder, obstruction of justice, witness tampering, and perjury. If convicted, she might spend the rest of her life behind bars. I'd heard a rumor that Austin Merkle had once again declared his love for her and planned to do everything he could to help defend her. Shanna's lawyer had already hinted at wanting a change of venue. Our office wasn't going to fight it. Shanna Clancy would soon be some other county's problem.

"If Kenya loses tonight, do you think the voters are just tired of the old guard? Her connection to your former boss, Phil Halsey, has been a stain on her record since the day his corruption came to light. Do you think it would have been better if Kenya had just stepped aside?"

"Enough!" Sam appeared out of nowhere. He towered over Dave Reese and put a protective arm around me. Though I appreciated the gesture, I wasn't so sure it wouldn't fuel even more speculation. But I was grateful for Sam's formidable presence as he weaved his way through the crowd and into the sanctuary of the back room.

"Thanks," I said. Sam had a table waiting. An empty, dark back booth. Kenya was at the front of the room, talking to some of her closest supporters and her campaign manager. She acknowledged me with a wave and tapped her watch, letting me know she was going to try to break away in a minute or two.

"She looks good," Sam said. "Keyed up still."

"She's been going the old-fashioned route, knocking on doors all week since the trial ended."

"It's gonna be close," he said. "But I wouldn't count Kenya Spaulding out just yet."

I looked around the room. Sam was the only cop here. Early last week, the sheriff's command union came out and once again endorsed Kenya's opponent. It had been a bitter blow and I knew Sam didn't agree. As acting sheriff, his presence here tonight wouldn't go unnoticed. It mattered. And it's exactly what Bill Clancy would have done.

"Where's Gus?" I asked.

Sam flagged a waiter and got us a pitcher of beer and two frosted mugs. He pulled out his wallet.

"No need," the waiter said. "These are compliments of that table over there."

I looked over Sam's shoulder. Mercy Gale sat with a group of her classmates. She raised her own beer mug to us.

"She shouldn't have done that," I said. "We should be buying a round for her."

Then I shouted, "We should be buying a round for you!"

Smiling, Mercy came over. She was already a little glassy-eyed. She'd gotten a head start on the rest of us.

"Thank you," I said.

"Oh, it's nothing," she said. "Paula's offering dollar pitchers tonight."

I laughed. "Well, thanks anyway. And I don't just mean for the beer. You've been invaluable during the Clancy case. You're sharp. Your dad should be proud."

Mercy's face fell for a fraction of a second, then she covered, smiling.

"Have you thought about what you want to do after you graduate?" I asked. "Things are in flux a bit until after the results tonight. But we could use someone like you on a permanent basis."

Mercy took a sip of her beer. "Thanks. But I'm not planning to stay in town. I've got ... um ... a family matter I need to look after."

She didn't elaborate, but by the dark look in her eyes, I wondered if something might be wrong with her father, the famous E. Thomas Gale, lawyer to the stars. It wasn't my business to pry.

"Well," I said. "I know how complicated those can be. So I wish you the best of luck with it. If you change your mind. Give me a call. And put me down as a reference. I'll give you a glowing recommendation."

"Mercy!" One of her friends at the other table called her back over. Mercy said a heartfelt goodbye, then went back to join them.

"I'll miss that one," I said. "She's the best intern we've had in years."

"I couldn't find any dirt on her," Sam said. I had a pang of guilt that I'd ever asked him to try. I realized then he'd never answered my question about Detective Ritter. So I asked again.

Sam set his mug down. "Gus is taking things pretty hard since the trial ended. He blames himself for a lot of the things that went wrong."

"He shouldn't."

"That's what I told him. But you know Gus. Anyway, I convinced him to take some personal time. He has almost six weeks' vacation banked plus some PTO on top of that. He's headed out west to visit his brother. He'll be back after the first of the year."

"It'll be good for him. But I'm gonna miss the guy. On the other hand, after tonight, I might be getting some personal time whether I like it or not."

I looked at the television screen over Sam's shoulder. With forty percent of the precincts reporting, Kenya was down by three points.

Sam looked too. "I wouldn't worry about that. It wasn't pretty, but you won. You can declare victory in Bill's case. You made national news. No matter what happens to Kenya, you're not going to be out of a job. Skip Fletcher would be a fool to send you packing. He's told me as much."

"You asked him? Why were you talking about my job with Skip Fletcher?"

I had my hand flat on the table. Sam reached over and took it in his. It was an intimate gesture. One that sent my heart racing. He stared at me and suddenly, I knew what he was trying to tell me.

"You've been offered a job yourself, haven't you? The county commissioners want to make you sheriff on a permanent basis, don't they?"

He took a breath, then nodded. "Yes. I wanted to talk to you about it first before I decided for sure."

"Sam," I said. "It's you. It was always going to be you. Even Bill wanted that. You'll be good at this. The county is lucky to have you."

"They'll have to hold a special election next year. My appointment is only good until the end of Bill's current term. I'll have to run in my own right."

"And you'll win. You'll have my vote."

"Mara," he said. "We haven't ... with everything that's been going on. I know we haven't really had a serious talk about where this is going. And I know the last thing you probably want is to be involved with another politician. So if you ..."

"Sam," I said. "Stop. Do you think I would ever ask you to give up your ambitions because of me?"

"That's the thing. I never thought this would be an ambition of mine. But now ... Bill wasn't done. He had a vision for this county and the department. A good one. I think I could help carry that forward."

"You can't do this for Bill. You have to do it for you."

"Yeah," Sam said. "I know that. And I believe in Bill's vision, but I have some of my own, too."

"Then you need to fight for them. When things hit the fan with Jason last year, do you remember what you told me? You said I wouldn't have to face that alone. Well, you don't have to do this alone either."

"Could you handle it though? This job ... it's going to take up a lot of my time. I might not be able to ..."

"Sam," I said. "If it's worth fighting for, then you fight for it."

Our eyes met. I knew what I meant. He knew what I meant. For now, that was the most either of us could say. I lifted my beer mug and gestured for him to lift his. "This calls for a toast."

Sam smiled, but sadness filled his eyes. "To Bill."

He was right. Bill Clancy would cast a long shadow. But Sam had a shining light all his own.

"To Bill," I said, clinking my mug against his.

A roar went up. Paula turned up the volume on the television. At the anchor desk on Channel 8, the announcement came.

"This is breaking news. With eighty-one percent of all precincts reporting in Maumee County, we can now call a couple of local races. Just hang on for one minute while we gather the results."

I met Kenya's gaze. She gave me a thumbs up, then pressed her hand to her breast. She turned back to the screen and I held my breath with her as the anchor called Kenya's race. I couldn't hear what he was saying. Too many heads blocked my view of the crawl across the bottom of the screen.

"Can you hear? Can you see?" I said to Sam. He shook his head no. The only answer I got was the collective gasp from those closest to the television screen. Then Kenya's face froze for a moment. She collected herself just long enough to order a double shot of bourbon from the bartender.

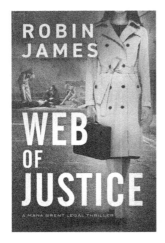

CLICK TO LEARN MORE

A MISSING CHILD. A WEB OF lies. A lone prosecutor must unravel the truth before it's too late.

The stakes have never been higher when the defendant in Mara's latest murder trial decides he wants to cut a deal. His freedom in exchange for information on the whereabouts of a high-profile kidnapping victim. Mara must match wits with one of the most dangerous criminals she's ever faced. This time, one misstep could cost an innocent child's life.

Don't miss Web of Justice, Book 7 in the Mara Brent Legal Thriller Series. https://www.robinjamesbooks.com/web

NEWSLETTER SIGN UP

Sign up to get notified of Robin's new releases, plus get *Crown of Thorne*, a FREE exclusive legal thriller ebook novella.

SCAN TO JOIN
ROBIN JAMES'S
NEWSLETTER

ABOUT THE AUTHOR

Robin James is an attorney and former law professor. She's worked on a wide range of civil, criminal and family law cases in her twenty-five year legal career. She also spent over a decade as supervising attorney for a Michigan legal clinic assisting thousands of people who could not otherwise afford access to justice.

Robin now lives on a lake in southern Michigan with her husband, two children, and one lazy dog. Her favorite, pure Michigan writing spot is stretched out on the back of a pontoon watching the faster boats go by.

Sign up for Robin James's Legal Thriller Newsletter to get all the latest updates on her new releases and get a free bonus scene from Burden of Truth featuring Cass Leary's last day in Chicago. http://www.robinjamesbooks.com/newsletter/

ALSO BY ROBIN JAMES

Mara Brent Legal Thriller Series

Time of Justice

Price of Justice

Hand of Justice

Mark of Justice

Path of Justice

Vow of Justice

Web of Justice

with more to come...

Cass Leary Legal Thriller Series

Burden of Truth

Silent Witness

Devil's Bargain

Stolen Justice

Blood Evidence

Imminent Harm

First Degree

Mercy Kill

Guilty Acts

Cold Evidence

Dead Law

with more to come...

SCAN FOR
ROBIN JAMES'S
COMPLETE BOOKLIST

MARA BRENT SERIES IN AUDIO

SCAN FOR INFO ON
MARA BRENT IN
AUDIOBOOK FORMAT

Made in the USA
Las Vegas, NV
12 May 2024

89854014R00218